David Alex Jones

THE NIGHT CLASS

An Alternative Tale of Reconciliation

Published by:
Apparently Normal Publishing
Waterloo, Ontario, Canada

ISBN (Paperback Edition) 978-0-9951963-6-0

Version 2022.12.15

The Night Class is a work of fiction. Any references to real-life characters, documents, locations, and events are made only to provide historical or political context, and are used fictitiously. The remaining characters and events in this book, like any other work of fiction, are drawn from a multitude of life experiences. Those characters are a composite of tiny snippets of physical or psychological characteristics drawn from a lifetime of interactions with a multitude of people. Thus, any significant resemblance of the fictional characters in this story to real-life persons, dead or alive, is purely coincidental.

In addition, every effort has been made to make characters of different races, portrayed in this story, realistic enough to make the story believable. However, in no way does the author claim to be an authentic voice for people of those races.

Finally, because the story contains elements of political commentary designed to raise discussion of issues related to reconciliation, the characters are purposely intended to be "politically incorrect" within the current Canadian social context. Some readers may find some of the words and actions of some characters offensive, or even psychologically triggering, at times.

LAND ACKNOWLEDGEMENT

This book was written in Southwestern Ontario, Canada, on land located within the Haldimand Tract, land that was granted to the Haudenosaunee of the Six Nations of the Grand River, and is within the shared traditional territory of the Neutral, Anishinaabe, and Haudenosaunee peoples

TABLE OF CONTENTS

FOREWORD

SINCE I BEGAN telling friends and acquaintances that I'm writing another fictional novel, this one set within the context of Indigenous Truth and Reconciliation in Canada, I've been met with a lot of silence, raised eyebrows, or comments like: "Have you checked with Indigenous sources?" or "How did you get the idea for your characters?" or "Can you be sure the story is authentic?"

I understand their concerns. They're all worried that I'm stepping into a racial and political minefield—and I agree with them. But I think it's a racial and political minefield that *somebody* in Canada has to navigate, in order to help raise awareness in the non-Indigenous public of the need to take an active role in helping to resolve the longstanding, complex issues related to Truth and Reconciliation.

Before I go any further, I want to make the disclaimer that I am definitely pro-reconciliation! As much as anybody, I want to see the wrongs of the past corrected, and I want to see our Indigenous brothers and sisters treated with fairness and dignity. But, despite that, I have observed that non-Indigenous Canadians continue to have a lot of questions about the political process of reconciliation. Thus, although *The Night Class* is a fictional coming-of-age story, it is also a political commentary about reconciliation. Will readers (both Indigenous and non-Indigenous) find this story controversial? Will *The Night Class* generate emotional reactions, some heated debate, and dialog about reconciliation? I certainly hope so, otherwise there's no point in writing the story.

At this point, you're probably asking yourself the same question as my friends and family: "Why is this guy crazy enough to tackle this controversial subject?" So, I'll try to answer that question as briefly as possible, after telling you a bit about my background.

My ancestors were colonial settlers in Prince Edward Island, Ontario, and Saskatchewan, Canada. As young children, my sisters and I often spent summer vacations at my grandparents' cottage in Saskatchewan's Qu'Appelle Valley, having to drive through the small village of Lebret to get there. I remember seeing a large building beside the road, with children playing in a playground, and I remember asking my parents and grandparents about the building, which I now know was one of Canada's residential schools. Their answer was that "this is where the Indian kids go to school." Since I'd already learned that most Indians (as we called Indigenous people then) lived separately on reserves, having separate schools for Indian kids made logical sense to my ten-year-old mind, and I never thought to ask any more questions about the schools. Non-Indigenous children my age simply accepted those explanations at face value. That was just the way things were for us back then.

However, as the years passed, non-Indigenous Canadians like myself have had our childhood naiveté systematically broken down by a non-stop flow of disturbing news stories about the ongoing problems in many Indigenous communities—problems and truths that keep repeating themselves time and time again. And eventually, I started asking myself: "Why does this keep happening?"

So, I started reading. And no matter what Indigenous topics I chose to read, they all ultimately pointed me in one direction—towards Canada's *Indian Act*. And the more I read about the Act, and the more I read about what Canada's Indigenous people were saying about it, the more appalled I became!

Then, over the past two to three years, I noticed that the words "Truth and Reconciliation" were popping up more and more frequently in the news. So I started reading key documents like the

United Nations Declaration on the Rights of Indigenous Peoples (UNDRIP), and the final report by Canada's Truth and Reconciliation Committee, with its ninety-four *Calls to Action*.

My reading prompted me to start talking with friends and neighbours about Truth and Reconciliation. But, when I raised the topic, something very surprising happened. Many of them were reluctant to talk about the subject, let alone ask questions or express concerns about what the word *reconciliation* actually means for Canadians. They were afraid to ask how long the process might take, or whether there is a goal or an endpoint for reconciliation. Most importantly, they were afraid that anything they said might be interpreted in a way that might brand them as racists. And given the current political and racial climate, especially in North America where there are apparently no grey areas, and where being branded a racist is a very all-or-nothing, unforgiving judgment, I don't blame them one bit for being cautious.

The only way I could get some people to openly express opinions about reconciliation was to link an informal, confidential survey about reconciliation for friends to access via my Facebook page. The results and comments were not only insightful, but they aligned completely with previous polls conducted by the Truth and Reconciliation Committee, as well as other reputable polling companies over the past few years. Despite the results of the Truth and Reconciliation Committee's 2015 findings and report, and despite the recent multiple revelations of finding the bodies of missing Indigenous children at Canada's residential schools, reconciliation is still only a priority for a small percentage of Canada's non-Indigenous population. Even worse, a majority of Canadians rated their level of knowledge about reconciliation to be very low.

Frankly, this is a shame, and I think it needs to change! How can we encourage First Nations and non-Indigenous people to engage in a dialogue about reconciliation, and to start moving that process forward, when a large part of the non-Indigenous population is afraid to talk about the subject? How can we increase awareness of reconciliation issues, when it isn't even a high priority for most non-Indigenous people? And most importantly, how can those of us who are non-Indigenous, help to raise awareness in our communities of the need to get reconciliation moving forward in a meaningful way?

Given the recent residential school revelations, which includes a ground search at the school that was located at Lebret, the need for moving Truth and Reconciliation forward in Canada is even more pressing. So, as a writer, I decided to use fiction as a vehicle to raise awareness in non-Indigenous people, and also to raise awareness in Indigenous people that much of the non-Indigenous population is either afraid to engage with them in meaningful dialog, or doesn't care about the issue. My aim is to raise awareness through storytelling, in a way that is entertaining, but also in a way that tells the story through characters representing the reality of Canada's ethnic mosaic. As such, *The Night Class* is both a coming-of-age story and a political commentary. It necessarily contains a certain amount of political incorrectness in order to raise awareness of issues and generate dialog. There is a long history of political commentary in fiction, beginning in ancient Greece and re-emerging in the sixteenth century. Like an independent media, these types of stories serve a necessary need in any society claiming to have free speech.

Thus, I hope this book will be difficult to read in places. *The Night Class* exposes biases and prejudices present in both Indigenous and non-Indigenous perspectives, with the intention of eliciting strong emotional responses and discomfort from both groups. I'll be presenting examples of racist attitudes that I grew up with, many of which still prevail today. I do not endorse those attitudes. Instead, I wish to expose them for what they are—myths and misconceptions about our Indigenous brothers and sisters.

THE NIGHT CLASS

While writing *The Night Class*, I did my best (as a non-Indigenous person) to research and make the experiences of the Indigenous characters in my story as realistic as possible. I also did my best to reach out to consult with members of the Indigenous community, to obtain critical feedback on the first draft of the manuscript. However, this is where I experienced another surprising phenomenon, when nobody I approached in the Indigenous community seemed motivated or interested in reading the manuscript and giving feedback. I was asked a pointed question by one young Indigenous lady: "Why are you the one to tell this story?"

On one hand, I completely understand that Indigenous people feel a deep need to reclaim their history, and to tell their own stories and truths along the road to healing and reconciliation. Non-indigenous people have been appropriating Indigenous stories and cultures for hundreds of years now. But, on the other hand, the experiences I described above have left me feeling like reconciliation is currently a one-way street, where there does not seem to be a lot of interest from the Indigenous community in engaging in frank, open dialog with an average, non-Indigenous Canadian about the process of reconciliation. Given that the definition of the word *reconcile* is to resolve differences and restore harmony between people, it's difficult for me to see how any path towards Truth and Reconciliation in this country can resolve differences or restore harmony without frank, two-way dialog, even if that dialog is sometimes uncomfortable for all parties involved.

Consequently, it is my hope that *The Night Class* provides a lesson in how both Indigenous and non-Indigenous peoples must learn to look at themselves and their approaches to reconciliation, how both groups must learn lessons from our past, and how we must make it a higher priority to learn to work together as one team in the present, if we all hope to move forward and live together in peace and harmony in the future.

At the end of the story, you'll find something that is a bit unusual for a work of fiction—a short list of recommended readings, for those of you who are interested in learning more about the issues raised in *The Night Class*. The list includes important documents such as the *UNDRIP* and Truth and Reconciliation Committee's findings and Calls to Action. I would particularly like to recommend three books: *21 Things You May Not Know About the Indian Act,* by Bob Joseph; *Indigenous Relations*, by Bob and Cynthia Joseph; and *From Where I Stand,* by former Federal Justice Minister Jody Wilson-Raybould. Together, these three books provide valuable insight for non-Indigenous people, into the First Nations' perspective on the *Indian Act*, and on the process of Truth and Reconciliation in general.

I hope you enjoy *The Night Class* and its cast of characters. And, if you also learn something that helps to raise your curiosity or your awareness of reconciliation and Indigenous issues, and causes you to think more about those issues—even better. Finally, if you enjoyed the story and it's messages of the need to build trust between Indigenous and non-Indigenous peoples, and the need for teamwork and compromise in rebuilding our nation, please use social media to recommend *The Night Class* to your friends and neighbours. We won't achieve reconciliation in our country unless we spread awareness of these complex and important issues to all Canadians, and until we all realize that *now* is the time for concrete action on the part of each one of us, Indigenous and non-Indigenous alike, to make reconciliation become a reality in our country.

David Alex Jones

December, 2022

CHAPTER 1—WEEK ONE

I OFTEN wondered why I continued going to therapy sessions every week back then. Don't get me wrong, Dr. Way was a really good psychologist. She was calm, understanding, and empathic. Sometimes she even let me call her by her first name, Barbara. But most importantly, she never judged me, even when I dyed my hair purple and showed up with a nose ring one week. She helped me curb my cutting habit and eating disorder, and she helped me through my first stressful year of grad school. But after a year of therapy, I still had a strange, lingering feeling that I couldn't explain … something Barbara never managed to help me find during those sessions. I had always had a feeling that something important was missing from my life.

Sure, my birth mother, Diane, physically and verbally abused me from a young age, and my sperm-donor dad ran out the door when I was three. But my uncle and aunt rescued me and gave me a loving home, and they provided anything I needed or desired. So things couldn't have been too bad, right? I couldn't have been the only teenager who rebelled and pushed back against their parents. And I can't be the only twenty-six-year-old grad student who still has flashbacks and a history of anorexia and cutting—who still feels like there's something missing from her life, or who is constantly in danger of flunking out.

Looking back, who would have predicted that it wasn't therapy that would finally give me the answer and save me from a lifetime of searching. Instead, it was a ragtag group of undergraduate students and a kindly, long-lost aunt, who would converge in my life and turn my world upside down over a period of only thirteen weeks. Together, they would school me and send me in a direction on my life's journey that I never could have imagined.

"I'M PROUD of how much you've improved over the summer," Dr. Way says. "You did some difficult work identifying some important inner voices … the angry and judgmental ones, the masochistic one, the fearful and abandoned three-year-old one, the intellectual and creative ones …"

"Don't forget my non-conformist and survivor voices," I add. "I rely on them a lot."

My eyes roam around Barbara Way's office. The room in the old sandstone building can only be described as neutral … institutional, at best. The light grey paint job is old and tired, and the blue-grey carpet shows signs of becoming threadbare. Barbara's attempts to warm up the room won't win any design awards. While the pillows on her grey couch have some orange and blue accents, they do little to brighten the space. The framed prints on the wall wouldn't be out of place in a hotel room. I chuckle to myself.

Did she decorate this way on purpose? With all the grey and neutral colours, did she turn the room into a three-dimensional Rorschach card experiment? Is she expecting me to project all of my conflicted inner voices onto the walls of this room?

"Yes, you do," Dr. Way answers, her voice waking me from my brief daydream. "Many of those EMDR sessions this summer were extremely intense and emotional. But you did well to keep yourself stable while you processed some very difficult memories. I guess I'm curious to see where you want to go next in therapy."

"Hmmh … I don't know," I answer honestly. "It took a few days to recover from some of those sessions. I don't think I can afford to have that happen, now that classes are starting up again. Things are going to be pretty stressful."

"I agree," Dr. Way says. "I think you need some time to consolidate your recent gains."

Uh, oh! Is she going to end my therapy? I feel my abandoned, fearful, inner three-year-old self coming alive and starting to panic.

"Does that mean you don't want to see me anymore?" I ask, almost on the verge of tears.

"Oh, no! Not at all," Dr. Way exclaims. "I was thinking we should still meet every week, just so I can stay up to date on how you're managing your stress. What do you think?"

My inner three-year-old heaves a huge sigh of relief.

"That would be great," I say. "I don't want to let things overwhelm me, like they did last year."

"I just want to make sure that you're still able to keep yourself stable … using your slow breathing, going to your safe place, and using lots of positive self-talk. If you keep using those skills, I'm confident you'll do fine this term," she says.

"I'll use them. I promise!"

"Speaking of big stressors," Barbara asks. "Have you heard back from your mother yet?"

"You mean about finding my biological father?" I answer. "No, and I'm not going to hold my breath waiting for her. I doubt if she'll ever follow up on that."

Dependability isn't one of Diane's strong points. In fact, I'm pretty sure my birth mother doesn't have any strong points. What can you say about a mother who still smokes, swears, and drinks like a sailor, who screamed and beat me anytime I cried as a child, and who left me home alone for hours on end, with little else other than goldfish crackers to eat?

"I'll probably have to stop in and see her this weekend," I continue. "She's been phoning and laying the usual guilt trip on me about not visiting enough."

"Is there anybody else you could contact for information about your dad? Any family members?" Dr. Way asks. "Or what about contacting Family and Children's Services?"

"I don't know. I don't have much for family. And now that classes are starting, I really don't need the added stress of dealing with Children's Services. I won't have the time …"

Time … Classes … Oh shit!

A quick glance at my watch tells me that my first class starts in five minutes, and I'm going to have to run all the way across campus. I jump to my feet, grab my bag, head towards the door, and shout over my shoulder to Dr. Way.

"I'm so sorry! Tonight's the first class of the term, and I'm going to be late! I'll see you next week! Gotta run!"

I bolt from Dr. Way's office, run down the hallway, and then I fly down a set of stairs. At the bottom of the stairs, I push the bar on an exit door and sprint into the September dusk.

MOMENTS LATER, I burst through a set of doors into a small lecture theatre, breathing heavily. I stop to catch my breath, stuffing a sheaf of papers and a book back into my bag, just before they fall to the floor.

All eyes in the room are immediately drawn to me—the woman with the purple hair and a nose ring who is causing the ruckus. Below, at the base of the theatre, sixty-five-year-old Dr. Eric Sanderson stands ready to begin his lecture. With his white hair tied back into a ponytail and his white beard, he comes across more as a grandfather than a professor. He is amongst the most popular professors on campus every year. He looks up to see what's causing the commotion and gives me the evil eye. I catch his glare, run down the stairs, and slump into a tiny desk in the first row, still breathing heavily.

As I catch my breath, I gaze up at the perfect domed ceiling in the old lecture theatre, admiring the architecture. We're in one of the oldest buildings on campus, and most students have no idea that the parabolic shape of the ceiling is acoustically perfect. Students in the back of the room can hear the lecturer perfectly without the need of a microphone. They can also hear whispers about last night's sexual encounters from students in the front row. But it works both ways. People in the front row, where I'm sitting, can also hear whispers from the upper rows. And right now, I hear them whispering about me.

"Who's that scatterbrain?"

"I wonder what group she's in? I hope she's not in mine!"

"Seriously? That babe can't keep her own shit together, let alone help us!"

My eavesdropping is interrupted by the sound of Dr. Sanderson clearing his throat.

"Welcome to *Team Building 201*," he begins. "This course is offered jointly by the School of Business and the Department of Psychology. We designed it as an option for students in *all* faculties, because we feel that learning to work as part of a team is an essential skill for anybody, whether you graduate from Business School, the arts, science, or any of the professional schools."

He clicks a remote control to bring up another slide, then walks across the front of the room, taking up position behind a lectern.

"In the past, before COVID, this course had a bit of a reputation for being an easy 'A'. Unfortunately for you, I took time during the pandemic to rethink and redesign the course to incorporate a team project, so you could all have an opportunity to apply what you learn in the course."

Moans and grumbles fill the room as Dr. Sanderson continues his introduction, raising his voice over the background noise.

I chuckle to myself. Little do the students know that Dr. Sanderson and I can hear every little derogatory comment they make.

"You'll see on your course outline that I've randomly assigned the thirty-two students in this class to four teams that will each complete a different group project, worth fifty percent of your final grade. The topic for each team is intentionally controversial and challenging."

Dr. Sanderson pauses and moves purposely across to the other side of the room.

"Each team will be responsible for doing research on your topic, writing a final report, and presenting your findings during the last lecture, during Week 13 of the term."

The background grumbling continues unabated while Dr. Sanderson brings up a new slide.

"Here are your topics. Team number one, your project is *What Did Humanity Learn from the COVID-19 Pandemic, and What Could We Do Differently Next Time?*"

The background grumbling gets louder and the students start shifting restlessly in their seats.

"Team number two: Systemic Racism in Policing: Would your team defund police forces to deal with the problem?"

Tough crowd! ... They're like a school of pirañha ... They could tear me apart if I'm not careful!

"Okay, settle down!" Dr. Sanderson shouts. "You can save your comments and questions until I'm finished."

He pauses and waits for the noise to gradually subside.

"Team number three, your topic is *Climate Change: What Would You Do to Help Canada Meet Glasgow Agreement Targets?* And finally, team number four: *What is Indigenous Truth and Reconciliation? (And How Can Indigenous and Non-Indigenous People Work Together to Achieve It?)* Okay, now. Any questions?"

The students resume talking to each other and the background noise rises in a steady crescendo. A middle-aged woman with curly, strawberry-blonde hair raises her hand and Dr. Sanderson nods to her.

"Your name and your question?" he asks.

"My name is Katya. How much information do you expect us to cover?" she asks, with a noticeable German accent. "It seems like a lot, especially when most of us haven't studied any of these topics. For instance, I've got the reconciliation question, and I wouldn't know where to start on such a big topic. How long will our presentations be?"

"Good questions. You're only going to have forty-five minutes per group for your presentation, so you will only have time to cover the major points in that amount of time. But I expect much more detail in your reports."

Dr. Sanderson pauses and moves back toward the middle of his platform.

"As for the second part of your question, remember that this is a team building project. I don't expect that you'll all become experts on your topic. I'm more interested in how you organize your team, your report, and your presentation, and in how well your team is applying the course material along the way. We want to see how well you listen to each other, whether you can learn to trust your teammates, whether you can reach a consensus, and whether you can all commit to the same goals."

The grumbling and discontent grow louder again.

"Oh, that reminds me … I forgot to introduce your TA, Samantha Bower, one of my grad students. She'll be running the tutorial session and will be grading your participation in your team's project. Would you stand up, Sam?"

He motions to me. But as I rise from my seat, I bump my overstuffed bag that's balanced precariously on the tiny desk. It hits the floor with a thud and spreads its contents … books, pens, phone, tampons, and sheaves of paper over the floor.

Nice work, Sam! Way to make a good first impression!

I hear the whispers and laughter from the upper rows, most of it expressing dismay that they're going to have to put up with me as their TA for the term. The heat in my face tells me I'm already crimson with embarrassment. I turn to face the class and give a timid wave, while I try to think of a way to salvage the situation.

"Just call me Sam," I say meekly. "I guess I'll be meeting you all next week in the first tutorial session … does anybody have any questions about the tutorial?"

Really? … That was so lame! … Is that the best you could do for a first impression?

I see a middle-aged, African-American woman with her hand raised. Eager to shift attention away from the mess I've just made, I point to her.

"Let's start with you, up there," I say.

"My name is Shanise. I work during the day, so I'm wondering if you have later office hours, in case any of us need some individual help?

"Good question," I reply. "I'll be available in my office for the hour just before the lecture each week. However, if you can't make it then, I'll hang around for a few minutes after each week's tutorial."

Feeling like the flush is slowly leaving my face, I feel a semblance of confidence returning. A young, darker-skinned man with curly black hair, raises his hand and I acknowledge him.

"I'm Uri," he says, with a noticeable Middle-Eastern accent. "Are we expected to stay for the entire two hours of the tutorial?"

"Another good question," I reply. "And the short answer is yes. Each team will get thirty minutes to meet with me every week, so I can answer questions and give you some guidance. The schedule will rotate, so some weeks you'll meet with me first, but other weeks I'm afraid you'll have to stay later. And when you're not meeting with me, we expect your team to use the time to work together on your project."

Groaning and grumbling starts to fill the room again.

"We're sorry for that," I add, raising my voice to be heard over the din. "But we understand that this is a night class, and many of you, like Shanise, work and have different course schedules. So we thought the easiest time to meet with your teammates would be after the lecture, during the tutorial session, when you're not meeting with me."

I see Dr. Sanderson pointing to his watch.

"If you have more questions, you can ask them when we meet next week," I say, then I nod at Eric to take over.

"Thanks, Sam. The first lecture and tutorial will be next Tuesday. Be ready to get down to work then, since you'll only have twelve more weeks until your presentations. If you don't have the handout showing which team you're on, I still have a few on the table down here. See you all next week!"

As students rise from their seats and start talking, I kneel down to gather my belongings, grateful that my first shaky appearance as a teaching assistant is now behind me.

STUDENTS CONTINUE to file out of the lecture hall while I'm still crawling around the floor, gathering my belongings and stuffing them back into my bag. As the room thins out, the noise levels gradually lessen.

Behind me in the second row, I see a young Indigenous man with twin braids of long black hair, and a middle-aged, blonde caucasian woman seated beside him, looking at each other and rolling their eyes. Unaware of the room's perfect acoustics, they start whispering about me.

"Are you kidding," the young man whispers. "That klutz is supposed to help *us*?"

"Hard to believe!" the woman whispers. "By the way, my name's Terri. What team are you on?"

"I'm Hunter. I'm on the reconciliation team. I wonder if Sanderson knew I was Indigenous when he picked the teams?"

Terri smiles and chuckles quietly. "That *is* funny! I'm on the reconciliation team too. Looks like we're going to be teammates."

I'm finally finished filling my bag, so I sling it over my shoulder and start making my way up the stairs towards the top of the lecture theatre.

You don't think I can hear you, do you? Something tells me that you two aren't going to make things easy for me this term!

Hunter gives me a furtive glance as I climb the stairs.

"How much do you suppose Sam knows about reconciliation?" he asks Terri.

She shrugs her shoulders and shakes her head as she looks in my direction.

"I don't know. How much do any of us really know about it?"

CHAPTER 2—WEEK TWO

HAVE YOU ever promised yourself that you'll never do something again, and then found yourself doing it again anyway? How does that even happen? I don't know how many times I've promised that I'm done with Diane, my biological mother. And yet, here I stand outside the old red brick, Sixties-era quadriplex, where she lives … if that's how you'd care to describe her existence. The instant I pull up in front of the building, I feel my heart pounding in my chest and every muscle in my body starts to tremble. The feeling is so aversive, I feel like putting the car back in gear and driving away.

And yet, I find myself walking up the sidewalk towards her apartment building, like a lemming being drawn towards the ocean. I press the intercom button and wait. Moments later, it finally buzzes and I hear a click as the front door unlocks and grants me entry. I descend a stairway to the ground level apartments, and then walk down a dark hallway where all but one of the fluorescent lighting fixtures on the ceiling are either flickering continuously, or burnt out. The odour in the hallway is a stomach-turning mixture of mold, old urine, and rancid cooking oil. I reach the end of the hallway and stop in front of the last apartment on my left. My heart continues to race and I feel my stomach churning as I stand in front of the door, torn between knocking and running away. Finally, I force one of my sweaty hands to knock.

"Door's open!" Diane shouts.

Reluctantly, I wipe my hand on my jeans, then I pull my hand back up into the sleeve of my sweater, allowing only the garment to touch the grimy looking doorknob. I give it a twist and, against my better judgment, enter the dragon's den. I see cigarette smoke coming from the kitchen, so I walk towards it, stopping as I reach the kitchen's entrance. My eyes scan the kitchen, and then Diane, leaving me in a state of disbelief.

She's a withered, grey-haired woman who looks at least ten years older than her real age of forty-five. I watch as she sits at her kitchen table with a cigarette dangling from her mouth. Empty liquor bottles line the counter, dishes are piled high in the sink, and the table is piled high with stacks of old mail and assorted paperwork, leaving only enough room for her glass, a bottle of rye, and a filthy plate for her ashes. The apartment reeks of a combination of old sweat, old urine, and stale cigarette smoke that makes my stomach want to heave.

"I told you I can't stay long, Diane," I say. "What was so important that I had to come over right away?"

"Grab yerself a glass an' pour a drink," she slurs. "Pull up a chair'n stay fer a while."

"Not today. I have to get to a meeting," I lie.

I really need to get out of this place before I vomit!

"That how ya treat yer ole' ma, 'specially after all I've done fer ya?" she answers.

"All you've done for me! When?" I retort. "You've never been a mother to me. Never! Name one good thing you've ever done that wasn't for yourself. All you ever did was beat a defenceless young child, leave me home alone all day, and then tell me you wished I was never born! You call that parenting?"

"Ya don' understan' nothin'! Ya don' know how hard it was fer me after yer no-good father walked out an' left me high 'n dry," Diane moans. She reaches for the bottle of rye and pours herself a refill. An ash falls from her cigarette and lands in her lap. She sweeps the hot ashes off her lap and onto the grimy floor.

"Here we go again!" I shout. "More of your 'poor me' sob stories! I'm not going to waste any time listening to you blame me and the rest of the world for your problems!"

"Ya know yer just an ungrateful li'l bitch," Diane slurs. "Can't even take a li'l time now 'n then t'come visit yer ol' ma!"

"Enough of the guilt trips!" I shoot back. "I thank God every day that Children's Services took me away to live with Uncle Bob and Aunt Melanie. They adopted me and took care of me. They'll always be my mom and dad! So, if you only called me over for another guilt trip, I'm not interested. I have more important things to do!"

Diane flicks another long ash from her cigarette onto the dirty plate, then she starts rooting around in a stack of paper on the table. She finally seems to find what she's looking for, and tosses a scrap of paper onto the table for me.

"What's this?" I ask.

"Don' say I never done nuthin' fer ya!" Diane answers. "Ya said ya wanted t'know who yer father is. That phone number's fer his sister. She still lives up north on the reserve."

The words seem to take an eternity to sink in. I'm completely speechless while my brain tries to process this new piece of information.

"Wha'sa matter? Diane cackles. "Cat gotcher tongue?"

She genuinely seems to enjoy this ... seeing me in a state of shock.

"Yer dad's Native ... Ojibwe ... don' know if he's alive, an' I don' fuckin' care," she says, and then she chortles. "Good luck trying' t'find the useless bastard!"

A STEADY STREAM of tears runs down my face, as I lean forward, head in hands, on the couch in Barbara Way's office. I'm sobbing so hard that I'm gasping for breath. I can't stop rocking involuntarily back and forth … the rhythm is strangely soothing … the only thing that's holding me together at the moment.

"It means I'm half Ojibwe!" I blurt between sobs. "Don't you see? … it could explain … that weird feeling … that emptiness … that's always been there … something missing … from my life."

"Let's slow things down, Sam," Barbara says. Her voice is calm and soothing, while her words are slow and reassuring. "Try taking deeper breaths to slow your breathing … you can do it …"

"I've been … having flashbacks," I say, still rocking back and forth slowly and still gasping for breath. "I can't explain … I think they're from … earlier … before Diane … before the beatings … they're not clear …"

Barbara purposely slows her breathing, setting a rhythm that my subconscious starts to follow.

"… Just dark shadows … crashing sounds … screaming … I'm so afraid," I continue.

Without knowing it, I've fallen into Barbara's rhythm of breathing. My breathing and my words are coming more easily, but the tears continue to stream down my face.

"I haven't stopped shaking … and crying … for two days," I tell her. "Haven't been to school … can't miss any more … please help me! …"

Barbara remains perfectly calm. Nothing I say or do seems to rattle her. She continues to talk in her slow, rhythmic monotone, always soothing and reassuring. I close my eyes and concentrate on my breathing. As it gradually slows, my sobbing and gasping start to subside.

"Just focus on your breathing … that's it … you're doing great … we're just going to do some things to help calm and stabilize you today … try to let yourself go to your safe place now," Barbara suggests. "Can you do that?"

I nod silently.

"How old do you feel?" she asks.

I frown and wrinkle my forehead, letting Barbara's question sink in.

"About three?" I say, as my brain tries to process the question.

"Is your survivor voice present there now?" she asks.

I nod again. I feel my panic slowly subsiding, as if somebody is opening a heavy, black curtain that's been shrouding my mind.

"How is she feeling right now?"

"Better … I'm not shaking or crying anymore," I answer.

"Which of your voices were shaking or crying?" Dr. Way presses gently.

I pause again as my brain sifts through my various inner voices.

"… I'm not sure …," I finally reply.

"Was it any of the voices you've talked about before? Was it three-year-old Sam?" she asks.

"… No … I think it's a new voice," I say. My voice sounds tiny, timid and afraid.

"How old does that voice feel?" Barbara asks.

" … So young … she can't explain … can't talk … she sees dark shadows … hears crashing and screaming … so afraid …"

"What does that little voice need right now, Sam?"

I go silent while my young self processes Barbara's question.

" … Somebody to hold her …," I answer timidly.

"Does one of your other voices feel like holding that little girl?" Dr. Way asks.

More silence. Finally my three-year-old speaks.

" … My caregiver?" She says tentatively.

"Can you imagine your caregiver taking that little girl in her arms … holding her … rocking her?"

My inner caregiver does as Barbara suggests. I imagine her holding my tiny, inner self. My sobs have slowed and turned into occasional tiny sniffles. My rocking motion has transformed into a slower, more subtle, and more relaxed rocking motion. My breathing feels more stable. I feel Barbara's presence, but I feel her giving me time to process the sensation of having that small, inner voice being held by my inner caregiver. Slowly and gradually, I feel a sense of peacefulness and calm settling over my body.

Finally, Barbara breaks the silence.

"You've done some really difficult work today. Does the three-year-old voice, and this very young new voice, feel calm enough to leave your safe place, and come back into the room with me?" she asks.

I pause while I check in with my assorted dissociative voices.

" … Yes … they feel okay now."

"Okay, then … just continue to take those nice slow breaths … and you can open your eyes whenever you feel ready …," Barbara says calmly.

I open my eyes after a couple more breaths, feeling somewhat disoriented, while my eyes take in my surroundings and check back into the present time and place in Dr. Way's office.

How are you feeling now?" she asks.

"Better … thank you," I reply, sounding much more like my adult self.

"I know you were feeling like your world was falling apart when you came in today. So, before you go, can you tell me some of the positive things you have in your life?" Dr. Way asks.

I pause, giving my brain a chance to change gears. It takes a moment before I can think of anything positive.

"I still have Uncle Bob and Aunt Melanie," I answer. "They feel like my real mom and dad. I know they're still there for me when things get tough."

"That's good. Anything else?"

I pause again.

"Well, I'm still in school … and I still have you to talk to!"

"That's very true. And you know I'm here for you. You're probably still going to have some flashbacks over the next few days," she says. "So remember, if you find you can't manage them, promise me that you'll call me and we'll do some more stabilization."

"I promise. Thank you!"

"Things will get better, Sam. If you're patient and you keep using all the skills you've learned, you'll be able to make it through this term. Maybe next week, if you're feeling up to it, we can spend some time talking about whether or not you're going to contact your aunt about your father."

I gather my jacket and bag, and start getting to my feet.

"I suppose so," I say reluctantly. "Thanks for being here for me. I'll see you next week."

I open the door and exit Barbara's office. As the door closes behind me, I stop and take a long, deep breath. I feel as if I've just run a marathon, so I push any further thoughts of contacting my biological dad aside for now.

I'm going to need a lot more than a week to build up my courage, before I'm ready to face that challenge.

I GLANCE at my watch as I walk through the Social Sciences Building toward my tutorial classroom. Eight-thirty … three teams down, with only Team Reconciliation to go before my first tutorial evening is over. In my other hand, I carry a large double-double coffee, intended to get me through this final meeting of the night.

I pause outside the door. This classroom and I have a history. The room itself is about the size of a small boardroom, with an oval-shaped table large enough to seat about ten people. But it's an inner office, with no windows and terrible ventilation. Once the door closes, if there are nine or ten people in the room consuming oxygen … well, let's just say I've been known to nod off during lectures. The walls are painted the same institutional light grey as Barbara Way's office, and the off-white conference table adds nothing to the decor that might help to keep people awake. The only other objects in the room are a tabletop lectern made of light birch, a pull-down projection screen, and a utilitarian grey cart with a portable projector chained to it. The fluorescent lighting fixtures contain cold white bulbs that are hard on the eyes, and their nearly subliminal buzzing sound creates an almost perfect ingredient for a catnap.

I take a breath, open the door, and walk into the room, putting my coffee on the table beside the lectern, which I then pick up and place on the floor in the corner of the room. I'm just here to supervise, not to lecture.

"Hello, everybody," I say. "Good to finally meet all of you in person."

A quick headcount tells me that everybody is present, except one. It doesn't take long to figure out that the missing team member is Hunter, one of the two students who were dissing me last week. Call me paranoid, but I've had an ominous feeling all week about Hunter and Terri—that their attitudes might spell trouble for the team and me.

"Let's give it a few more minutes until the team is all here," I say. A prolonged silence fills the room, and I note everybody's discomfort. While we wait, I can't stop my mind from drifting and thinking about phoning the number Diane gave me.

Why can't I get that man out of my mind? ... What if he wants to meet me? ... Or worse, what if he doesn't?

I push thoughts of finding my father aside and I see that nobody amongst the seven team members appears ready to break the ice. The silence is becoming unbearable.

I glance at my watch again and note that we've all been waiting for over five minutes, so I decide to start the meeting without Hunter. But, sure enough, just as I get ready to start, the door opens. He saunters into the room, taking a seat to my right, so I give him a moment to get settled.

"Welcome, everybody!" I say cheerily. "It looks like we're all here now, so let's begin. Like I said last week, I'm Sam, your TA. I thought we could start things off by introducing ourselves … maybe telling the team where we're from and what we're studying. I'll go first, and then we'll go around the table … so, I'm in my second year of grad studies in industrial/organizational psychology, and Dr. Sanderson is my supervisor. I grew up here in the city."

I turn and nod to Hunter. He pauses for a moment to think, then he clears his throat.

"My name is Hunter, and I'm Haudenosaunee, from the Six Nations of the Grand River. I spent six years with the Canadian Forces, first in Afghanistan, and then in Northern Iraq, helping the Kurds fight ISIS. I'm in pre-law, and I'm interested in Constitutional Law as it relates to my Indigenous people."

The remaining team members are quiet, looking around the table at each other. I see a mix of different emotions on their faces, given the team's reconciliation-related topic: surprise, understanding, and even appreciation, but the room remains quiet. I jump in to break the awkward silence.

"Thanks for sharing that with us," I respond. "And welcome to the team. With your background, and with your academic interests and goals, I'm sure we're all going to benefit from your perspective on this project … now, who's next?"

I nod to a tall, slim, brown-skinned man in his early twenties with black hair, seated on Hunter's right.

"I'm Arjun," he says. "My parents immigrated here from India when I was just a kid. They both worked two jobs while I was growing up, so they could give us a better life and a better education. Now I'm in my second year of pre-med."

"Thanks, Arjun," I say. "Welcome to the team … and the lady next to you?"

I look to a middle-aged woman with dark complexion and a multi-coloured hijab, which covers her shoulder-length black hair. Streaks of grey show in some exposed areas of hair around her face.

"I am Fatima. I study history part-time, and I am particularly interested in Middle Eastern history. My husband and I are from Northern Iraq. We immigrated to Canada when we saw what ISIS was going to do to our country. We are fortunate to have a fast food business that keeps us very busy."

Fatima turns to Hunter and makes eye contact with him.

"We thank you so much for what you did to fight ISIS, and to help the people in our homeland," she says. She holds her hand over her heart and nods to Hunter in a gesture of appreciation.

"Thanks for sharing, Fatima," I say. "Welcome to the team … who's next?"

Seated next to Fatima, I notice the curly-haired, blonde, middle-aged woman who stood to ask questions in last week's introductory lecture, with her German accent.

"I'm Katya," she says. "I came to Canada from East Germany with my husband in 1989, when the Berlin Wall came down. My husband is an engineer, and I stayed home to raise our two children. I'm here because now it's my time to go to university. My goal is to get a degree in psychology."

I notice that the team members gradually seem to be feeling more comfortable with each other. Some of them, especially the women, applaud lightly to show their support for Katya. I feel pleased to see them starting to come together.

"Welcome, Katya," I add. I look across the table at a tall, slender, Asian woman in her early twenties, seated next to Katya. She has long, straight, dark hair and brown eyes. "Next?"

"My name is Mandy. I am from Hong Kong and I am in my second year, studying anthropology and history. My parents have bought a home in Canada, and they will hopefully be moving here to join me as soon as their status is approved.

"Welcome, Mandy," I reply. "Thanks for sharing."

The next team member is a tall, middle-aged African-American woman with long, dark hair woven into dreadlocks. I remember her from last week's initial lecture, and I give her a nod to proceed.

"I'm Shanise," she says. "I work full-time in the HR department of a large insurance company. I'm taking this course to learn more about how we can improve teamwork in our workplace. I came to Canada with my husband from Curaćao twenty-five years ago, so we could give a better life to our children."

"Thank you and welcome, Shanise," I answer.

I recognize the next team member as the tall, blonde woman with a ponytail who was dissing me, along with Hunter, at last week's lecture. Although she is middle-aged, she is slender and in excellent physical shape. Her blonde ponytail makes her look a good five to ten years younger than her likely age.

"I'm Teresa," she begins. "But you can all call me Terri. I own a dance studio in Edmonton, but my husband just started a two-year Oral Surgery program here at the Dental College. I never had a chance to go to university when I was young, so I figured 'What the Hell!', and here I am."

"Welcome to the university and the team, Terri," I reply. "Okay, last but not least …"

I acknowledge the young man to my left, who has darker skin and dark curly hair. I also recognize him as one of the students who asked questions in last week's lecture.

"I'm Uri," he says. "I come from Israel and I'm in my second year, studying physics. Besides school, I enjoy astronomy, science fiction, and going to nightclubs."

"Thank you, Uri," I answer. "Welcome to the team."

I pause and take a deep breath, feeling a sense of relief.

Well, that went better than I thought! Maybe this group isn't the school of piraña I thought they might be!

"So, before I turn the session over to you folks to start organizing your team, are there any comments or questions?"

Terri puts up her hand, and I acknowledge her with a nod.

"I'd just like to say to Hunter that I'm appalled and disgusted by everything that happened to all those children at the residential schools! I'm just glad that they're all closed now, so everybody can move on and put that behind us!"

I see the other team members, apart from Hunter, nodding and expressing their agreement together. Then I turn to Hunter on my right, and I see my first signs of trouble. His jaw muscles are tense and I see fire in his eyes.

Uh, oh! I knew this was too good to be true! Please ... No conflict!

I feel my own body tense, preparing for trouble. My feet and legs start to vibrate up and down in response to alarms of foreboding that are ringing throughout my body.

Hunter looks around the table at each team member, then starts shaking his head slowly from side to side.

"Truth and reconciliation is *not* just about the residential schools!" he begins. "It's about colonial oppression and the continuing efforts of the Canadian Government since 1867 to commit cultural genocide against Indigenous peoples! It's about the systemic racism that's built into the colonial government's systems for dealing with us! And above all, it's about the trauma that my people have suffered over the past seven generations since Confederation, and the healing that must take place before reconciliation can happen!"

I see Terri roll her eyes and hear her let out a large, audible huff. She jumps to her feet. My head starts pounding as my impending feelings of dread turn into reality.

"Come on, Hunter!" Terri shouts. "The residential schools are all closed now! Look around this table. We're all in agreement that what happened to your people in the past was wrong. But genocide? Really? Do we look like murderers who are trying to kill your people off?

Terri stops long enough to catch her breath.

"What our ancestors did was wrong. I get it! But I refuse to take responsibility or apologize for the sins of my forefathers! That's like asking me to go to prison for crimes my father committed. It's time to get over it and move on!"

I feel myself growing increasingly fidgety, agitated, and anxious as Hunter's voice grows louder.

"That's easy for you to say, with your European colonial privilege and your dance studio! Every one of you around this table is a privileged, entitled, settler on our lands!"

Hunter pauses to look around the table at each team member.

"You … Mr. Israeli … your country is the modern day example of colonial expansion, settling on the land of Palestinians! And you … from India and Hong Kong … your parents bring their money and their privilege here to settle on our traditional lands! And Katya, you escaped from hardship in Communist Germany, but look at what your European privilege has given you!"

I feel myself starting to panic. I feel like somebody is sitting on my chest, my heart is pounding, and my head is throbbing. My legs are vibrating up and down like a pair of out-of-control jackhammers. Somewhere in my brain, a voice is telling me to step in and stop the confrontation. But another part of me overrides it and orders me to freeze.

Please! Somebody make him stop!

Hunter continues his verbal bombardment, this time returning his focus to Arjun.

"And how would you have felt when you came to this country as a child, if the Government had taken you away from your parents? … If they taught you that your parents … your language … your customs … were worthless?"

Finally, Hunter turns his attention to Fatima and unleashes his wrath on her.

"And you," Hunter shouts. "I feel sick that I went to Afghanistan and your country to protect people, and I witnessed no end of horrific shit, only to come home and see privileged settlers like you building wealth! Meanwhile, my people are still living as second-class citizens, many of them in poverty, with no hope for the future!"

Hunter pauses his barrage to take a breath, then continues his assault on Fatima.

"How would you feel if the Government showed up on your doorstep and took your children away tomorrow?" he continues. "There can be no reconciliation until you settlers understand the truth, join us in our grieving, and help with our healing!"

Their voices are growing more distant and I feel as if my mind is starting to check out of the room. Terrifying flashbacks of adults, arguing and fighting, are forcing their way into my consciousness, and I feel helpless to stop them.

"Stop trying to bully us into your version of reconciliation!" Terri shouts back. "We know what happened in those schools! You don't have to beat us over the head with story after story. We're not stupid! We get it, and we'll grieve it in our own way!"

Run, Sam! ... Hide! ... Make it all stop!

I feel completely disconnected from my body, which is in the midst of a full-blown panic attack. I feel myself pushing back my chair, jumping to my feet, throwing open the door and running into the hallway, unaware of where my feet are taking me … not caring, as long as it's far away from the shouting!

Team Reconciliation stares in disbelief as I flee the room.

"What's happening?" Terri asks. "What's wrong with her?"

I FEEL like somebody's sitting on my chest as I burst through the door into the washroom. I need air, but I can't take the deep breath I really need. Instead, I feel myself starting to hyperventilate. I hear myself reciting Barbara Way's words in my head.

Slow down your breathing ... Talk to yourself ... Positive thoughts ... Nothing dangerous is happening ... Reassuring thoughts ...

I feel like a fool as I start talking out loud to myself between gasps.

"You can't let ... Hunter's arguing ... trigger you ... this way," I hear myself saying. I finally manage a breath that is slightly slower and deeper.

"... he's got ... nothing to do ... with the dark shadows ... the scary sounds ... from the past ...," I continue.

I take another slightly slower and deeper breath. I feel the weight starting to ease slowly off my chest. I struggle to keep my mind from straying back into the distant past.

"... maybe ... finding my father ... just too much ... right now ..."

I'm still struggling, but I feel my breathing starting to slow. I hear a distant voice ... my survivor voice ... calling to me from somewhere deep inside.

Keep talking ... More reassuring thoughts ... You can manage the panic ...

I continue talking out loud to myself.

"You can't afford ... any more time off school ... you have to help those students succeed ... you can get through this ... you can get your doctorate ... you *can* be a professor someday ... just focus on the present ... nothing bad is happening right now!"

The washroom door opens unexpectedly. My body starts and I inhale sharply. I recognize Shanise from Team Reconciliation.

"Are you alright, Sam? What's going on?" she asks. Her face shows genuine concern.

I feel my face flushing with embarrassment. A pregnant silence ensues as I search for words.

"I guess ... I guess that argument was just getting too intense for me ... I've never been good when people argue," I tell her.

"Was it Hunter?" she asks. "Did you feel like he was bullying everybody? Is that what caused you to leave?"

I nod in agreement, but I'm still too embarrassed to make eye contact with Shanise.

"I think I know how you feel," she continues. "I've suffered from PTSD and panic attacks before, mostly because of bullying and discrimination in my workplace. I felt myself getting triggered by Hunter too."

I still can't force myself to make eye contact with Shanise. Instead, I look in the mirror, turn on a faucet, and start splashing water on my face. I turn off the water, reach for a paper towel, and begin blotting water from my face.

"Yes … maybe … but I'm feeling better now," I answer. "Thanks for asking …"

I quickly blot the remaining water from my face with the paper towel, throw the wet towel into the trash, and rush towards the washroom door. I just need to be alone right now.

CHAPTER 3—WEEK THREE

I STILL can't believe how severely I've been affected by Hunter's angry outburst the other night … not only by the panic that it triggered and how quickly things spun out of control, but by the terrifying, dark memories from my past that took over complete control of my mind. I think that was the scariest part of it all … that it happened instantaneously … and that I had no control over what was going on in my brain. I hate feeling that much out of control … I think it's probably the worst feeling I've ever experienced! If anybody, including Barbara Way, had told me how much present day events could trigger those dark memories from my past, I never would have believed them. But the events of the past few days have definitely made a believer out of me!

"I'm proud of you," Barbara says. "I think you did a great job of using the tools that you've learned, to manage your panic!"

"Thanks," I reply self-consciously. "But it sure didn't feel that way at the time."

"You can't expect yourself to end the panic attacks completely yet," she cautions. "It takes practice. But once you get more confidence that your tools work, you'll find that it gradually gets easier."

I find myself nodding, trying to share her optimism.

"I sure hope so," I reply.

An awkward silence fills the room while Barbara waits for me to say more. Finally, she breaks the silence.

"Have you been thinking much this week about whether you might start looking for your father?" she asks.

I knew you were going to ask that question again ... Didn't I tell you already that I don't have time this term?

"Actually, I don't know why I ever thought I wanted to find him," I answer. "He abandoned me and left me with Diane. He had to know that she was beating me and leaving me alone without enough to eat! Who would do that to their little girl?"

I feel my eyes watering. A tear manages to escape onto my cheek before I can wipe it away.

"It's natural to feel angry … or to feel sad," she replies. "In fact, it would be natural for you to feel a lot of mixed emotions from your inner voices …they can be extremely confusing at times."

"I'm not sad, I'm just angry!" I retort. "I don't understand why I ever wanted to reach out to him in the first place, when all he did was shut me out of his life, and leave me with that self-absorbed witch!"

"It's up to you whether you decide to meet him or not," she responds, her voice remaining as calm and reassuring as ever. "I'm certainly not going to force you to do something you're not ready to do."

"Thank you!" I say, before giving a defiant huff.

"But, I'll leave you with one word of advice to consider," Barbara continues.

I knew it ... There always has to be a 'but' ... Why do we have to complicate things?

"You need to know that avoiding a big issue like this could very likely stall your progress in therapy, or even cause you to regress. And that would be too bad, especially since you've made such good progress lately."

I feel myself starting to feel pressured, and I feel the anxiety starting to mount inside. My brain looks for a way to escape the situation. I find myself abruptly getting to my feet and grabbing my bag.

"I have no use for that man!" I shout. "I won't do it! I don't want to talk about it anymore! I'll see you next week … maybe! …"

The fearful and angry parts of me are pissed at Barbara for pressing me on the issue. And I feel guilty … why do I always feel like there's something wrong with me? But, on the other hand, my survivor voice knows Barbara's right. And that just pisses me off even more and leaves me feeling embarrassed. I avoid eye contact as I stomp out of her office.

I'M TRYING desperately to keep my feet and legs from vibrating and giving away my anxiety. I look around the table at the members of Team Reconciliation, noting the obvious absence of Hunter. My eyes shift to Terri, looking for clues as to her current state of mind. If she's still harbouring any animosity towards Hunter, it's too soon to tell, given his absence. I watch as she talks and laughs with Katya and Fatima. I rehearse my planned script for the session in my head, then I take a deep breath.

"As you've learned in Dr. Sanderson's lectures," I begin. "It's important for teams to learn how to feel comfortable expressing differing opinions, and how to deal with conflict. And, because I'm sitting in on your team meetings, that goes for me as well."

The door to the classroom opens and Hunter strides into the room. I can't help but notice Uri, Terri, and Mandy looking at each other and rolling their eyes. Hunter takes a vacant seat across the table from me.

"So, before you get on with setting up an organizational structure for your team, I'd like to take a few minutes to finish last week's very animated discussion," I continue. "But hopefully, we can proceed this week with more emphasis on listening to each other."

I feel the strain in my chest and limbs as I move my eyes towards Hunter and make eye contact. I try to take a deep breath, but it's anything but smooth. My tense breathing muscles stretch open grudgingly, and then close in a jerky motion, reminiscent of my first inept attempts at driving with a clutch.

"Hunter ... would you like to start?" I ask. "If reconciliation isn't just about the residential schools, what does it mean to you?"

Hunter inhales deeply and looks around the table, stopping to gauge Terri's reaction. He remains seated and seems intent on speaking more calmly to his teammates.

"Thanks," he replies. "For me, reconciliation covers a lot of issues, especially addressing the inherent Indigenous rights to lands we've lived on since time immemorial, and also our rights to self-government, that are both entrenched in the U.N. Declaration."

He pauses to look around the table, before taking another breath and continuing.

"Most importantly, it means decolonizing the way the Canadian Government deals with Indigenous peoples, and ending the policy of cultural genocide."

I look around the table at the rest of the team. Everybody still looks calm and rational.

That wasn't so bad!

I allow myself to let out a sigh of relief.

"Alright, thanks Hunter," I answer. "So what does the team think of Hunter's perspective? ... Mandy? Any comments?"

"Hunter, I'm interested in your claim that Indigenous people have lived on your land since time immemorial. Recent genetic evidence appears to contradict that claim, showing that Indigenous peoples are genetically related to people from Northeast Asia."

Mandy looks at me to see if she should continue. I nod, giving her the go-ahead.

"So, it may be more correct to call your people the 'first migrants' or 'first colonists' of the Americas. Can you comment?"

Hunter's eyes narrow and I notice his facial muscles beginning to tense. He starts to rise from his seat to address Mandy.

"Just a minute, Hunter," I interject. "Can we hear from the rest of the team first? You'll have a chance to address their comments later, okay?"

He reluctantly takes his seat, but it's clear from his body language that he's not happy and his anger is building. I also notice the tension starting to build again in my body.

"Anybody else?" I ask.

Katya puts up her hand.

"Go ahead, Katya."

"I was also offended last week when you called me a privileged settler. You have no idea what it is like to live under a Communist government, or what it is like to leave your own country to start your life over, with only a suitcase and a few thousand dollars in your pocket! I am proud to be an immigrant, and I am proud to have built a new life in Canada from practically nothing!"

Before I can respond, Shanise jumps into the conversation. The discussion is starting to feel like a runaway train.

"I also object to you referring to me as a 'settler', when you know that my ancestors were brought here against their will to be slaves!"

I see Hunter's facial muscles starting to bulge, and his face turning red. I feel my own body tensing and starting to freeze once again. My mind is drifting and voices are starting to sound distant.

"Hey, everybody," Uri answers. "Don't you think you're being a bit hard on Hunter? After all, his people were here first, regardless where they might have come from. It's like in Israel … Jewish people just want to live in the land that was given to us by God."

"Surely, you are not going to use your Zionist views to justify Israel displacing millions of Palestinians from their homes!" Fatima shouts.

"I agree with Fatima," Hunter answers, his voice booming over the others. "Make up your mind, Uri! If you agree that Indigenous people occupied their lands first, then you can't possibly condone Israel's policy of cultural genocide against the Palestinians! They were living there long before shiploads of Jewish war refugees re-colonized it!"

"Aren't you throwing around the word *genocide* rather loosely, Hunter?" Arjun interjects. "To me, that sounds a lot like the pot calling the kettle black, when you consider that the Iroquois almost completely wiped out the Huron people in the seventeenth century."

No longer able to contain his anger, Hunter leaps to his feet.

"This is all bullshit!" he yells. "Organize yourselves! I won't be part of this racist, colonial crap!"

In the distance, I hear Terri shouting.

"Don't you dare walk out on us again!"

My mind is already checked out and I'm powerless to stop it. I'm vaguely aware of Hunter grabbing his things and stomping out of the classroom, slamming the door behind him. As it slams, another wave of sounds and images from the distant past floods into my mind … a man's bellowing … dark shadows … breaking glass … a woman screaming … cries of pain …

Make it stop! … Please, make it stop! …

I feel my body jumping up from my seat and rushing to the door. It opens the door, bolts from the room, and runs out into the hallway again. I leave the rest of the team behind me, deeply divided and in stunned silence, for a second week in a row.

I'M FIGHTING a losing battle against the panic that has taken control of my brain and body. In the washroom's mirror, I see myself pacing back and forth frantically, sweating heavily, fanning myself, and struggling to breathe. I try to bring up pictures of

Barbara Way, trying to remember the skills she taught me. I keep trying to take deep breaths, but my breathing muscles are clamped tight. I feel like I'm going to suffocate and my panic only worsens. Somewhere deep in my consciousness, Barbara's distant voice is telling me to talk to myself. But my inner voices are in chaos, unable to hear her words.

I try to keep my eyes glued to the image of myself in the mirror. If I don't, the flashbacks renew their attempts to creep in and take control over my consciousness. I see glimpses of those dark shadows and keep catching fragments of sound clips from the past … breaking glass … cries of pain … and then the worst of all … silence … and with the silence comes an overpowering sense of loneliness.

I hear a tiny, distant voice … a small child …

Mama? … Mama? … Where are you?

I hear that tiny voice sobbing with despair and I feel overwhelmed by a sense of combined loneliness and fear.

I stare into the mirror again, desperately trying to find a way to anchor myself back in the present. Seeing the taps, I turn on the cold water, lean over the sink, and start splashing cold water over my face.

But my attempt to bring myself back to reality, and to control my panic, fails miserably. I'm still gasping, trying to snatch short breaths of precious oxygen, but I'm losing the battle. New images and feelings penetrate the dark shadows in my mind.

The tiny, sobbing voice won't leave … my body feels rigid and cold … I feel myself shivering … I feel hunger deep in the pit of my stomach … the feeling grows stronger and more aversive … I feel it transforming into nausea …

The feeling of nausea continues to grow … smaller waves gradually picking up momentum … I feel like I'm a small ship, being tossed and battered mercilessly by a storm that is unabating …

Suddenly, I feel myself wheeling away from the mirror … my legs start moving beneath me … I'm running … throwing open the door of a cubicle … dropping to the floor … staring down into a giant white porcelain bowl … just as I feel the wave of vomit erupting …

I retch wave after wave of vomit, until there's nothing left but dry heaves. Only then, do I feel the panic slowly releasing its intense grip over my body and mind. My body starts to relax, and I finally feel small breaths of cool, fresh air finding their way into my lungs. I rest my head on the cold, porcelain rim of the toilet … and I hear myself beginning to weep.

As the panic in my body slowly recedes, it is replaced by a single overwhelming feeling … I feel totally isolated and alone … weeping uncontrollably … my loneliness inconsolable.

I STILL haven't recovered completely from last night's panic attack. Okay, I know it was more than just a panic attack. Barbara Way would have called it a dissociative episode. It's her clinical way of saying that I came unglued again in front of my students. I feel completely embarrassed to be sitting in Eric Sanderson's office, unable to make eye contact with my supervisor. My body is tense and I feel my feet and legs vibrating up and down rapidly.

My eyes survey Eric's office as he takes a seat at his desk. He makes a weak attempt to clear some of the mess from his desktop. His office is a disaster. The bookshelves in his office have been overfilled for years. Stacks of books and scientific journals fill the space between the bookshelves and ceiling, while other stacks take up most of the room's floor space. In short, Eric is a legitimate hoarder of knowledge. Visitors to the office have to find their own path through the stacks in order to gain access to the only other chair in the room, apart from Eric's.

"I don't think I can do it, Eric!" I blurt. "The reconciliation team is out of control! I don't think I can bring them together!"

I pause, making a conscious attempt to slow my breathing. I know that if I try to take a breath that is too deep, I risk having my breathing muscles tense up again, possibly triggering another panic attack. As my breathing slows, I muster the courage to tell Eric the whole story.

"But that's not the only thing that's going on," I say. "I found out recently that I'm actually half Indigenous myself. My biological father, a man who abandoned me in childhood, is Ojibwe … Anishinaabe."

Eric raises his eyebrows, and I finally find the courage to look him in the eyes.

"Really!" he exclaims. "That's interesting, given that you're having such trouble with the reconciliation team. How do you feel about that?"

"I'm not sure yet," I answer. "I guess I feel confused. There's a lot of things for me to unpack now. First, there's anger … some days I'm really angry towards him. But, on other days I feel compelled to reach out to meet him. And then there's the whole Indigenous thing … never did I imagine that I would have some Indigenous blood in me … Barbara … er, Dr. Way … says it's natural to have a lot of conflicting emotions."

"I understand," Eric replies. "You've certainly got a lot of stress in your life these days. But, this is a critical year for you. You still have to decide on a thesis topic by Christmas."

"I know," I say meekly. I find myself looking down at my feet again, and I try to stop them from vibrating.

"And being my TA this term is a big test of how suitable you are for the I/O Psychology program. I'm expecting big things from you in mentoring the four project teams," he says.

"I'm doing okay with three of the teams," I answer, in my defence. "Because the COVID restrictions really polarized people, Team Pandemic has had to work through some disagreements. But they've managed to be respectful and to find places where they agree. It's only Team Reconciliation that can't agree on anything or work together. They haven't even organized their team, and we're almost at the end of September!"

Eric pauses. I watch him stroke his beard while he mulls things over.

"You're still continuing your therapy with Dr. Way, right?"

I nod my head. My legs continue to vibrate up and down while I wait to hear what Eric has to say.

"I'd like you to make sure you continue your therapy with Dr. Way. And I agree with her that you should think seriously about meeting your father. The longer you sit on the fence trying to make a decision, the more anxious you're going to become, and the more likely that you'll become paralyzed in your ability to make a decision. Does that make sense?"

"I guess … sort of," I reply.

"If you don't resolve this, one way or the other, it could very well interfere with your ability to fulfill your academic duties. Do you think you can do it?

I can't stop my legs from vibrating. I take a few seconds to gaze out the window while I think things over.

"I really don't know."

Eric pauses for a moment, and then exhales.

"How about taking it one small step at a time," he says. "What about just contacting your aunt first? What's the worst that could come from that?"

I take a moment to consider Eric's suggestion, my legs still vibrating rapidly.

"Not much, I guess."

"Okay, then," he answers. "Will you promise me that you'll at least try to do that?"

Finally, I swallow hard and force myself to look into Eric's eyes before I answer.

"I just don't know, Eric. I'll have to think about it."

CHAPTER 4—WEEK FOUR

I FOLLOW the signage that eventually leads me and my vintage Yaris into a gravel parking lot. To my left is a breathtaking view of Georgian Bay. The late September sky is deep blue, with occasional fluffy cumulus clouds dotting the sky. A few isolated patches of red and yellow leaves stand out against brilliant green hillsides and rocky cliffs along the shoreline. The lake is almost perfectly calm, reflecting a mirror image of the shoreline's autumn foliage.

I still can't believe I got up the courage to call Aunt Rose. But it was my talk with Eric that tipped the scales. He made me see the writing on the wall … if I don't get my act together this term, I'm finished in grad school … and I don't have a 'Plan B'. I have to face my past, or I risk having it torpedo my goals for the future.

I step from the car and I take a deep breath of crisp fall air, a subtle harbinger of what is to come over the following months. The mixed scents of the lake and the nearby forest bring my senses alive.

I turn around to gaze at the imposing, two-storey log structure behind me. The *Healing Lodge* is obviously relatively new, as the logs still retain much of their natural yellow-orange tint. The building's steel roof is rust in colour. Together, the roof and the logs blend into the forest beyond, with its early patches of yellow, orange, and red foliage. I also notice a number of small log cabins that appear to be clustered behind the lodge, at the edge of the forest. As I take in the beauty of the natural setting around me, I take a couple of deep breaths to gather my courage. Finally, I force my shaky legs to start walking towards the lodge, where I make my way tentatively up the front steps and into the building.

The air inside the lodge is just as calming as outdoors, with the fragrance of wood permeating the air. My olfactory senses also detect a distinct herbal, smokey scent … possibly sage … coming from my right, where there is a large gathering space with an open-beam ceiling that extends to the full height of the lodge. A group of about a dozen people are gathered in a circle around a woman who is conducting some kind of a ritual.

To my left, I see a gift shop where two women, one middle-aged and the other in her early twenties, are talking. I'm immediately attracted to the colourful articles of clothing and brilliant works of Indigenous art that adorn the clothing racks and walls of the shop. I gather myself and approach the two women.

"Ummh … can you help me?" I ask shyly. "I'm looking for Rose Sinclair. I was supposed to meet her this afternoon."

The middle-aged woman's face lights up in a warm smile.

"Boozhoo … Hello … I'm Rose," she replies. "You must be Samantha! Welcome to our *Healing Lodge*. Did you have a pleasant drive up here?"

Rose's voice is soothing, empathic, and motherly, and it has an immediate calming effect on me.

"Yes, I did," I answer. "The scenery was stunning and the traffic wasn't too bad."

"I'm glad to hear that. I'm sure that being here under these circumstances must be a bit overwhelming for you," she continues. "Can I show you around?"

"Thanks, I'd like that," I answer.

"We might as well start here with the gift shop," Rose begins. "We try, as much as we can, to feature local artisans and artists. If not from the immediate area, at least from First Nations within the province."

"Can I touch?" I ask.

Rose's face flashes another warm smile.

"Of course, dear. Be my guest."

I pick up a beautiful pair of high top moccasins, feeling the soft, smooth hide, the fur lining and trim, and admiring the intricate, colourful beadwork adorning the footwear. I raise one moccasin to my face and inhale the fragrance of the leather.

"They're so soft and they smell wonderful!" I gush.

"Don't they?" Rose says. "They're made by a local family. I couldn't resist having a pair of my own!"

I put the moccasins back on the shelf and gaze at the artwork on the walls.

"I love the art too!" I add. "Especially those … the ones showing the islands!"

Suddenly, I remember what I'd forgotten to bring with me today.

"I can't believe I didn't think to bring my good camera today. I need to come back some time so I can capture some of this area's natural beauty."

Rose places her hand gently on my shoulder.

"That would be lovely. You're welcome here anytime! Come," she says. "Let me show you the rest of our facilities."

Rose leads me out of the gift shop towards a staircase, and then she leads me up the stairs to a second floor balcony. I gaze out over the prayer circle that I'd seen on my way into the building. At this point, the group is singing traditional chants, and some of the group members are also playing traditional drums.

"When I came into the building, I saw a woman waving smoke over the other people with a feather. What's that for?" I ask.

"It's called smudging," Rose replies. "It helps to get rid of negative spiritual energy around you, that makes you feel uncomfortable, on edge, or afraid. It's a cleansing ceremony, often done to purify spaces, individuals, healers, and even ceremonial objects."

"It had a distinct fragrance," I add. "Do you know what that was?"

"That was sage," Rose answers. "In addition to getting rid of negative energy and bad spirits, it also has healing qualities. It's one of our four sacred medicines."

"What are the other three," I ask.

"Tobacco, sweetgrass, and cedar or cypress," she replies.

"And what's the significance of the feather?" I ask.

"It's a ceremonial object, but not necessary," Rose answers. "A person can use one's hands instead. They help to wave the smoke over the mouth and eyes, the head, the heart and body, and the ears. We usually combine it with prayer that states what needs to be cleansed, to express gratitude, or to help us speak directly to the spirits."

Most of the people here are healing from intergenerational trauma from the residential schools, like your father and me," Rose continues. "Smudging is part of the healing process."

Rose's words hit me like a falling brick, leaving me momentarily tongue-tied and wide-eyed. It never occurred to me that Rose and my father could have been residential school victims.

"You were both sent to the schools?" I ask.

"Yes," Rose answers. "I came back to my people to heal. But Charlie … your dad … he didn't do well back here, you know. He was angry and felt like he didn't belong anymore. He was drinking a lot and moved away to Toronto. I heard he met someone and had a daughter, but he never said anything to me about that."

"He and Diane, my mother, were both angry people," I explain. "There was a lot of arguing, fighting, and screaming when I was really young … I guess you'd say there was a whole lot of negative energy back then. Since I found out about him, I've started having a lot of scary flashbacks of those times. I haven't been doing well lately."

"I'm sorry to hear that, dear," Rose replies.

"What else do you do for healing here at the lodge?" I ask.

"We have two different programs, one focusing on survivors with alcohol or drug abuse problems, and the other focusing on survivors of sexual abuse. We have prayer circles, individual counselling, sweat lodge ceremonies, full moon ceremonies, and more," Rose replies.

"It all sounds really interesting," I say.

"We're a residential healing centre, " Rose continues, raising her arm and pointing to a number of doors along the second floor balcony. "We have a dozen rooms here in the main building, and a number of small group lodges outside. Follow me."

As Rose leads me back down the stairs to the main floor, I hear a healer talking to the people in the prayer circle. I don't recognize the language.

"Is she speaking Anishinaabe?" I ask.

"Yes, she's telling traditional stories in our language," Rose says. "We also have language programs here. It's one of the things that the residential schools tried to take from us."

We exit the building through a doorway at the rear of the lodge, emerging onto a grassy area where the smaller lodges are located.

"These lodges each sleep up to four people," Rose explains. "At the moment, we can house up to thirty survivors in the main lodge and these smaller lodges. It's not nearly enough. We keep asking for more funding from the Government so we can expand, but getting money from them for healing has been like pulling teeth."

Rose leads me towards a creek, where she turns onto a path that follows the creek into the forest.

"There is a small pond back here where we have the sweat lodge, and where we conduct other outdoor ceremonies," she says.

After a few moments, we emerge from the forest and into a clearing, where we come upon a dome-shaped structure beside the pond that's covered in a thick layer of blankets. Beside the dome, I notice a firepit surrounded by wooden benches.

"This is our sweat lodge," Rose explains. "A fire keeper tends the fire and uses it to superheat sacred stones from the creek. Then he takes the red-hot stones over to heat the sweat lodge. The sweat lodge ceremony is a place where survivors come to cleanse themselves of spiritual weight and demons they have been carrying on their shoulders for a long time, and wish to shed."

"That's so interesting," I say. "I'd like to learn more about that."

"Do you think it's something you might like to do sometime?" Rose asks.

"Maybe," I answer. "What other ceremonies do you do here?"

"We also do full moon ceremonies around the fire," she replies. "We have another one coming up in October … *the falling leaves moon.* That might be a very good one for you to attend, if you want."

"I would," I answer, genuinely curious to find out more about my newly-acquired heritage. "I think I'd really like that."

We start walking back along the path through the forest, towards the lodge.

"I'm glad you're interested," Rose says. She puts a hand on my shoulder again, and I feel her warmth and sincerity. "I realize that this must be a lot for you to take in. You can call me anytime you have questions, or if you just need somebody to talk to."

My mind is spinning as we walk in silence, trying to process what I've learned today … trying to connect dots … to find a way to integrate it with my previous life experiences. Suddenly, I stop walking and I turn to Rose beside me.

"If my father was a victim of the residential schools, that makes me a product of intergenerational trauma too, doesn't it?" I ask.

"I'm afraid so, dear," Rose replies.

I pause again for a moment, deep in thought. This new information pretty much clinches it for me.

"I don't think there's any turning back for me now. Can you find out how I can contact him?" I ask.

"Are you sure?" Rose says, once again placing a reassuring hand on my shoulder.

I pause again, swallow hard, and then take a deep breath of fresh air.

"It's scary … but I think this is a path I need to follow," I say, finally.

Rose wraps her arm around my waist and gives me a gentle hug. It feels warm, genuine, and reassuring.

"Then I'll ask around the community to see what I can find out. I'll call you when I know more."

I FIND myself staring at my computer monitor again, my mind off in another world. I see the same three sentences that were on the screen half an hour ago, still waiting for me to complete my notes on the latest research article I've been reading. I haven't been able to concentrate since yesterday, after Rose passed along a possible phone number for my biological father. Apparently, it didn't take the residential school survivor's grapevine long to find somebody who was still connected to Charlie, and for that person to get back to Rose. I'd left the Healing Lodge late Saturday afternoon, and Rose had a number for me by Sunday evening. My eyes drift again to my cell phone, laying on the desk beside my keyboard. I take a breath and then exhale slowly. Tired of fighting the distraction, I stand up, pick up the phone, and stare at Charlie's number with my finger poised above the dial icon.

After what seems like an eternity, but is probably only a matter of seconds, I put the screen to sleep and resume pacing back and forth across the tiny office, trying in vain to avoid obsessing over my dilemma, while my conflicted inner voices continue to battle each other.

I share my windowless office, probably about the size of the average prison cell, with another grad student. Fortunately for me, she's finishing up her thesis and she spends most of her time working from home this year. I glance at the stacks of research journals that I've piled high on my office mate's desk, and I wonder for a moment if I'm becoming a hoarder like Eric Sanderson.

Just phone him, Sam ... Get it over with! ... What if he wants to meet me? ... What if he doesn't? ...

I pick up my phone, open the home screen, and once again stare at Charlie's number in my contacts list.

What's the worst that could happen? ... If he says no, your world stays the same ... nothing changes ... No big deal, right? ...

I turn and pace back in the opposite direction. Once again, I raise a hand, ready to touch the *dial* icon. But my arm and hand remain frozen, still unable to follow through.

A sudden knock on my partially-open door causes me to jump and to inhale sharply.

Shanise, from Team Reconciliation, pokes her head into the room.

"Are you okay?" she asks. "I'm sorry I startled you."

I exhale slowly to help calm my jittery nerves.

"Ummh … yeah, I'm alright … can I help you?" I answer, still rattled.

I catch Shanise's eyes sizing up my office.

"Nice posters," she says. "You have good taste. Where did you get them?"

"Thanks," I reply. "They're just from the annual poster sale that comes to campus each fall. They're nothing special. With no windows in the office, I needed to inject some colour in here. They're both by Matisse … the one on the left is *Woman Beside the Water*, and the one on the right is called *Pastoral*."

"What about that small picture above your computer?" Shanise asks. She points to an image with six silhouetted figures rowing a traditional West Coast Indigenous canoe, set against a light purple dusk sky.

"It's one I picked up at a garage sale," I answer. "I don't know why, but I loved it the moment I saw it. And the price was definitely right."

I glance at my phone to see how long we have until Dr. Sanderson's lecture.

"You had some questions?" I ask, bringing the subject back to the reason for Shanise's visit.

"Oh … yes," she says. "I just had a couple of questions about last week's lecture."

I cast an anxious glance at my phone, and Shanise catches me in the act.

"But if you're busy, I can talk with you after tonight's class," she says. "Are you sure you're okay? Does this still have something to do with Hunter?"

"No, it's not that," I answer.

I pause to think. On one hand I feel leery about opening up to Shanise. But on the other hand, I sense her motherly nature and I feel like I can trust her. Finally, I motion toward the open office door.

"Can you close the door?" I say.

Shanise closes the door and turns to me.

"You look like a bundle of nerves. What's happening?" she asks.

"Ummh … well … it's like this … my father … my real father … left me and my mom when I was little … and I recently found out how to contact him."

"Wow!" she exclaims. "How do you feel about that?"

"Torn!" I answer. "Every time I get ready to dial his number, I can't go through with it. I'm just too scared!"

"That's understandable," Shanise replies. "I think I'd be terrified too if it was me."

She pauses to think for a moment.

What do you think you're most afraid of?" she asks. "Was he abusive to you and your mom?"

"It's hard to remember," I say. "I don't think he beat me, but I think he beat my mom … and he was always angry and shouting."

"That can be just as bad," Shanise says. "Are you afraid he'll hurt you now?"

"No, it's not that," I insist. "I don't know … I think I'm just afraid he'll say no to me, and I'll feel abandoned all over again."

Shanise nods her head up and down.

"I get it," she says. "You really want to meet him, but you're afraid he'll reject you. No wonder you feel stuck and afraid. Is there anything I can do to help?"

I take a deep breath and pause to think about it.

"Thanks for the kind offer," I reply. "And thanks for listening … but I think maybe I still have some more work to do on this issue before I'm ready to do this."

I glance at the time on my phone.

"We've still got some time before the lecture. Let's take a look at those questions you had.

ON A POSITIVE note, I've been so preoccupied with whether or not to call Charlie, I haven't had time to be anxious about meeting with Team Reconciliation again tonight. However, having fled the room in a state of panic two weeks running, I realize that I've already got two strikes against me. As I approach the classroom, double-double in hand, I feel my body growing tense and my stomach starting to churn. The door is closed, so I knock tentatively before opening it a crack and sticking my head into the room.

"Are you guys ready for me yet?" I say meekly.

As I interrupt them, I notice that the entire team is still seated around the conference table, apparently discussing how to organize their project. Because Dr. Sanderson's lecture ended over half an hour ago, I take the entire team's presence as a good omen.

"Yes! Your timing is perfect," Fatima replies.

"Good," I say, as I set my coffee on the table and take my seat in the only remaining chair. "Are you guys making any progress?"

"As a matter of fact, we are," Arjun answers. "We chose Fatima as our chairperson. We all felt that she has the most real-life experience, because she's constantly dealing with a team of people in her business."

I glance at Fatima, who confirms Arjun's statement with a nod.

"That sounds like a wise choice," I say to Fatima. "Congratulations! Any other decisions yet?"

"Yes," Fatima replies. "After that, we decided to split the team into three subgroups: Research, Plan of Action, and Presentation. So far, Hunter, Arjun, and Terri have volunteered to do research, and I'll pitch in where needed. Katya and Mandy will compile the report, and Uri and Shanise will work with them on the Powerpoint presentation and the final report. We were just about to discuss who would work on the Plan of Action."

Is this too good to be true? Can this really be happening?

I find myself exhaling, and I feel some of the tension in my body letting go.

"Well, don't let me stop you," I say. "Do you mind if I sit and observe?"

"Of course not," Fatima answers. She turns to the rest of the team.

"I see creating a plan of action as the most difficult job!" she begins. "It will involve sifting through all of the research team's information, choosing the most important points, and then recommending a reconciliation plan to the team as a whole. Do we have any volunteers?"

There is a prolonged silence, and I realize quickly what is happening. With all of the team members already volunteering on the Research and Presentation teams, nobody is willing to volunteer to take on more work. Nobody wants to be the workhorse while others on the team slack off and take credit. I'm just about to intervene when Katya puts her hand up.

"Katya?" Fatima says.

"It seems to me that the people who do the research are the best people to work on the Plan of Action," she says. "They would already be familiar with the research, where the rest of us would not. It will save a lot of time."

"I agree," Hunter says. "I think it's essential to have my perspective on both the research and any recommendations we make."

"I think that makes a lot of sense," Fatima says. "Any other opinions?"

I look around the table, especially at Arjun and Terri, to see if they're on board with taking on extra work.

Uh, oh! Terri doesn't look happy.

I feel the hairs on the back of my neck starting to stand up, and my chest beginning to tighten up once again.

"I'm sorry, Hunter," she begins. "I disagree. Just because you're the only Indigenous person on the team, it doesn't mean you're entitled to special treatment. You're going to start bullying people until they see everything your way, just like you've done every week in these meetings!"

Terri glares at Hunter. I feel my legs and feet starting to vibrate up and down, and I feel the blood draining from my face.

"I'll volunteer, but I won't do it if I have to work with Hunter," she says.

Hunter immediately turns to me. The muscles in his face are tense and the familiar anger has returned to his eyes.

"There she goes again, Sam!" he shouts. "If anybody on this team is prejudiced, privileged, and thinks she's special … and if anybody is going to bully the team, it's Terri. I refuse to work with her and her racist lies! So what are *you* going to do about it?"

I feel my mind starting to check out again, and I feel helpless to stop it … I sense my terrified three-year-old self … laying all alone in my bed … dark shadowy images of a man and woman … screaming at each other … intruding into my consciousness … I see the shadows dancing ominously on the walls … in the distance, I hear a young child's voice wailing unconsolably … at the same time, I also hear Hunter's voice in the distance …

"I've had it!" Hunter shouts, glaring at me as though I'm a deer caught in a car's headlights. "I'm out of here until you and this group get your shit together!"

He stomps from the room, throwing the door open so violently that it slams against a doorstop and bounces back towards the doorway.

The sudden slamming sound jerks my mind back into the present … back into the room. I feel disoriented for a moment, until I see Shanise's familiar face across the table from me.

"It is alright, Sam," she says reassuringly. "He's gone now."

The sight of her face and the sound of her voice give me something familiar to latch onto, and to help anchor myself to the present. I become aware of my shallow breathing, and I remember and feel Barbara Way's familiar rhythm of breathing. Then I hear my inner survivor voice talking to my three-year-old self.

It's not happening now, Sam … You're safe here … The angry ones are gone now …

I feel my mind gradually reconnecting with my body again. I look around the room and see the remaining faces of Team Reconciliation staring at me, especially Terri … I see her expecting me to bolt from the room again … expecting to see me swing and miss on strike three …

You can do this, Sam! … Show her that you're in charge! … Don't give her the satisfaction!

I dig deep, take a long, slow breath, and then exhale. It still feels jerky, but I feel my breathing muscles relaxing slightly as the air flows out of my lungs.

"Well, I'm sorry Hunter feels that way," I manage to say. "But it *is* normal for group members to have strong opinions and a lot of conflict, especially in the beginning … that's probably enough said for tonight. We can talk about ways to help resolve this conflict when we meet next week, when everybody is hopefully more calm and rational."

As the team members pick up their belongings, and some start chatting while others go their separate ways, my inner voices pick up where Terri and Hunter left off … arguing amongst themselves.

Why don't you feel any sense of relief or accomplishment, Sam? … So you managed to end a dissociative episode … Big deal! … You only barely avoided disaster … Sure, you didn't strike out … But you didn't hit anything either … It's like you just got hit by a wild pitch … You should have seen it coming … You deserved to get hit … You deserve to feel emotionally drained …

CHAPTER 5—THE SWEAT LODGE

I CAN'T BELIEVE I'm actually doing this—standing around outside on a chilly mid-October afternoon in my swim suit, while I wait for my first sweat lodge ceremony to begin! Fortunately, Rose brought a blanket for me to wrap myself in. We stand in a circle, along with seven other people, watching a man tend a roaring fire and its red-hot embers. Four piles of stones, collected from the nearby creek, stand beside the sacred blaze. Rose tells me that the man is a ceremonial fire carrier. I turn around and see the same dome-shaped sweat lodge that I'd seen on my first visit to the Healing Lodge.

"This is for your offering," Rose says, as she hands me a small bundle of ceremonial tobacco, wrapped in yellow cloth and tied in twine. We join with the others in throwing our tobacco into the fire, and then we join with them in smudging ourselves with fragrant smoke from smouldering sage. I notice another man walk over towards the fire to talk with the fire carrier.

"Who is that?" I ask Rose.

"He is the healer who will be conducting the sweat lodge ceremony," she says. "His name is White Owl."

White Owl finishes talking to the fire carrier, and then he turns to address us.

"The sweat lodge ceremony is a purging or purification ritual," he says. "The lodge represents the womb of Mother Earth, and the heated stones represent the embodiment of our ancestors and their wisdoms. The fire, in which the rocks are heated, represents the everlasting light of the world, and the steam we create will help each of you bring your intentions to life. There will be four rounds, where we add seven hot stones each round. If you're ready, you may enter the lodge now. Please keep to the left on your way in a circle around the steam pit."

The remaining participants, four men and three women, shed their blankets. Any skin not covered by a swim suit is now exposed to the chilly October air.

"Here, I'll take your blanket," Rose says.

I shiver as I lose my protective layer, instinctively clutching my arms close to my chest in a futile attempt to warm myself.

"Are these people all from your community?" I whisper. "I feel like I'm an imposter … like I don't belong here."

"Don't worry, dear," she says quietly. "We feel it's important to share our ways with others. Everybody has different reasons for wanting to be here. It's not for us to judge the intentions of others."

"I'm scared," I answer. "I don't know if I can do this!"

"You're in good hands," she says. "Remember, the heat usually peaks in the third round. So, if you have trouble breathing, put your head down in your lap, or lay on your side. I'll be waiting here until you're done. Off you go."

I fall in line after two men and a woman. One at a time, we kneel down and crawl through the lodge's entrance.

As I enter, it takes a moment for my eyes to adjust to the darkness. Once they adapt, I see how the lodge is constructed. Its inner skeleton is comprised of willow saplings, each one anchored into the ground and then bent over and tied together with another willow from the opposite side of the lodge, thus forming a number of arches. Four rows of horizontal saplings circle the dome. They are tied to the upright arches to stabilize the skeleton. Layers of blankets, fastened to this wooden frame, keep any light from entering the structure and also keep the heat from escaping.

In front and to my right, I see a deep pit dug into the ground in the middle of the lodge. We crawl around the pit, finding our positions, and we end up sitting cross-legged in a circle around the pit. I end up stuck at the far side of the circle, opposite the entrance. Reality sets in when it dawns on me that I'll have to crawl over everybody else if I need to get out of here.

I feel my heart beating faster now that the ceremony is becoming real. I take a deep breath and exhale slowly, then I try to swallow the large lump I feel in the back of my throat.

Nowhere for you to hide now, Sam ... Looks like you're here for the duration ... Take nice, slow breaths!

White Owl crawls into the lodge behind us and takes his place around the fire. I notice that he has a bundle of sage in one hand, and a pipe in the other. He looks around the circle at each of us before he addresses us as a group.

"I will say a prayer in our native Anishinaabe language," he says. "And then, before we close the lodge, I will pass around a pipe with tobacco for you to share. I will ask each of you to introduce yourselves, and to say your intentions for what you hope to receive from this sacred ceremony."

The fire carrier appears at the sweat lodge entrance. He hands a container of disinfectant wipes to White Owl, who passes them to the man beside him.

"We live in a new world today," he says. "With the recent pandemic, we've learned that we need to adapt our sacred ceremonies to keep ourselves safe. Please take a wipe and cleanse the pipe well after you have used it."

White Owl then closes his eyes, raises his arms with his palms turned upwards, and begins his prayer. I feel a nudge in my side from a woman next to me. She leans closer and whispers in my ear.

"Do you know Anishinaabe?"

"No," I reply, still feeling like an outsider.

"He says his prayer is to the spirits of all the residential school children who didn't survive," she says. "He hopes that they will eventually find peace in the spirit world. He also prays for the school survivors, that they may heal and find peace in this life."

"Thank you," I whisper, touched by the woman's kindness.

The fire carrier appears again, this time carrying a single white-hot stone between two large wooden sticks, which he deposits on the ground at the opening. White Owl picks up two wooden sticks of his own, and transfers the stone to the steam pit. The fire carrier hands a bundle of sage to White Owl, who then touches the bundle to the stone. The sage ignites instantly, causing it to smoulder and display orange embers at the end of each sprig. The fragrant aroma of sage fills the dome, as White Owl uses the embers to expertly light his pipe. He inhales, holds his breath, and exhales a cloud of tobacco smoke. He then wipes down the pipe, and passes it along to a middle-aged male participant beside him. He nods for the man to proceed.

"My name is James," he says. "I'm here at the *Healing Lodge* because I'm an alcoholic. I came to the sweat lodge to cleanse myself … to pray to the spirits for help in fighting this disease … to help me heal my relationship with my wife and kids."

James takes a puff from the pipe, wipes down the mouthpiece thoroughly, and then passes it along to the woman next to him, who appears to be about Rose's age. The aroma of tobacco mixes with the lingering scent of sage.

"I'm Victoria," she says. "And I'm a survivor of the schools … I was raped over and over as a little girl. I come here today to unburden myself … to cleanse myself of the demons that still live inside."

She inhales from the pipe, cleanses it, and passes it along to a young man sitting beside her.

"I'm Mike," he says. "I'm here to cleanse myself of my anger … anger towards my parents … I didn't know they survived the schools … anger at myself for taking it out on everybody around me."

Mike takes a long drag from White Owl's pipe, cleanses it, and passes it to the young woman beside me, who had so kindly translated White Owl's prayer for me. She appears to be about my age, in her late twenties.

"My name is Willow," she says. "My intent for coming here today is to help shed the burden of my addiction to drugs … mostly heroine and fentanyl … I'm doing well in my program here at the *Healing Lodge* … I hope that the sweat lodge will help cleanse my body of its need for these drugs."

Rose was right. We all have baggage we're carrying around. I guess I'm not the only one whose life is screwed up!

Willow cleanses the pipe and then hands it to me. I pause for a moment as I collect my thoughts. Finally, I put the pipe to my lips and feel the pungent air enter my lungs, holding it for a few seconds. As I exhale the sacred smoke, I feel myself relax slightly.

"I'm Samantha," I say. "I recently discovered that I'm a survivor of intergenerational trauma from a victim of the schools … I've been carrying that trauma on my shoulders for most of my life … I'm here to help cleanse myself of that burden."

I wipe down the pipe's mouthpiece and pass it along to a middle-aged man beside me.

"I'm Chris," he says. "I am also a school survivor … abused in almost every way imaginable … I came to the *Healing Lodge* for help with sexual addiction … I'm here today to help cleanse myself of this disease … and for help in making amends to my wife."

He cleanses the pipe and passes it along to the middle-aged woman beside him.

"I'm Heather," she says. "I'm here to support my husband, Chris … to cleanse myself of my anger towards him … to become more understanding of how the school damaged him."

Heather wipes down the pipe and hands it to the last participant, a young man in his twenties.

"I'm Liam," he says. "I'm here for help in acknowledging that I am two-spirited … to cleanse myself of the expectations of others … to learn to be more accepting of myself."

Liam wipes down the pipe and returns it to White Owl.

"Thank you, everybody, for sharing your intentions," he says. "May the spirits help you realize them, and help you cleanse your own minds and bodies. Remember, round one is a round for yourself."

White Owl then motions with his hand to the waiting fire carrier outside the entrance.

"Stones, please," he says.

THE FIRE carrier delivers the final stone and White Owl uses his own pair of wooden sticks to add it to the steam pit. The fire carrier then closes the entrance flap and the sweat lodge is plunged into near darkness, the only light coming from the yellow-white glow of superheated stones in the firepit. White Owl pours two ladles full of water over the stones, which hiss angrily and eject clouds of steam into the air. I make the mistake of trying to take a slow, relaxing breath just as the cloud of steam reaches me. My lungs seize up instantly, making it impossible to breathe. Instinctively, I lunge forward and bury my head in my lap, covering it with both arms. Only then do I dare to take a slow, tentative breath of protected air. My lungs gratefully accept the slightly cooler air and resume taking shallow, cautious breaths.

I feel the temperature within the dome climbing steadily. My body breaks out in sweat. I feel it dripping down my chest between my breasts, and I find myself constantly wiping it from my forehead. White Owl begins singing a traditional song, and some of the others start singing along with him. I try to follow Willow's voice without much success. The heat continues to rise and I feel my head expanding like a balloon, while my heart rate accelerates in my chest. My body feels much the same as it does when I'm overwhelmed by my panic attacks. But, paradoxically, simply thinking about my fear of having another attack actually starts to trigger one, creating a self-fulfilling prophecy of panic. I feel overwhelmed by an urgent need to bolt from the tent, but I know that I'd have to either climb over the superheated rocks or over the other participants to do so.

I'm trapped! ... Let me out of here!

The colour of the rocks has changed from yellow-white to orange. White Owl adds another two ladles of water and the stones hiss again in protest, not quite as loudly as with the first dose of water. My head dives instinctively for my lap again, and I create another pocket of cooler air with my arms over my head. The temperature within the dome continues to feel more oppressive.

"White Owl ... can't do this ... too hard," I call out, after briefly uncovering my head.

"Have faith, sister," he says calmly. "You're almost there."

Almost where?

White Owl begins chanting another traditional song, this time to the rhythm of a small traditional drum. I wipe the sweat from my forehead yet again, and then quickly cover my head with my arms. I close my eyes and try to focus on the rhythm of White Owl's song and drumming. After a few moments I realize that my breathing has fallen into the same beat as the drumming, much like it does when Barbara Way uses her own rate of breathing to set a pace for me.

Just focus on the drum, Sam ... Nice slow breaths ... You can do it ...

The chanting and drumming finally comes to an end, and I hear White Owl clear his throat.

"That's the end of round one. You should all be proud—you did well!"

He taps against the entrance flap, and the fire carrier opens it. My lungs rejoice at feeling the cool, refreshing air that rushes into the lodge. I wipe the sweat from my forehead, and for a few minutes, it stays away.

I did well? ... Is he kidding? ... It sure didn't feel that way to me!

"PLEASE CLOSE the door," White Owl says to the fire carrier, then he turns his attention to us. "Round two is for the mother."

The temperature inside the dome starts building instantly. I feel my heartbeat starting to quicken and sweat is already emerging on every exposed surface. My swim suit, already soaked after the first round, starts dripping with sweat. My skin feels as though it's on fire.

I see White Owl reaching for a ladle full of water, and my head dives instinctively for my lap, bracing myself for another onslaught of superheated steam. I hear the rocks hiss loudly, and then again as a second ladle full of water vaporizes and fills the dome.

Once again, my head starts pounding and feels like it's going to explode.

"In this round, we each pray for the mother," White Owl says.

An image of Diane enters my mind, and I feel myself start to panic.

I will not pray for that woman! ... Pray for Aunt Melanie instead ...

I hear James begin his prayer to his mother in the background, while I try to compose a prayer for Aunt Melanie. But inspiration won't come, and I feel like I'm forcing it. Then, seemingly out of nowhere, I hear the distant voice of my inner caregiver.

What about Aunt Rose?

I try to recall moments from the time I've spent with Aunt Rose recently ... my first images of autumn foliage on Georgian Bay ... feeling and smelling leather moccasins in the *Healing Lodge*'s store ... the brilliant Indigenous paintings of Georgian Bay ... that first whiff of burning sage from the prayer circle ... walking along beside the nearby stream ... the quiet, reassuring sound of Rose's voice ...

I'm jolted from my inner world when I hear Willow's voice beside me, saying a prayer for her estranged mother.

"I know she did the best she could for me," Willow says. "Being with her wasn't always bad … there were good times too … we used to sing together …"

I hear Willow sniffling and her voice quivering as she talks.

"… If you're happy and you know it, clap your hands … If you're happy …"

Willow's voice trails off and turns into sobs.

"… She left this world too soon … I pray that she's at peace in the spirit world."

I lift my head, open my eyes, and reach for Willow's hand. I give it a squeeze to let her know I understand and feel her pain. She squeezes back to show her thanks.

Our moment is interrupted by the sound of White Owl's ladle filling anew with water, followed by the stones hissing their protest at being doused once more. I drop my head back into my lap and cover my head yet again, while the fresh cloud of steam permeates the dome. In the background, I hear White Owl's voice.

"Samantha," he says. "You have a prayer to the mother?"

I try my best to fill my lungs, and then I lift my head and sit up. The heat is oppressive and my head feels like it's swelling once again. I wipe away the sweat that drips from my forehead and tries to make its way into my eyes.

"This is for my Aunt … for Rose … I pray to the spirits, thanking them … thanking them for bringing her into my life … for her wisdom … her calming voice … her listening without judgment … for being with me in spirit right now … like the mother my inner child always longed for."

I feel myself getting dizzy from the heat, and I feel my mind starting to disconnect from my body. I feel like I'm floating, looking down on myself, Willow, and the ceremony happening below. I see myself plunge my head back into my lap and cover it again. I feel the searing heat, far in the distance. I watch passively from above as Chris, Heather, and Liam say their prayers to their mothers.

Finally, I see White Owl tap on the opening flap. Seconds later, it opens, letting in daylight and precious cool air. Gradually, I feel myself reconnecting with my body. My lungs drink in cool, refreshing air with breath after deep breath.

"That's the end of round two. You're half way there!" he says. "I'll pass around some bottles of water. Try not to drink too much at once, and save some for the next round."

Only half way? I don't think I can last that long!

And then I remembered Rose telling me that the third round is the worst!

WHITE OWL places the last of the seven new stones in the steam pit, and once again I feel the temperature climbing. The air is filled with smoke from another bunch of sacred sage that White Owl has ignited. He pours two ladles full of water over the new stones, and they hiss their protests once again.

"Round three is for the father," White Owl announces. "This time, we give our prayers and intentions for our fathers. James, will you begin?"

The new mixture of steam and smoke is more than my lungs can take, easily overwhelming me. My head drops down into my lap again and I cover myself with my arms. My swimsuit is wringing wet. Sweat pours off my hair and forehead, and then down over my face, leaving a constant taste of salt on my lips. I feel a steady stream of hot liquid running down between my breasts again. I reach for my bottle of water and suck back a couple of large gulps.

My skin feels scorched and my head feels like it's going to explode, despite the limited protection from my arms. I hear James, but his voice is distant. I feel myself getting dizzy and disoriented. I sense that Willow has keeled over beside me, lying on her side with her head close to the muddy earth, where the air is coolest.

I remember the rest of Rose's warning: "Lie down on the ground if it gets to be too much." My body gives up the battle and tumbles over, leaving me lying on the ground next to Willow.

I feel my mind disconnecting from my body again … floating over the scene … watching James and Mike saying their prayers and intentions … seeing Willow and myself lying side-by-side on the earth in fetal position.

The stones in the pit cast their orange glow onto the inside surface of the dome. Shadows dance on the walls every time one of the participants moves … my mind makes a connection between the shadows and the terrifying images of fighting adults from my childhood … the two sets of images seem to merge in my mind … a surreal blend of past and present … dark, distorted, terrifying images looming over me on the lodge's ceiling … lost in time …

Suddenly, the entrance flap opens. The images disappear abruptly as daylight and cool, refreshing air flow into the lodge. I feel a breeze cooling my soaked skin and swim suit. Willow and I sit up, both dazed and disoriented, reaching for our bottles of water and gulping the precious liquid.

My body feels drained … both physically and emotionally.

I can't do this again! Let me out of here!

Willow's voice helps to bring my mind back into the present.

"We missed out on the father intentions," she says.

Secretly, I feel a sense of relief at missing that part of the ceremony, given my mixed emotions around meeting my biological dad.

And then a realization hits me like a bolt of lightning! Having my mind leave my body and hallucinating, is helping me to see the links between my past and the present. The hallucinations helped me survive the notorious round three!

I CAN do this!

THE FIRE CARRIER closes the entrance flap after delivering his final load of seven superheated stones. We're plunged into near darkness for the last time. I feel the temperature rising quickly again after White Owl ladles water onto the stones. They hiss again and rapidly fill the dome with steam. I gulp the last of my water to hydrate myself for another assault on my body.

"This is the final round," White Owl says. "The wisdom round is a time for each of you to be with yourself, in total silence."

I look at Willow and see her smile at me. I reach over and take one of her hands in mine, giving it a reassuring squeeze. Then, we let go and leave each other to find our own, unique wisdom.

This time, as the heat scorches my skin once again, and the rivers of sweat run rampant over my body, I focus on the yellow-orange glow of the stones and the dark, distorted figures dancing on the walls of the dome. This time, I purposely let my mind disconnect and float over the scene, watching myself, White Owl, Willow, and the others meditate in silence.

I allow my mind to connect with the terrifying images from my past, once again allowing those images to merge with those that are dancing on the walls of the dome … dark, silent images … no yelling or screaming … I'm weirdly fascinated by how the dancing images are distorted by the curvature of the dome … but I feel no emotions … no fear or loneliness …

A sudden realization coalesces in my mind.

The old childhood images … They have no sound or emotions attached anymore … They're not real … They're over now … They're like harmless shadow puppets … I don't have to let them control me anymore!

I feel a sense of peace descend upon my body, unlike anything I've ever felt before. Despite the oppressing heat and humidity in the sweat lodge, I feel myself growing stronger as the fourth round continues. I allow myself to enjoy my newly found revelations and feelings. I am oblivious to the passage of time.

White Owl starts chanting a traditional Anishinaabe song in time with his drum, and the others join in with him. I watch Willow's mouth closely, trying to imitate the sounds she's making. But I don't feel like an outsider this time. We smile at each other, laughing and holding hands while we sing.

And then, the fire carrier opens the entrance flap for the last time.

"Congratulations," White Owl says. "You've completed the final round of the ceremony."

I wait for the others to start crawling out of the lodge, and then follow. When I emerge, Rose is standing outside the entrance. She holds out my blanket and then wraps me up in it.

"How was it?" she asks.

It's a simple question. But, I can't find words that can adequately describe such an overwhelming sensory, emotional, and spiritual experience.

"Awful," I begin. "Overwhelming … both physically and emotionally … terrifying at times … but also amazing! … I feel cleansed … energized … and stronger."

I let my blanket fall open, then I reach out to give Rose a big hug.

"Thank you so much for inviting me!" I say, and then I laugh. "Oh, my God, I'm getting you all sweaty. I'm so sorry!"

Rose joins in my laughter.

"I'm happy for you. I knew it would help you grow," she says. "Let's get you back to the lodge. I'll make you a nice hot cup of Ojibwe tea, and you can tell me all about it."

I pull the blanket tight and Rose puts her arm around me. I feel at peace as we walk along the path back to the *Healing Lodge*, hearing the sound of rippling water from the creek, and the sound of our feet in rustling leaves, anchoring me firmly in the moment.

CHAPTER 6—WEEK FIVE

I'M ENJOYING the warm sunshine on my face on this unseasonably warm mid-October day, as I make my way towards the Student Union Building to get a bite to eat. After my weekend up north at the Healing Lodge, I feel energized and eager to finish my research readings, so I can finally decide on a thesis topic.

What's the commotion up ahead? ... Probably some guest speaker that the Student Union has brought to campus.

As I get closer to the commotion, I detect two familiar voices, both of which sound angry.

This is no guest speaker ... Oh, shit ... That's Terri's voice ... And Hunter's!

"Trying to walk away again? Afraid to look me in the eye, big man?" Terri shouts.

"I don't have anything to say to you," Hunter answers.

I arrive at the scene and work my way through the gathering crowd until I'm within a few feet of the combatants.

Hunter tries to walk around Terri, but she blocks his way.

"What's the matter, are you afraid of me? Are you just a big pussy?" Terri shouts. "Don't you dare walk away from me again when I'm talking to you!"

Hunter stops in his tracks and glares at Terri.

"I'm tired of your privileged white arguments. I don't have to listen to this!" Hunter shouts.

Terri steps closer and gets her face right in front of Hunter's.

I feel my body starting to tremble, and my stomach starting to churn.

Damn! Not this again!

"Well, I'm tired of this country's Indian problem, and all the special treatment you people get!" Terri shouts. "And I'm not the only Canadian who feels that way!"

I feel the crowd growing and pressing from behind me, as more passersby stop to see what's causing the ruckus.

"All that 'special treatment'," Hunter says, sarcastically, "Is nothing but white myths, generated by ignorant, privileged settlers like you, who know nothing about the *Indian Act* and the misery it has inflicted on us! We don't have an 'Indian problem' in this country—we have an *Indian Act* problem!"

"You think I'm privileged?" Terri shrieks. "Growing up dirt poor as the oldest kid on a farm in Northern BC, with a drunk for a father who treated me like his own personal Cinderella? Living with that selfish prick, who made it my job to take care of my sick mom and seven other kids when I was only ten? A filthy pig who made me take the place of his wife in *every* possible way, if you know what I mean!"

Terri's face is now red with rage, and she starts wagging her finger in front of Hunter's face. As she does, I feel my inner infant and three-year-old voices growing increasingly restless and afraid. The dark images from my past threaten to intrude into my consciousness again. The trembling in my body grows worse.

"I walked out that door the day I turned sixteen, took a bus to Edmonton, and didn't look back!" Terri screams. "I had to start stripping to make a buck. And, yes, I did tricks on the side just to make ends meet, and coke became my best friend! I even did six months for theft! The only thing that saved me, was meeting one person in prison who believed in me, and showed me how to believe in myself. When I got out, he loaned me enough money to start my own exotic dance studio. I worked my butt off to build my business, and I paid back every penny after twelve months! So don't tell me I'm privileged!

"Right!" Hunter bellows. "Any chance that guy was a privileged white male?"

Stop it! Please stop it!

I feel my mind trying to disconnect and slip away … trying to avoid seeing and being vicariously traumatized by the verbal onslaughts. My body freezes, and I feel helpless to act.

"Give me a break!" Terri shouts. "You think *every* non-Indigenous person is privileged? That guy grew up poor like I did, and he worked his butt off to educate himself. So, go stuff your white privilege accusations up your anally-retentive ass!"

Terri turns, as if she's going to walk away. Then, it looks like another thought changes her mind. She wheels around and gets right back in Hunter's face before he can leave the scene.

"You don't want to talk about the privileged treatment *your* people get?" Terri shouts. "What about the forty-billion dollar payout that Ottawa is shelling out to Indigenous kids over the next few years? Where is all that money going to go? When is the waste going to stop?"

"You can't be serious!" Hunter shouts. "Being sent into the settler child welfare system was just another version of the residential schools! Those people need to be compensated for being taken away from their Indigenous communities!"

Terri refuses to back down, and stays right in front of Hunter's face.

"You know as well as I do where all that money is going to go," Terri shouts. "Alcohol and drug sales are going to skyrocket, and you know it!"

Hunter shakes his head, temporarily lost for words. But I see the muscles in his jaws and fists tensing, and that familiar fire returning to his eyes.

"It's attitudes like these that make it necessary for my people to resort to passive resistance," he shouts. "It seems to be the only way to get you people to pay attention and take our problems seriously!"

"Passive resistance?" Terri shouts. "Are you kidding? Is that what you call burning down churches, desecrating statues, and blocking railways and pipelines? You may think it's passive, but it's nothing more than a form of aggression … aggression masquerading as peaceful protest. Canadians have had enough of it, and we're not going to take it anymore!"

My inner infant and three-year-old are growing more terrified with every angry word. My mind is just about to disconnect again … then something unexplained happens. In the distance, I hear my angry inner voice … the voice that has always been so angry at Diane and my father … the voice I've always been ashamed of, and kept to myself. It's heard enough of Hunter and Terri's verbal conflict and it can't remain silent any longer … its voice rapidly becoming loud and clear.

I find myself rushing from the crowd.

"Stop! That's enough!" I scream.

I see a look of shock on both Hunter's and Terri's faces. I insert myself between the two combatants and push them apart.

"I expect *both* of you to be at tonight's team meeting, and we'll settle this there!"

Hunter slowly turns and walks away, while I hold onto Terri to keep her from following. She glares at me, and then turns on her heels and walks away in the other direction, just as we see two campus cops arriving on bicycles.

Feeling more of that same sense of power that I experienced in the sweat lodge, I turn my attention to the crowd and the campus cops.

"That's all, everybody. The show's over—nothing more to see here!"

I turn away from the crowd and head for the Student Union Building, resuming my quest for something to eat. I feel proud of what I just accomplished, and I love the sense of power I feel from using my angry voice. And yet, at the same time, I feel my old nemesis, guilt, lurking in the background. It's telling me that showing my anger is wrong, and I should feel ashamed of myself.

Slowly, self-doubt and hopelessness start to creep back into my mind. I find myself growing preoccupied with tonight's team meeting, and I realize that my appetite has disappeared.

They're doing their best to tear Team Reconciliation apart ... What am I going to say to stop them? ... How am I ever going to get that pair to work together? ...

I PACE back and forth in the hallway outside the tutorial classroom, rehearsing what I want to say while waiting anxiously for the whole team to gather. As I take a sip of soothing hot coffee to calm myself, I see the last team member arrive. I collect my thoughts and walk briskly to meet Fatima before she enters the classroom.

"Can I have a word with you?" I ask.

"Sure, Sam. What is on your mind?"

"I don't know if you heard about the big ruckus on campus earlier today," I say. "But I stumbled upon Terri and Hunter having a big blowout outside the Student Union Building. They were screaming at each other ... it was really ugly!"

"Oh, no!" Fatima replies. "Thank you for telling me. I would have walked into that room completely naive."

"If you don't mind, I'd like to address the team before you take over the meeting. I'm going to lay some ground rules for dealing with any future conflict within the team."

Fatima nods in agreement.

"Please do," she says.

She opens the door for me and follows me into the room, then we both take our seats without saying a word. I take one last sip of coffee, then I clear my throat.

"Before I turn this meeting over to Fatima," I say, "I have some issues to address."

You're tentative and shaky, Sam. You sound scared. Where's that angry voice from yesterday? It's time to show them who's in charge here!

I put on my stern face, take a breath, and then exhale to calm myself.

"As your TA," I begin. "I shouldn't have to intervene in team issues. I'm really only supposed to be sitting and watching. You've learned in lecture that conflict within your team can be healthy, as long as team members listen and respect each others' opinions. But, unlike the other three teams in this course, this group is dysfunctional beyond belief!"

I look around the table and see sheepish looks of embarrassment on many of the faces. In contrast, both Hunter and Terri have looks of defiance on their faces. Their crossed arms and closed body posture show me that I have my work cut out for me. I look at each of them and give them a penetrating glare.

"The name-calling and lack of respect I've seen from certain members of this team has to stop!" I say, raising my voice. "So, I'm laying some ground rules for this team moving forward."

I stop to look around the table at each individual.

"From now on, no more use of emotionally-charged words like Indian, redskin, privileged, settler, colonist, or terms such as genocide, even if those words are used by others in some official documents! Those words only make people defensive and less likely to listen. Instead, can we agree that this team will use less emotionally-charged words like Indigenous, non-Indigenous, immigrant, or assimilation in our conversations, and in your presentation and report?"

I feel my body trembling slightly in anticipation as I look around the table. I see nods of agreement from everybody, except for Hunter and Terri. I glare at each one of them for a few seconds, until Terri finally relents and nods silently in agreement. Hunter follows a moment later. I allow myself a relaxing deep breath and then exhale slowly.

"Good!" I say with relief. "Fatima, the meeting is yours."

"Thank you, Sam," Fatima says. She looks around the table at each of her teammates.

"We still have some unfinished organizational business," she explains. "We must come to a consensus on who is going to be on the Plan of Action committee."

Fatima makes eye contact with Terri, and then with Hunter.

"Hunter and Terri," she says. "You both want to be on this committee, and you both have some very different perspectives on reconciliation. Like Sam said, we have to expect team members to have different opinions. But, what I need to know from each of you is this: Can you two make an effort to at least *listen* to each other's opinions, and try to find some common ground?"

She makes eye contact with Terri, and then with Hunter, pausing to give them time to consider her question.

"I'll give it a try," Terri says. "As long as Hunter is willing to abide by Sam's ground rules too."

Hunter swallows and pauses to look at me. We make eye contact and I make sure to maintain the stern look on my face. Finally, Hunter turns his attention back to Fatima.

"Okay, I'll try," he says.

"Thank you," Fatima says. "Now, because the Plan of Action committee is a big job, does anybody else want to add their voice to this committee? I'd like one more person, if possible."

Fatima looks around the table for volunteers. Finally, Arjun raises his hand.

"I'll work with them," he says.

"Thank you," Fatima says, with a noticeable look of relief on her face. "One last item to discuss for tonight. Hunter has suggested that he could arrange for the team to visit a local Indigenous support centre for victims of intergenerational trauma. I think this is an excellent idea. How many of you would be available two weekends from now?"

Team members look around the table at each other and gradually raise their hands, one by one, until they are all on board. Fatima turns to address Hunter.

"Excellent!" she says. "Please tell them that we look forward to visiting with them, and let us know more details once you have worked them out."

She looks around the table at the rest of the team.

"That will be all for tonight," she says. "Research team, be prepared to report on your progress next week."

Fatima glances at me. Both of our faces share a look of relief. She stays behind while the remaining team members start talking and gradually filing from the room.

"That went better than expected," Fatima says. "Thank you for setting those ground rules. If they can abide by them, maybe there is some hope for this team after all."

"Maybe," I reply. "Time will tell."

But you've learned the hard way before, Sam ... Don't get your hopes up, waiting for people to change!

I TRUDGE up the last few stairs towards the second floor and my cramped little bachelor suite, carrying a bag of groceries in each hand and breathing heavily.

Too much time in the library and in front of my computer. I have to make time to get back to the gym!

I finally reach the second-floor landing and put down one of the bags while I search for my keys and let myself into the apartment. I pause for a moment to catch my breath.

The room is silent, apart from the hum of the refrigerator, so I pull my laptop out of my handbag and set it up quickly on the table in my eating area. I browse the internet for the local TV station and start streaming it, before picking up the grocery bags and depositing them on the kitchen counter, next to the fridge. The voice of Kevin Murphy, local TV news anchor, keeps me company as I start restocking the rather barren-looking refrigerator shelves.

"Visitors to Victoria Park this morning confronted an unidentified Indigenous man who had scaled the statue of Queen Victoria and poured red paint over the Monarch's likeness, with help from two other men," the news anchor says.

The news report reaches my ears, but doesn't really register as I place my eggs in the egg keeper.

"Onlookers and the three alleged perpetrators hurled insults at each other, before police finally intervened and separated the two groups. A police spokesperson indicated that no charges were pressed against either the alleged perpetrators, or the onlookers, to avoid escalating the situation. We have Jessica Chen reporting."

As the station switches to Jessica's report, I hear voices taunting each other behind her. My ears suddenly pick out the sound of a familiar voice, and I spin around to see Jessica approach one of the young men responsible.

"I'm here at Victoria Park with one of the men alleged to have covered the statue of Queen Victoria with red paint," she says. "Can you tell me why you came here today?"

Oh, my God! It's Hunter! What the ...

"We're here today to tell the truth about the colonial governments and their racist treatment of Indigenous people since European contact," Hunter begins. "We demand that this statue, and others like it, come down as part of decolonizing this country's shameful history!"

My phone starts ringing and vibrating on the table beside my computer.

It's Fatima ... what does she want?

"Hi, Fatima. What's up?" I say.

"Are you watching the local TV news?" she asks.

"As a matter of fact, I am," I answer. "Why on earth is he doing that?"

"I do not know," Fatima replies. "But this is just another example of his angry, disrespectful behaviour that has sabotaged our project from the beginning! What are we going to do about him?"

As we talk, I watch Jessica Chen winding down her interview.

"This is Jessica Chen reporting from Victoria Park."

I mute the volume on my computer.

"Sorry, you were saying?" I ask, having been distracted by the end of the interview.

"I am concerned that this is just more of his angry, disrespectful behaviour," Fatima says.

I understand," I muse. "But, are we really sure this will have any effect on your team's project?"

"What if the rest of the team sees this?" Fatima says. "They already feel like he is disrespecting them, with his bullying and showing up late for team meetings. They are just going to see this as another sign of disrespect!"

"Unfortunately, it seems like that's the least of his concerns," I reply. "But it could be the least of his problems too. He's applying for Law School this year … does he have any idea how something like this could affect his chances, if they hear about it?"

"Exactly! Is there anything you can do about it?" Fatima asks. "Especially after you laid down your ground rules for respect this week?"

I pause again to think things over. I recall Hunter's and Terri's argument about Indigenous passive resistance and desecration of monuments.

"Even though it seems disrespectful, and could affect his relationship with the team," I reply, "What he does outside class time isn't my responsibility, and it isn't really any of our business."

The pause on Fatima's end clearly signals her disappointment.

"I think the only thing we can do, is to wait and see whether he continues to bring that attitude to class," I conclude.

"I suppose you are right," Fatima says, reluctantly. "Thank you for listening. I am sorry I bothered you."

"Not a problem, Fatima," I say. "I'll see you in class on Tuesday. Good night."

"Good night," she says, and her call disconnects.

I stare at my phone, still processing this unexpected turn of events.

Hunter, you're a hard guy to figure out ... What are you thinking? ... Why are you so angry? ... Just don't screw things up for me and the team ... Please ...

THEY SAY it's a good thing to take time to let your mind wander freely. They say it helps with creativity, planning, and internal problem solving. If that's the case, I'd like to know who they are, and how they do it! When my mind wanders, it's usually because I'm talking to myself. And that usually happens when I'm juggling too many balls ... when my brain is preoccupied with too many things that I'm worrying about.

... Are you going to contact your father, Sam? ... Are you prepared for tomorrow's tutorial sessions? ... How is Team Reconciliation going to react to your new ground rules? ... What's going on with Hunter? ... What does Diane want from you now? ... What's Eric going to think of your new thesis idea? ...

That's the state I'm in as I scurry across campus, late as usual for my weekly Monday morning meeting with Eric. Suddenly, a distant voice from behind me calls my name and jolts me out of my internal reverie.

"Hey, Sam!"

It takes a moment for the voice to register.

Oh shit, it's Hunter! ... What does he want? ... Is this going to turn into another public shouting match?

I hear his footsteps running to catch up to me.

"Hold up for a minute!" he shouts.

I turn around as he reaches me. I'm still flustered and unsure what to say.

"Hi there," I answer.

Are you kidding me? ... Is that the best you can do?

"Do you have time to join me for a coffee?" he asks.

"Sorry," I say. "I'm on my way to meet with Dr. Sanderson."

"Too bad," Hunter says. "How about some other time?"

My mind continues to race, resulting in a pregnant pause.

Really? ... Is he hitting on me? ... Has he found out that I'm half Indigenous? ... Is he going to cause a big scene? ...

I'm flustered and confused. I realize that part of me is flattered by his invitation. But my guilty and fearful voices quickly jump in and take over.

"Are you asking me out on a date?" I ask. "Or is this about the team's project?"

"Neither," he replies. "I just wanted to talk about why you won't take my side in class."

I take a quick glance at the time on my phone and figure Eric won't notice if I'm a bit late. He's usually got his nose in a new journal article and loses track of time anyway.

"It's not about taking sides, Hunter," I say. "It's about how you say things. You can't keep blowing up at the team, or walking out on them, every time somebody disagrees with you."

"I realize that you and some of the others are upset with my opinions," Hunter says.

"That's a bit of an understatement," I reply. "But I get it. I know you're frustrated with them too."

"Of course I am," he blurts, his exasperation rising to the surface. "It must be pretty obvious that I've got a lot of firsthand knowledge I can share with the others about my culture and history. For one thing, the others are all obsessed about time deadlines."

Guilty, as charged.

I resist the urge to look at the time on my phone again.

"They don't understand that Indigenous people have a different concept of time. We don't see it as being linear, and we don't like to be rushed," he says.

"I understand where you're coming from, probably more than you realize. And I admire your commitment towards working for changes that benefit your people," I reply. "Remember, your team's goal is to learn about reconciliation. They know nothing about it right now. But, as they do research and learn, they'll probably become more open to your perspectives. Does that make sense?"

"It does," he answers slowly.

"So, do you think you can try to be more patient with the others, and learn to trust that they have the same goals as you in this course?" I say.

Hunter pauses for a moment to digest my comments.

"Since you put it that way," he says. "I guess I can try. Thanks for listening."

"No worries," I say.

I pause for a moment.

Okay, Sam. Do you address the elephant in the room now, or do you risk having it come up in tutorial tomorrow?

I decide there's no time like the present.

"There's one more thing," I say. "Have you got another minute?"

"Sure," he answers.

"I saw you on the news on Saturday," I announce. "So did members of your team. What are you going to say to them tomorrow night if they say something?"

"What do you want me to say," he answers. "What I do outside of class is none of their business!"

Hunter's defences are coming up and I realize I need to tread carefully.

"Technically, that's true," I reply. "Except in this case, your actions are relevant to the team's project, and you know how at least one of them is going to react. People on that team are going to take what you did as an attack on their values, and they're going to take it personally."

"That's their problem, not mine!" he says.

"Think of it this way," I counter. "When I laid down my ground rules last week, I asked you all to listen and talk to each other with respect. But remember, actions often speak louder than words. Non-verbal communication—your actions and body language—often have far more impact than your words."

"If you're telling me I need to stop being actively involved with my people in working for change, I won't do it!" he says.

"I'm not asking you to stop," I answer. "I'm asking you to pause and think about your actions. You're applying for Law School this year, right?"

"Yeah, so what?

"Do you think people on the Admissions Committee don't watch the local news? Do you think some of them don't have biases like Terri?" I argue. "There are times when you want your name in the news, and there are times when you don't! Just think about the big picture before you act … that's all I'm saying."

He pauses for a moment, and I almost think some of my words might have reached him. I glance at my phone while I wait for him to react.

"Oh, shit!" I shout. "I'm really late! If there's anything else, can you save it for the tutorial? I gotta go!"

I rush away and leave Hunter standing behind me. As I run, I start replaying the encounter in my mind. My sense of panic gradually softens. I exhale a huge sigh of relief at having avoided a major confrontation with Hunter. And then I begin to feel an unexpected sensation inside … a sense of accomplishment … growing self-confidence … and I really like the feeling!

CHAPTER 7—WEEK SIX

I DON'T know what I expected after yesterday's surprise encounter with Hunter. I saw a different, softer side of him that caught me completely off guard. They say that the best predictor of future behaviour is past behaviour. So why did I let myself start to think that maybe … just maybe … he'd turned the page on his 'mister tough guy' image? Did I really expect him to show up on time for tutorial, even when he pretty much told me that his clock doesn't run on colonial time? So, here I sit at the table with all of Team Reconciliation, except for Hunter, waiting for him to make an appearance. Who was I trying to fool, anyway? … apart from myself!

I make a promise to myself to just be an objective observer today …

Don't say a word, Sam … Even if he shows up fifteen minutes late! … No judgments … No interfering!

" I was hoping Hunter would have been here," Fatima begins, "So he could give us the details on our visit to *Spirits of the Seven Generations* on Saturday. But, since he's late again, I suppose we should start discussing what the research team has been doing over the past week."

Fatima looks around the table at the team.

"Terri, would you like to start?"

"Sure," she says. "I'm just starting to work my way through the *Indian Act*. Pretty damned dry reading, if you ask me. I also found a book by a Chief Joseph—it supposedly tells us about things we never knew about the *Indian Act*—but I haven't had time …"

The classroom door opens suddenly. Hunter saunters casually into the room and settles into the only remaining empty chair.

"Sorry I'm late," he says. "Couldn't help it."

I watch the team members' body language—icy stares, rolling eyeballs, and a couple of huffs—that betrays their collective frustration. Fatima jumps in to break the awkward silence.

"We were just starting to discuss the research team's progress before you arrived," Fatima says. "But, before we continue, have you confirmed details of our visit to the *Seven Generations* support centre?"

"I just finished talking with Ruby," Hunter replies. "Everything's all set. She'll meet the team at the centre on Saturday at ten A.M."

"Thank you," Fatima says. "The team was just saying how much we're looking forward to the visit … okay … where were we? … oh, yes … how is your research going?"

"I'm carrying most of it around in my head," he says. "But, don't worry. I'll get it written down in good time."

Fatima's expression turns into a skeptical frown.

"I see," she says. "Just a reminder that we only have four or five more weeks until we have to hand off our research and recommendations to the Plan of Action and Presentation teams."

Fatima turns her attention back to Terri.

"You were talking about the *Indian Act*? …"

"Oh, yes. I was just saying that it's a tough read. So far, I've found out that the 1876 Act consolidated the many regulations for managing Indians and reserves that came after Confederation."

Terri stops to look at Fatima.

"This is pretty boring stuff … do you want me to continue?" she asks.

"Try to keep it short, okay?" Fatima replies.

"Right," Terri says. "The Act gave Indians … as they're called in the Act … lands for reserves, created a system of government, provided for education, and made provisions for more modern housing."

"So you're saying those are good things?" Hunter interjects.

Terri's head snaps around and stares at Hunter, a look of disbelief on her face.

"Of course!" she says. "Since when was providing land, education, and housing a bad thing?"

Hunter rolls his eyes and shakes his head slowly from side to side.

Oh, no! ... Here it comes ... Let them work it out themselves ... Whatever he says, don't intervene ... Unless you absolutely have to!

"From the beginning, that's when!" Hunter bellows. "They only gave us a fraction of our land … often not even our own traditional land … and often land that couldn't grow decent crops. The government and housing were colonial, instead of Indigenous. And education? Really? I suppose you're going to say the residential school system was a good thing?"

I see Terri's face growing red as the confrontation escalates. I feel the familiar old sensations in my body … tight muscles … churning stomach … sweaty hands. I remember Barbara Way and I start slowing my breathing.

"The government has spent billions, maybe even trillions, of dollars on Indians since Confederation!" Terri counters. "We gave you special treatment when it comes to hunting and fishing, and we gave you free housing and education. So kindly explain what you and your people have done with all that money, and why they keep clamouring for more and more!"

Unable to contain his anger any longer, I watch helplessly as Hunter leaps to his feet and wags his finger at Terri.

Slow breathing Sam ... slow breathing ...

"If that's all you understand from reading that Act, then you either need new glasses, or you need to stop interpreting it through your racist, settler's eyes!"

"Stop!" Fatima shouts. "Just stop it!"

She slams a textbook on the table. Everybody in the room jumps in surprise, including me, followed by an immediate silence.

My heart is pounding. I see looks of shock on the faces of every team member, after the totally unexpected outburst from their normally calm, controlled leader.

"Hunter, sit down!" she shouts. "Do I have to remind you and Terri about Sam's ground rules? Like she said, you're both free to disagree, but we expect you to have the courtesy to show respect, to listen to each other, and then back up your points with research —*not* emotions! Understand?"

Fatima glares at the two offenders.

Wow, Fatima! ... I'm proud of you for grabbing back control of the meeting! ... I didn't know you had it in you!

"And while I'm talking about respect," Fatima continues. "Showing up late to team meetings is getting to be a bad habit that is disrespectful to everybody else on the team."

"Well, my clock and calendar don't run on colonial time," Hunter shoots back. "What about respecting my customs?"

We all stare in dismay as Hunter starts picking up his things.

"See you guys at Seven Generations!" he snaps, and then he abruptly walks out of the meeting.

"Isn't that just typical," Mandy blurts, rolling her eyes. "Is that all for tonight?"

I turn to Fatima, shake my head slowly, and shrug my shoulders. I feel sorry for her because I think she did her best to manage the meeting. She deserved better.

You were right to be suspicious, Sam ... Why would you expect him to change?

YOU'RE PROBABLY saying that I did pretty well with managing my anxiety at this week's tutorial session with Team

Reconciliation, despite Hunter's latest outburst. And you're probably partly right. I did manage to use the skills I've learned from Barbara, and I didn't panic in the face of Hunter's anger. A moral victory, right?

I wish life was that simple … that dealing with people was that easy! Just when I thought I'd made some progress in dealing with Hunter, it seems like he's taken two steps backwards. Why do the people in my life always seem to be sabotaging their lives? Even worse, why do they keep trying to sabotage my life too? Am I wearing a big sign on my back that says *Kick Me*? When I get thinking this way, I realize it's time to check in with Barbara, one of the few people I know who truly *does* have my back … but in a good way.

"I really think Hunter is trying to sabotage the team," I say, as I let out some of my pent-up frustration. "He's usually late for team meetings, he hasn't done any research yet, and all he does is stir up conflict within the team!"

"I understand your frustration, Sam," Barbara replies. "But sometimes people who've been abused—and that certainly includes Indigenous people—can become passive and non-assertive over time."

She pauses to let me digest her comment.

"And if those abuse victims try to become more assertive," she says. "They often overcorrect, and their actions can feel very aggressive to others. Does that make sense?"

"I think so," I answer, not too convincingly.

"Try to be patient with him," Barbara says. "Take time to listen, and try to model empathy. Find ways to show that you understand where he's coming from. See if that helps him change."

"Okay, I'll try."

"Good," she says. "Now, before you go today, I wanted to ask —how are your meetings with your Aunt Rose going?"

"Really well," I reply. "She's so calm and understanding … just like you. She listens and doesn't judge me at all. I feel really comfortable talking about Diane and my dad with her … did I tell you I went to a sweat lodge ceremony?"

"No, you didn't!" Barbara answers, her face reflecting her surprise. "What was it like?"

"It was hard … but amazing!" I say. "At one point, I didn't think I'd live through the heat. I'm pretty sure I was hallucinating … or maybe dissociating … I don't know which. All I know is that when it was over, I felt stronger … both mentally and physically!"

"Do you think you're feeling more like you could meet with your father?" she asks.

There it is … She trapped me! … I should have known that question was coming!

"I don't think I'm ready for that yet!" I snap. "I'm still feeling torn … I really want to find out more about my Anishinaabe heritage … but, I'm afraid it will trigger more flashbacks and panic attacks."

"I understand your fear," she says, calmly. "The flashbacks and panic feel overwhelmingly terrifying, don't they?"

I nod silently.

"Just remember to use the skills you've learned here," she continues. "Just like you did in this week's tutorial. And remember that inner strength you found in the sweat lodge ceremony. Close your eyes and see if you can re-create that same feeling in your body when you replay the memory. I know you can do it!"

I still feel torn. My younger, terrified inner voices are feeling pressured, crying for help from my protective caregiver and my angry voice, who are both rushing to the younger voices' defence.

Don't push us too hard … We're not ready! … Don't make us do it if we're not ready …

"I don't know," I mumble. "I'll have to think about it some more."

And then I feel it … that one voice that really pisses off the others, and causes all of the trouble!

You're not strong enough! ... What's wrong with you? ... How hard can it be? ... You're a loser who can't get her shit together ...

Yup! My guilty voice. Just when I thought I was getting stronger.

In the distance, I hear Barbara clearing her throat to help bring me back into the present. I see her glance at her watch.

"That looks like our time for today," she says. "We can talk about it again next week. Let's see what I have for appointments …"

THERE'S NOTHING like a good therapy session to stir shit up, and to throw a wrench into things! Even though my body is physically present in my office, sitting at the computer, I find myself staring right through *Woman Beside the Water*, while my mind leaps back and forth from one worry to the next. My brain feels like a busy Cirque-du-Soleil show, with little sideshows going on all over the stage. All of the newly-found energy I'd brought back from the sweat lodge ceremony seems to have disappeared, and I definitely feel stuck in a confused funk.

What IS keeping you from calling your dad, Sam? ... What's the worst that could happen? ... He hasn't been part of your life since you were three ... If he doesn't want to meet you, you haven't lost anything ... What do you have to lose? ...

Seems like it should be a no-brainer, right? But then there's the other competing voices.

What if he rejects you again? ... Why would you expect him to want to see you again? ... Why would he want to be with such a loser!

A sudden knock at my door causes me to jump, and yanks my mind back into reality.

Fatima pokes her head into the office. Her facial expression is serious.

"Come on in," I say.

"Do you have a few minutes?"

"Sure," I answer. "Have a seat. What can I do for you?"

Fatima slides into a chair beside my roommate's desk.

"The whole team … not just Terri … is extremely upset about Hunter, and they've asked me to talk to you. They feel like he's very passive-aggressive, and they also feel like they're being bullied whenever he gets angry."

"Go on," I say.

"So far, he hasn't brought any research for the team to consider, and term is half over. If this keeps up, I can't see the team coming together in time to finish our project."

Fatima pauses, looks down, and swallows nervously.

"They've asked me if it's possible for a team to expel a member," she says.

I pause and exhale slowly while I digest Fatima's unexpected request.

"Wow," I say. "I didn't know the team felt so strongly! … I have to admit I feel the same frustration and hopelessness when dealing with him. But, I feel like expelling him would be seen as insensitive and racist. And then, wouldn't we just be proving him right?"

"We didn't think about that … so what are we going to do about him?" she asks. "What do I tell the team?"

Thanks for putting me on the spot … I haven't even figured this dilemma out for myself yet … I haven't even had a chance yet to try what Barbara suggested in therapy … Barbara's suggestions … That's it!

An image of Barbara Way pops into my head, and I find myself recalling her words from this week's therapy session.

"Ask the team to take time to listen … I mean *really* listen … to what he says," I say, remembering Barbara's words. "Ask them to try to focus on *anything* that they can agree with, and try to be more patient and understanding of where he's coming from. See how he reacts to the team being more empathic. Maybe he'll start to trust them a bit more, if he feels you're all making more of an effort to understand his perspective."

Fatima takes a moment to mull over my comments.

"I'll talk to the team and ask them to try that," she says. "But we don't have much time, Sam. What if it doesn't work?"

"Let's give it a week or two," I suggest. "If he's still not pulling his weight with the team by then, I'll have to talk with Dr. Sanderson. We can't let him sabotage the team and take them down with him."

Fatima stands, seemingly satisfied with my temporary solution.

"Thank you," she says.

"Don't worry," I add. "I'll be watching him closely in our next meeting."

Fatima bows and nods slightly to me, then turns and quietly lets herself out of the office, leaving me alone and deep in thought. I let out a long, slow, sigh.

What ARE we going to do about you, Hunter? ... Especially if this doesn't work?

HAVE YOU ever had one of those days when you wake up feeling really optimistic, full of energy, and looking forward to doing something special? And then everything you own breaks down at the same time? Or everything that can possibly go wrong, goes to crap all at once? Well, that's the way my day has gone so far. They call it Murphy's Law … yet, when it happens to me, it almost feels normal … like I don't deserve for things in my life to go right.

Today wasn't supposed to be that way. I woke up feeling rested and full of anticipation, anxious to get on the road to the *Healing Lodge* for tonight's *Full Moon Ceremony*. I'm just tossing my overnight bag into the car, ready to get behind the wheel, when my phone rings. I notice that it's Fatima calling, and I'm immediately torn.

Decision time ... Are you going to let this go to voicemail and call her back tomorrow night? ... Or are you going to call her back right now?

After my recent meeting with Fatima, the call somehow feels ominous. That's when I remember that this is the day of Team Reconciliation's visit to *Spirits of the Seven Generations*. My phone continues to ring.

Shit! This can't be good.

I tap the answer button and I hear the call connect.

"Hi, Fatima. Sam here. What's up?"

"We are here at *Spirits of the Seven Generations* for our tour, but I cannot believe it—Hunter has not shown up yet! What should I do?"

I glance at my watch and do some quick time calculations in my head.

You don't have to be at the lodge until late afternoon ... You've got plenty of time.

"I live really close to the centre. I'll be there in a few minutes."

SPIRITS of the Seven Generations is located in one of those old Tudor-style houses that were once home to the city's upper class, almost a century ago—the kind of home that few individuals can afford to maintain, and are usually occupied by high profile professionals, especially law firms or charitable foundations. On display on the porch is a memorial of teddy bears wearing orange t-shirts, along with many pairs of empty shoes to commemorate the lives of children who didn't survive the residential schools. I pause to pay my respects, remembering what it was like to be an abused child. Without warning, I feel my inner three-year-old, and

I feel her overwhelming mixture of loneliness, fear, and sadness. After a moment, I manage to wipe my tears away and I take a deep breath, ready to face Fatima and the team waiting inside.

As I enter the building, I see and hear Ruby Smith, the centre's director. She's already talking to team members at the far end of the room.

Fatima and Katya break away from the group and walk in my direction.

"I cannot believe he has not shown up yet! He is twenty minutes late!" Fatima says quietly.

"This is *so* embarrassing," Katya whispers.

I pause to listen to Ruby, who is describing the centre's services to the team.

"We're here to provide support for Indigenous People who are feeling the effects of intergenerational racism and trauma."

Arjun raises his hand.

"You have a question?" Ruby asks.

"Yes. Can you tell us more about those effects?" Arjun asks.

"Of course," Ruby replies. "We hear about them all the time on the news. Poverty, alcohol and drug abuse, the disproportionately high number of Indigenous People in the prison system, youth suicide, family and child welfare problems … do I need to go on?"

Arjun and the remaining team members look at each other and collectively shake their heads.

"We provide services for all age groups," Ruby continues. "Rock climbing and martial arts classes for children and youth, assistive aids for seniors, food supports for those living in poverty, cultural and language programs, legal services, …"

I notice Terri raise her hand.

"Go ahead," Ruby says patiently.

"What kind of legal services? Do you have lawyers on staff?" Terri asks.

"That's a great question, and it's something very close to my heart," Ruby says. "I lost my way a few years ago and ended up in jail for stealing to support my drug habit. I couldn't afford a lawyer or bail. So I sat in jail for weeks, while other women who had committed worse crimes, like murder, got out on bail."

Terri shakes her head, and I see a side of her I hadn't seen before.

"I understand your pain," Terri says. "I've been there and done that. But, compared to you, I guess I was lucky. I had somebody who believed in me enough to bail me out."

"It happens all the time," Ruby says. "So, our centre connects inmates to lawyers who understand Indigenous issues, to agencies who can provide emergency housing, and we also provide food support. I was lucky enough to be on the receiving end of these services … they helped me to feel accepted, and they helped me to heal and to find purpose in my life again."

I'm happy to see Ruby continuing to engage the team members and answer their questions. On one hand, I'm grateful to Hunter for arranging the tour. But on the other, I'm furious at his blatant disrespect for Ruby and his teammates.

Fatima looks at her watch and shakes her head in disgust.

"It has been half an hour … he is not going to show up. It looks like I am going to have to apologize and make excuses for him," she says. "Unless you want to do it, Sam."

"I can't believe how rude and inconsiderate he is!" Katya echos.

I feel my phone vibrate in my pocket and I huff impatiently at the intrusion. I take it out of my pocket, and my eyes pop open in surprise.

What the? …

"I've got to take this!" I blurt. "It's Hunter!"

I leave Fatima and Katya behind, staring at each other with stunned looks on their faces.

I tap the answer button.

"Where are you?" I whisper tersely. "You were supposed to meet the team here half an hour ago! … What? … Again? … The Court House? … Why me? … Twenty minutes? … Okay, I'll see you then!"

I look at my watch, my mind doing rapid calculations to see if I can still make it to the *Healing Lodge* in time. I wave to Fatima and Katya.

"I'll tell you about it later! Gotta run!" I say, before spinning around and hurrying from the centre.

Shit! This is going to be close! ... Why did I bother getting out of bed this morning?

SITTING IN a courtroom, waiting for Hunter's preliminary appearance in front of a Magistrate, is most certainly not the way I thought I'd be spending this crisp, clear, sunny October Saturday afternoon. I can't stop myself from looking impatiently at my watch, eager to get on the road to reach the tranquility of Rose and the *Healing Lodge*. I've arrived just in time to see a woman in black robes take her seat on the Bench, at the front of the room.

"All stand!" the bailiff calls out. "The Honourable Judge Amy Garcia presiding"

As Judge Garcia takes her seat, I glance around the room and see only a handful of local news reporters, the bailiff, and another woman in black robes who is seated at the Crown Prosecutor's table. A door opens at the front of the room, revealing Hunter, who is ushered by the bailiff to the Defence table. Hunter seats himself in a chair behind the table.

"First case!" Judge Garcia announces.

"The Crown versus Hunter MacMillan," the Bailiff answers. He glares at Hunter, sending non-verbal instructions for him to stand up.

Hunter rises back to his feet.

"Your Honour," Hunter says, acknowledging the Judge.

Judge Garcia looks over the top of her glasses towards Hunter.

"Mr. MacMillan," she begins. "You're charged with vandalism and public mischief. How do you plead?"

"Not guilty, Your Honour," Hunter replies.

"I see that this isn't the first time you've been involved in something like this. Do you have access to Counsel?" the Judge asks.

"No, Your Honour, I'll be defending myself," he says. His voice sounds confident, verging on cocky.

She looks up over her glasses at Hunter again.

"I would advise you to reconsider, Mr. MacMillan," she says. "Do you have anything to say in your defence today?"

"Yes, Your Honour," he says, confidently. "I'm an Indigenous person, just a university student, who was expressing my Constitutional right to freedom of speech and expression."

Judge Garcia looks up over her glasses again, this time at the motley group of spectators in the room.

"Is there anybody in the room who can vouch for you, Mr. MacMillan?" she asks.

"Yes," he answers. "One of my university instructors … Samantha Bower."

Oh shit! Is that why he wanted me here?

I'm suddenly conscious of my appearance—torn blue jeans, dyed purple hair, and my nose ring. I feel Judge Garcia's penetrating stare, and I feel like crawling under my seat.

"Ms. Bower?" she calls, looking over her glasses at me.

I swallow, trying to clear the giant lump I feel in the back of my throat.

"Yes, Your Honour," I manage to say.

"You're his instructor?" Judge Garcia asks.

"Yes, Your Honour," I reply. "I'm his teaching assistant in a Team Building course at the university."

Judge Garcia pauses for a moment, and I see a wry smile on her face as she catches the irony in my answer. I wait for a sarcastic comment about Hunter's lack of team play, but the Judge wisely decides to take a pass on grabbing such low-hanging fruit.

"Can you vouch for Mr. MacMillan … that he'll appear in court on this matter?"

I pause and turn my gaze to Hunter. I see him watching me closely, his eyes pleading with me to say yes.

You'd better hope I don't regret this!

"I can, Your Honour," I answer, trying my best to sound confident and professional.

Judge Garcia turns her attention to the Crown Prosecutor.

"Any objections to bail from the Crown?" she asks.

"No, Your Honour," the other robed woman replies.

The courtroom is silent as Judge Garcia shuffles some papers and does some writing. Finally, she lifts her head and looks over her glasses again.

"Mr. MacMillan," she announces. "You're to appear in this Court on December 10th of this year. Bail is set at five hundred dollars, and a condition of your bail is that you stay away from the statue in Victoria Park until your next appearance. Is that clear?"

"Yes, Your Honour," Hunter replies.

"Good, see the office on your way out to make the bail arrangements. This case is adjourned."

Judge Garcia bangs her gavel.

"Next case!" she says to the bailiff.

The bailiff nods to Hunter, signalling that he's free to go. He makes his way to where I'm sitting at the back of the room, and we exit together in silence into a corridor. I stop and turn to face Hunter. My angry inner voice is primed and ready to unleash itself at him.

"I'm sorry, Sam," he says. "My sister's away this weekend, and I didn't know anybody else I could call today."

"And you thought that maybe I might be available, because I might be just a few minutes away at *Spirits of the Seven Generations*? You've got a lot of nerve, organizing that tour and not even bothering to show up to introduce the team to Ruby! Do you think I didn't have other things I needed to do today?"

I see Hunter's mouth start to open.

"Don't say a word!" I scream. "Defacing statues isn't an act of reconciliation—it's an act of retribution! All it does is generate push-back and animosity from the non-Indigenous community. I'm so pissed off, I don't even want to talk to you! Especially after I already warned you last week!"

Hunter hangs his head. I'm surprised to see that he actually looks embarrassed.

"Are you stupid, or just plain deaf!" I shout, continuing my rant. "Can't you see that I'm just trying to keep you from sabotaging your own future? If you really want to help your people by becoming a lawyer, smarten up and start behaving like one!"

I pause long enough to take a breath, before I continue my verbal assault.

"And you'd better stay away from that statue, and be here on December 10th," I shout. "I don't want to look like an idiot for vouching for you. Now, if you don't mind, I'm late for something really important!"

I see Jessica Chen, the local TV news reporter, coming our way. I wheel around and stomp away in the opposite direction.

He'll regret this even more if I don't make it to the Healing Lodge in time! ... And he'd better be smart about what he says to that reporter!

A quick glance at my watch tells me I need to run to my car and hit the road without any more delays. I may have just enough time to get to the lodge. That is, of course, unless Murphy's Law strikes again ... like causing my car to break down, or whatever else Murphy might have planned for me.

As I approach my Yaris, the feeling of foreboding in my gut comes alive as I see the long, yellow sheet of paper under my windshield wiper, flapping happily in the breeze.

"Perfect! Just friggin' perfect!" I shout to Murphy and the parking gods, as I rip the parking ticket out from under the wiper blade.

I throw open the driver's door, throw the ticket onto the passenger seat, and turn the key in the ignition. Thankfully, the engine roars to life and I accelerate out into the flow of traffic. Feeling the tension in my chest, I finally allow myself to sigh—letting out a long, slow breath as I glance at my watch.

Can this day possibly get any worse?

CHAPTER 8—FULL MOON

I TWIST the ignition key to turn off the engine in my trusty little Yaris, and then I allow myself a major sigh of relief. Although the nondescript silver car may soon be an antique, she thankfully didn't succumb to Murphy's Law today, getting me to the Healing Lodge just in time. I look out the window toward Georgian Bay, and I see the last dying glow of daylight on the horizon. The sky is turning a deep, dark blue hue, with Venus and some brighter stars twinkling. It's a good omen for viewing tonight's full harvest moon.

I exit the vehicle and grab my overnight bag from the back seat, before walking across the parking lot and up the stairs to the *Healing Lodge*. Rose sees me through the window and comes running to the front door to open it for me.

"You made it!" she shouts, her face beaming with joy. "Come to my office. You can change into warmer clothes there. Would you like a cup of Ojibwe tea to help you relax?"

"That would be perfect," I answer. "I've been stressed out and angry all day. You remember that Indigenous student I told you about last time?"

"Yes, I do," she says. "Is he the one who poured red paint on the Queen Victoria statue?"

"That's the one," I reply. "He was at it again today."

"I know," Rose says. "That news item has gone national. He's drawing a lot of attention to Indigenous issues."

"Well, he's making my life a lot more difficult in the process!" I blurt. "Why is he so resistant to listening to the other team members' opinions? Why does he insist that his view of reconciliation is the *only* view when it only seems to create more pushback from the rest of the team?"

Rose sighs and then smiles. I admire her calm demeanour and the fact that nothing ever seems to fluster her, not even my frustration.

"Be understanding," Rose answers, as we continue walking towards the lodge. "Help him to understand that his words are like small seeds … they will need time and patience before they can germinate and take root in people's minds. But, as those seeds grow, the others will slowly open their eyes and their minds, and they will begin to see new possibilities."

"That makes sense," I say. "But what about the rest of the team's points of view? They make some good points … if their ideas are like seeds, will Hunter ever give them a chance to take root in his mind?"

"Be patient … give them time," Rose responds.

"But we're running out of time. They've wasted half of the term, and they only have a few more weeks to get their act together! There must be something more I can do to get everybody to reach some sort of a compromise!"

Rose smiles again and puts her hand gently on my shoulder.

"In your therapy with Dr. Way, when do you find that you make the biggest insights and gains … when she lectures you, or when she gives you a bit of new information and then asks questions?"

"Like you're doing now?" I answer. We both smile and have a good chuckle. "When she asks questions … it guides me in a certain direction and forces me to think, so I come up with my own answers."

"Exactly," Rose replies. "Just because Hunter and the rest of the team disagree with each other, it doesn't necessarily mean that they don't respect each other. Be patient, give them time, and be prepared to ask questions and guide them when necessary. Do you think you can do that?"

She's telling you to take a step back and get out of the team's way!

"Patience isn't my strong point, but I suppose I can try," I reply sheepishly.

"Good. We have some time before we have to leave for the ceremony," Rose says, as we arrive at her office and she closes the door. "Would you like to smudge? You might find it helpful in cleansing yourself of the negative energy you're feeling right now."

I take a moment to mull over Rose's offer and to remember my first experience with smudging during the sweat lodge ceremony, while Rose boils water and begins the process of steeping our Ojibwe tea.

"Sure," I reply finally. "I could use anything right now to relieve the stress I've been feeling all day, but I'm not sure I remember how to do it."

Rose picks up a large white shell containing a small bundle of sage, and then she lights it carefully. The ends of the sage start to glow orange, and wisps of fragrant smoke start to rise and swirl in the air. She picks up a large feather and begins making a circular fanning motion, directing the sacred smoke over our torsos, then over our mouths, and finally over our heads.

"Focus on all the negative energy in your body," she says. "Then pray to the creator to take it away … to replace it with positive energy and intentions."

I follow Rose's lead, breathing in the fragrant air a number of times, and then exhaling tension and negative energy each time.

"Now, you try it," she says.

She hands me the shell with the burning sage and the feather. I feel awkward and clumsy as I begin fanning smoke towards me with the feather.

"Start with your heart," she says, as she watches patiently. "That's very good. Now fan it over your lips … then your ears … and finally, your head …"

Rose says a prayer in her native Anishinaabe language as I finish smudging my head. When she's finished her prayer, I hand the shell and its smoldering sage back to Rose.

"You did very well. You're a natural," she says. I notice a sense of pride and joy on her face. She pours me a cup of the tea that has been steeping while we smudged.

"Here you go," she says. "When you're done, change into your warmer clothes and we'll leave for the ceremony."

I take a sip of Ojibwe tea and allow myself to unwind even further, grateful that Murphy's Law appears to be in my rear view mirror for now. Finally, I allow myself to feel a glimmer of hopeful anticipation for the ceremony that I'm about to experience for the first time.

DRESSED FOR the crisp, cool, mid-October night, Rose and I carry our camp chairs through the forest trail, towards the same firepit that was used for the sweat lodge ceremony. We join a group of women who are already gathered around a fire, which is tended by a fire keeper, the only man present. I look up at the perfectly clear sky, where more and more bright stars are appearing as night falls. The air is still, and I hear the sound of coyotes in the distance. I turn my attention back to the women around me. Most of them are attired in traditional ribbon skirts, along with more practical winter jackets, boots, toques, leggings, and mittens. The skirts are adorned with ribbons of black, red, yellow, and white that circle the bottom portion of the garments. Rose pulls two yellow objects from a small bag that she is carrying.

"I've tied up some tobacco in two small squares of yellow fabric for you," she says. "It's customary to give one as a gift to the fire keeper, and to throw the other into the fire later on, as an offering to Grandmother Moon.

She hands one of the yellow bundles to me, and I carry it over and offer it to the fire keeper. After I return to Rose, she hands me the other bundle to put in my pocket for later. Then she steps inside the circle to begin the ceremony.

"We gather around this sacred fire tonight," she begins, "to celebrate Grandmother Moon and the tenth moon of this year—the *Falling Leaves Moon*. This is the time of year when Mother Earth honours us with Her grandest colours."

Rose spreads her arms wide and turns her body slowly in a circle, paying tribute to the beauty of the natural vista surrounding us.

"We bring our gifts, our intentions, and our offerings to Her to celebrate the miracles of Creation around us, and to give thanks for everything that gives us life," she says, completing her greeting.

Rose returns to stand beside me during a moment of silence, while the remaining women think on their intentions and make their prayers to Mother Earth. Then, one-by-one, the women begin lighting sprigs of sage or small clumps of tobacco inside shells or bowls. Some use feathers, while others simply use their hands, to smudge the sacred smoke over their offerings, the food they brought for the post-ceremony feast, and themselves. Rose and I join in, smudging our offerings first, and then smudging ourselves again as part of the ceremony.

The smudging complete, the women step up to the fire, one-by-one, and gently throw their yellow offerings into the flames.

"I have some food back in the lodge for us to contribute to the feast," Rose whispers, while we step up to the fire to make our offerings. We then return to our place around the fire with the other women.

With the offerings now made, the attendees begin drumming out a rhythm on hand drums, and they begin chanting traditional songs towards the eastern sky.

"I noticed some women who remained seated and didn't make an offering," I say to Rose, raising my voice over the songs and drumming. "Is there a reason for that?"

"Those women are on Moontime … their sacred time of the month. It's a time when they relax and take it easy, while others take care of them and do their work for them," she says. "It's a time for women to cleanse themselves … physically, emotionally, and spiritually … a time when they can ask Grandmother Moon for healing energy … and a time when some women often feel like they are their most powerful."

At that moment, an enormous autumn moon begins to peek slowly over the eastern horizon.

Wow, it's huge! This is so beautiful!

"The *Full Moon Ceremony* is about letting go," Rose says, "so that we no longer carry around the things that we no longer wish to have as burdens. We are asking Grandmother Moon to shine her moonlight on us for strength and guidance."

I stand, completely still, in awe of the ceremony's spectacle, now unfolding in front of me. I allow myself to bask quietly in the warm feeling of celebration. Then, unexpectedly, I find myself swaying to the rhythm of the drums and trying to sing along with the songs. Before long, I feel myself slipping into a semi-hypnotic trance, lost in the almost non-stop singing and drumming that continues until the moon reaches the height of the tree line. At that point in time, the chanting and drumming stops. I open my mind and body to soak up the moment of natural silence that follows. I feel calm, serene, and at peace.

"The ceremony will be over soon," Rose whispers. "Let's walk back to the lodge, and you can help me arrange the food for the feast."

We fold up our camp chairs, Rose picks up her bag, and we begin walking back through the forest, guided by the light of the full moon.

"What did you think of the ceremony?" Rose asks.

"It was beautiful … almost magical," I answer. "This may sound crazy, but I feel like I'm starting to see the world through two sets of eyes at once these days. During the ceremony, I felt as if there was a wave of energy flowing through my body … sort of like how I felt after the sweat lodge … I feel stronger … yet I also feel lighter, if that makes any sense … like there's less weight on my shoulders."

I pause for a moment to think, and then I turn to face Rose.

"I think I'm ready to call him," I say.

Rose places a hand on my arm.

"I'm glad," she says. "Just remember one thing. Many of the survivors don't like to talk about their past, especially their time at the schools. It's just too painful for them. So don't get your hopes up too high … meeting with you might be too painful for him."

"I understand," I reply. "But I'm pretty sure I'll regret it for the rest of my life if I don't try."

I GIVE Rose a long, warm embrace, and then she holds the door open as I pick up my bag and exit the Healing Lodge. I stand on the front steps for a moment, trying to psych myself up for going back to the city and all the stressors I'd left behind for the past couple of days. I look out over Georgian Bay and I notice that the sky is clouding over and the wind is picking up. I hope it's not an omen of what my upcoming week is going to be like. I walk to my car, throw my bag in the back seat, and slip in behind the wheel. I sit silently for a few moments, before I take my phone from my purse. I stare at the new contact that I just typed into my phone … it feels like an eternity while I sit staring … then I toss the phone into the passenger seat.

I lean my head against the steering wheel and close my eyes.

Get it over with, Sam … No sense putting it off any longer … You can do this!

Moments pass while my inner voices battle for control. Finally, I sit up, reach over to the passenger seat, pick up my phone, and tap the send button. I realize I'm holding my breath while the phone rings. Finally, I hear it connect.

"Hello?" I say, meekly.

My voice is so shaky I can barely speak.

"Is this Charlie? … Charlie Mitchell? … This is your daughter … Samantha."

CHAPTER 9—WEEK SEVEN

I'M TRYING to be a better TA this week. The peace and tranquility of the Healing Lodge, especially being around Rose, has helped me to realize that I've been getting too personally involved in Team Reconciliation's conflicts, and I need to take a step back. I've often wondered what it's like to be a fly-on-the-wall in many situations, so this is my opportunity to practice.

So far, Fatima's done a good job of starting off the meeting. She told me that she wasn't going to call out Hunter for missing Saturday's tour of *Spirits of the Seven Generations*, and she also didn't want to draw any attention to his involvement in the second vandalization of Queen Victoria's statue. As if the rest of the team hadn't heard about it already! I agree with her wise decision.

"Article 26 of the *United Nations Declaration* states that we have an inherent right to the traditional territories that we've lived on since time immemorial," Hunter begins.

He looks in my direction and tries to make eye contact, but I look down at the table and pretend I'm taking notes.

"Article 26 also states that we have the right to own, use, develop, and control those traditional lands, or any lands that we have acquired since," he continues. "Finally, the article declares that countries must give legal recognition to these lands and resources in a way that is consistent with our customs and traditions."

He looks around the table at the rest of the team.

"So, if Europeans hadn't settled here, we would still be occupying and managing those traditional lands," he concludes. "And, because those rights are now recognized in Section 35 of

Canada's *Constitution Act*, the federal and provincial governments must recognize these inherent land claims."

"Maybe you'd still be occupying those lands … maybe not," Uri says. "Are you familiar with Heisenberg's *Uncertainty Principle* in physics?"

"I don't see how that's relevant here," Hunter says, his facial expression signalling his skepticism.

"Bear with me," Uri replies. "The principle states that the very act of observing an object changes it. So, even if the Europeans had only made a brief appearance in the Americas, it could have changed Indigenous cultures in many unpredictable ways over time, even without colonization."

"Yes, and one could argue," Mandy adds, "that once the land bridge with Northeast Asia disappeared, your people were fortunate to have been spared countless waves of human migration due to climate, war, famine, or overpopulation, that the rest of mankind experienced for thousands of years. You could call it a sort of 'Indigenous Privilege'."

I see Hunter's body stiffen, and he shifts in his chair.

Oh, damn! … He's getting angry again … Try to restrain yourself, Sam.

"This is what I've been talking about," Hunter says, trying to restrain himself. "It's always about the European view of history! Before there can be reconciliation, there has to be a truthful retelling of history!"

I sense the old familiar muscle tension and churning stomach trying to hijack my body again.

"So, you just want to ignore the genetic and archaeological evidence?" Mandy responds. "That's your version of the truth?"

Hunter leaps to his feet, unable to hold himself back anymore. He looks directly at me, and I feel my body start to tremble all over.

"Say something, Sam!" he pleads. "I feel like I'm banging my head against a wall with this bunch of racists! If you can't do something, I'm out of here!"

I feel both my body and brain freezing up. I can't seem to get my thoughts straight or find any words to say.

"That is enough!" Fatima shouts. She glares at Hunter. "Is that how you deal with everything in your life? Every time you disagree with anybody, you just run away? Or you show up late, or do not even bother to show up at all? How do you ever expect others to respect and listen to you?"

Hunter turns in my direction and glares.

"So, what's it going to be, Sam? Are you going to side with them?"

I notice my internal angry voice gathering in strength, overruling my fear. I dig deep and suck in a big breath, pausing while I search for the right words, and then I exhale.

So much for being a fly on the wall!

"I think you've raised a lot of significant and valid issues with the team, Hunter," I answer.

A look of smug satisfaction appears on his face, as he looks around the table at his teammates. The look is short-lived.

"But," I add. "I think your fellow team members have made some good points as well. It isn't about who's view is right and who's is wrong. Team building is about learning to listen to others and to find respectful ways to disagree. When you keep walking away from the team, or when you're late, or when you simply don't show up, you're disrespecting them!"

Hunter sits down abruptly, crossing his arms across his chest, clamping his mouth shut, and closing himself off from the rest of the team in an act of defiance.

Like I did in the courthouse on Saturday, I'm suddenly discovering a surprising source of strength in my angry inner voice. But tonight, I feel like some of my other inner voices are also starting to sit up, feeling some of that same strength.

"*Nobody* owes *any* of us respect," I continue. We have to earn it by respecting others first. If you want this team to respect you and take you seriously, you're going to need to start respecting and trusting them. Give the team a chance … trust them … they might surprise you and find ways to compromise. What do you have to lose?"

With my newly-found sense of self-confidence, I look around the table at the other team members.

"And that goes for the rest of the team too," I conclude. "Time's running out for you guys. You either get your shit together soon, and start applying to your project what Dr. Sanderson is teaching in the lectures, or you're all in danger of failing this course!"

I work my way around the table, giving each team member a few seconds of my newly-found evil eye. I don't have time or patience to deal with their dysfunction anymore. I've got other, more important things on my mind these days … like Charlie … wondering what it's going to be like to meet him … wondering what we'll talk about … and most importantly, wondering if we'll be able to accept each other into our lives again …

CHAPTER 10—WEEKS EIGHT & NINE

I'M GROWING more comfortable with the idea that I'm starting to see the world through two sets of eyes. My therapy sessions with Barbara Way have helped me learn to manage my panic, my cutting habit, and my eating disorder. And learning to see the world with the help of Barbara's eyes, has also helped me become more comfortable with having a number of different inner voices. But meeting Rose, and visiting her at the Healing Lodge, has opened a second set of eyes I never knew I had. Learning about Indigenous culture and learning to see the world from that perspective, has given me a new way of seeing myself that balances and complements the insights I've gained through Western psychology.

"The *Full Moon Ceremony* was beautiful!" I tell Barbara. "It was energizing … just like I felt after the *Sweat Lodge Ceremony*."

"I'm definitely seeing a difference in you lately," Barbara says. "Can you put it into words?"

"I don't know for sure," I say. "It's hard to describe … but every time I go to the *Healing Lodge*, I feel more like I belong there … like I know myself better. It's helped me to feel stronger."

I pause to gather and sort out more thoughts as they continue to stream through my consciousness.

"In some ways, I don't feel as angry towards Charlie lately, knowing that he was a residential school survivor. I think the *Full Moon Ceremony* helped me to realize that I need to focus more on the positive things in my life … like how lucky I was that my uncle and aunt adopted me and gave me a good home … how I

managed to stop cutting myself and restricting my food intake …
how I made it to grad school."

"Do you think that translates into an increase in your self-
confidence?" Barbara asks.

"Definitely," I reply. "It's given me confidence in knowing
that there are times when it's okay to be angry … times when
people are treating you, or other people, in ways that aren't okay
… as long as I don't *act* in anger."

I look at Barbara and laugh.

"I'm still having trouble with that part!" I say. "Just ask
Hunter and the rest of Team Reconciliation after my outbursts last
week."

"I'm proud of you for having the confidence to face your
anxiety and to call Charlie," she says. "But, I want to caution you
not to get overconfident. I see that happen often … people start
feeling better and forget that life is still going to throw surprises at
them … then they're at risk of crashing again when something bad
happens."

I shake my head and laugh again, this time more tentatively.

"Don't worry," I counter. "I'm still anxious about meeting him
this weekend. I don't feel the least bit overconfident."

"Well, I just want to remind you to stick to the basics, and to
keep using the tools you've learned here," she says. "They'll help
you get through the meeting with Charlie, and help you deal with
any surprises when they happen. By the way, how is it going with
the reconciliation team? You had some angry outbursts?"

"Things aren't good with them, and it's extremely frustrating,"
I answer. "But I think you would have been proud of me last week.
I managed to confront Hunter on his disrespectful behaviour. I
think I surprised myself … and the rest of the team too! I just need
to learn to be less angry when I confront people from now on."

"How did Hunter react?" Barbara asks.

"I'm not sure if it did any good," I say. "He just sat there and
didn't say a thing for the rest of the meeting. But, I also pointed

my finger at the others too. I warned them that time's running out on all of them, if they don't get their act together!"

Suddenly realizing that I've lost track of time, I glance at my watch.

"I'm sorry, I'm going overtime," I say. "Same time next week?"

"Same time," Barbara says. "I'm looking forward to hearing how things go with Charlie. I hope you have a good week."

I gather my things and get up to leave, but I stop with the office door partly open.

"I will," I answer. "And thanks for everything."

I close the door behind me and make my way out of the building. A strong gust of cold, damp northwest wind greets me. I shiver, then zip my coat all the way up, pull my toque down over my ears, and put on my gloves.

Time to get back to your office. That thesis proposal isn't going to type itself.

As I approach the Student Union Building, I make a quick detour.

It may not type itself, but a double-double should at least help to keep me awake!

I'VE CONCLUDED that gathering together all of my readings, and typing a reference list for my thesis proposal, is indeed the most boring task on the planet. My double-double has not been the least bit effective in preventing me from sitting at my desk, and staring at the monitor like a deer, caught in the glare of a set of high-beams. Instead, I'm preoccupied with my upcoming visit with Charlie … what will I say? … what will he say? … will he ever want to see me again? … what should I wear? … will he even be interested in my life and what I'm doing? … should I say anything about his past or the residential schools? …

I reach for my coffee and realize there's only a slurp left at the bottom.

More coffee ... Sounds like a good reason to take a break.

A knock on my office door startles me out of my daydream.

"Come in," I call out.

The door opens and Fatima pokes her head into the room.

"Is this a good time?" she asks.

"Sure, I needed a break anyway," I say, grateful for any excuse.

She opens the door and I notice that Shanise and Katya are standing behind her.

Uh, oh. This doesn't look good!

I look around my cramped little office.

"Sorry, I only have one extra chair," I say, shrugging my shoulders.

"Not a problem," Shanise answers. "I can stand."

"Me too," Katya adds.

"I can stand too," Fatima says. "We shouldn't be long."

"Well, at least take off your coats and make yourself comfortable," I say. "You can throw them on the spare desk."

With their coats comfortably stacked on the desk, Fatima clears her voice.

"It has been two weeks since we last talked about Hunter, and nothing has changed. He simply will not discuss things unless they are on his agenda!" she states.

"After you scolded him in that last meeting," Shanise adds, "did you notice how he went all passive-aggressive and said nothing? He just sat there and pouted like a little child!"

"I'm beginning to think that he wants us all to fail, just to make a point and to show he's in control," Katya says.

"Last time we met, you said that you would do something if things did not get better in the next two weeks," Fatima recalls. "Two weeks have passed, and the team is no further ahead."

I pause to digest their concerns.

"I feel your frustration," I say. "But, to be fair, Terri has been a problem too. It's a difficult situation, and I want you to know it's been on my mind a lot over the past two weeks. I'm trying to think of a solution so we don't have to get Dr. Sanderson involved."

I reach for a sheet of paper on my desk, and I show it to the three team members.

"I looked up some of the classic psychology experiments on overcoming racism in different groups of people. We've learned that, by far the best way to get people to break down stereotypes, to accept each other, and to work as a team, is to put them in situations where they must work together in order to succeed."

"But Dr. Sanderson already did that for us," Katya replies. "And it's clearly not working!"

"Clearly," I repeat.

I look at each one of the women in turn, my eyes silently looking for hints that one of them might have a suggestion. The room remains silent.

"Any ideas for how we can bring this team together?" I say bluntly. "We're getting desperate, so no idea is too crazy."

An uncomfortable silence descends on my office.

Come on! ... Somebody! ... Don't leave this all up to me!

Finally, Shanise breaks the silence.

"When I was a little girl in Curaćao, whenever we needed to get something done in the community, we would have a large dinner where every person brings something ... what do you call it here?" she asks.

"You mean a potluck dinner?" Katya says.

"Yes! That's it," Shanise answers. "But, in this case, we could get each team member to share a dish that is important to their culture."

I take a moment to let the idea sink in.

"You know," I say. "That's not a bad idea ... everybody loves food ... and food has always had a way of bringing people together. Just look at the multicultural festival every summer in the

park. The different ethnic foods draw people from all cultures …
but, would that be enough?"

"What about music?" Fatima asks. "They usually have
entertainment at those international food fairs."

"Also not a bad idea," I say. "But where would we find some
cheap entertainment? Remember, we're all just students."

More silence. I can almost hear the gears turning slowly in our
collective brains.

"What about asking team members to share something about
their interests or hobbies?" Fatima asks. "It might be a way to get
to know each other better … as fellow human beings."

"I think you may be onto something, Fatima," I say, my mind
still thinking her suggestion through. "It would also give us
something to do after the dinner … but where would we hold the
event? … does anybody know if there's a place on campus that we
could book?"

"We could do it at my home," Fatima offers. "My husband and
I love entertaining, and we have the space. A home would be a
more intimate setting than any room on campus. It might help to
make everybody more comfortable."

My mind connects with images of the drab grey walls in
Barbara Way's office and in the tutorial classroom on campus.

"You've got that right," I say. "That's awfully kind of you to
offer. Thank you."

I turn to Shanise and Katya.

"I think we might be onto something here," I add. "What do
you two think?"

"I'm not so sure," Katya says. "What if some people don't
come? It can only be effective if everybody attends, don't you
think?"

All three women look at me while I consider Katya's
comment.

"You're absolutely right," I say, finally. "We need everybody to attend, or we're wasting our time and energy. But, unfortunately, as your TA, I can't force anybody to attend."

I turn my attention to Fatima.

"On the other hand, you're the chairperson of the team. How you deal with attendance at team meetings is up to you. If you're willing to host the dinner, you can announce it at the next tutorial as a team function, and see how they respond," I say. "I just have one more question: When do you think we should do it?"

"This coming weekend is very short notice," Shanise answers. "What about the following Saturday?"

"My husband and I are free that evening," Fatima says. "Would that work?"

I look around the room and see everybody nodding their heads up and down.

"Are we in agreement, then?" I say.

More nods of affirmation.

"Alright," Fatima concludes. "My house, a week from Saturday. But, when I announce the dinner at this week's meeting, I will remind everybody that our levels of participation within the team will likely be reflected in our final grades."

FROM THE STREET, the coffee shop in downtown Toronto appears as weary and downtrodden as the patrons I see seated inside, next to the grimy windows. An ancient, red, flickering neon sign does its best to beckon newcomers inside.

This is it, Sam! ... You've come too far to turn back ... You can do this!

I approach the door and manage to wrestle it open, despite its poor fit and years of neglect since it last saw any lubrication.

The shop is long and narrow, with red-coloured vinyl booths lining the entire length of the wall on my right. The two booths on my immediate left are the ones I observed from the sidewalk. A serving counter, with a number of matching red-upholstered diner stools, takes up much of the left wall. Four more booths take up the remainder of the wall on my left at the rear of the shop. The floor boasts cream-coloured and red, asbestos-style, fifties-era floor tiles, laid in no discernible pattern. Many of the tiles are almost completely worn through in the highest traffic areas. A short-order kitchen, along with hand-made washroom and exit signs at the rear of the shop, complete the interior decor. The air is heavy with the aromas of coffee and freshly-grilled bacon and eggs.

Almost every booth is occupied, most of them with only one or two patrons. I inspect their faces, looking for somebody who might look vaguely familiar, even though my three-year-old self doesn't have any clear memories of Charlie's face. Finally, I see a man who looks like the most likely candidate, sitting by himself in one of the booths. I feel my body trembling with anticipation as I start walking in his direction. His face is grizzled, his clothing rumpled, and his hair dishevelled. However, he looks much older than Charlie's probable age of about forty-five. He's already sipping from a large porcelain mug of coffee.

"Excuse me?" I ask. "Are you Charlie?"

The man looks up, momentarily startled.

"Ahhh … I 'spose so," he says.

I feel the man's eyes studying me, and then I see them turn red and start to water. Unsure of what to do next, I extend my hand.

"I'm Samantha … your daughter," I say. "Thank you for meeting me … I'm sorry … I'm just a bit nervous …"

Charlie ignores my hand and motions to the other side of the booth.

"Have a seat," he says. "I won't bite."

A waitress appears beside our table and looks in my direction.

"I'll just have a large coffee … double-double," I answer, then I look across the booth at Charlie. "Do you want anything else? Something to eat?"

Charlie shakes his head, so the waitress rushes away, placing bills on a few tables before heading back to the serving counter.

"Yer probly still pissed at me fer leaving' ya with Diane back then." He mumbles. "Wouldn't blame ya if ya was."

Shit! He sure gets right to the point. What do I say to that?

I feel the inner struggle between my angry and guilty voices almost immediately, leaving me temporarily tongue-tied. Finally, I think I've found some appropriate words.

"I'd be lying if I said I wasn't angry," I say, cautiously. "Especially when I was younger. But, I guess I'm just curious now. That's why I contacted Diane, and then Rose."

Charlie reaches for his coffee and takes a sip while he pauses to think for a moment. Finally, he sets the cup back on the table.

"I was young when they booted me outta th' residential school, ya know," he says. "Had a lotta demons back then … still do from that place … an' Diane was young … too young."

"I know," I reply. "Rose told me about the residential school. I'm sorry you had to go through that."

The waitress reappears with my coffee.

"Thank you," I say to the waitress, who then hurries to the back and disappears into the kitchen.

I take a cautious sip of coffee to calm my nerves. It's hot, but surprisingly tasty.

"They brainwashed us y'know," Charlie continues. "They tol' us our language an' our customs an' our parents were nuthin'. They made us feel 'shamed when we was sent home fer holidays."

He stops to take a sip of coffee, and I see a distant look in his eyes, as if he's drifting back in time.

"Made us feel like shit at school, an' made us feel like shit at home too," he adds. "Din't feel like I b'longed nowhere. So I jus' felt angry 'bout everythin'."

My eyes are watering, and I can't swallow. I feel overwhelmed by sadness for what Charlie must have endured.

"I think anybody would be angry if that happened to them," I say, my heart full of compassion.

"Damn right!" Charlie says. "So, after you come along, I seen m'self takin' out my anger on you an' Diane, an' I figured you was both better off without me. I done it fer ya, Sam. Trust me … ya was better off without me."

Tears fill Charlie's eyes, and I'm fighting to hold mine back as I search for the right words to respond. My guilty self jumps at the opportunity.

"I'm so sorry for what you went through," I say. "I feel ashamed that I've been so angry at you all these years."

"Ain't nuthin' t'be 'shamed of … looks like ya survived yer mom an' turned out alright," he says. "She was quite a piece o'work too, ya know."

"Don't I know it," I reply. "They eventually took me away from her. Her brother and his wife, Uncle Bob and Aunt Melanie, raised me. They were really good to me and made sure I got a good education. I even made it into grad school. I'm studying psychology."

"I don' know nuthin' 'bout psychology, an I ain't learnt much in my healin' over th'years. But, I'm still workin' on it," he says. "An' one thing they tol'me is this … it ain't wrong t'feel angry 'bout people doin' ya wrong … but it sure ain't right takin' it out on others either … an' it's my curse that I never been able t'git that right."

I find myself both surprised and sad at this unexpected insight … something my own angry voice could certainly benefit from. The insight, and my emotional reaction to it, draws me closer emotionally to Charlie. I feel my eyes starting to water.

I notice Charlie starting to shift in his seat, his hands and his eyes signalling increased restlessness. I sense that Charlie, and probably myself, may be approaching the limits of our comfort with intimacy for today.

"That's probably enough of my stories for one day," I say. "But, if it's okay with you, I'd like to get together with you again. Would that be okay?"

I notice a hint of sparkle in Charlie's eyes, and I feel hopeful.

"I might jus' be 'greeable t'that, young lady," he says. "Ya got my number, right?"

"I do," I reply. "I'll give you a call soon, and then I can tell you all about my visits with Aunt Rose at the Healing Lodge."

I feel the urge to take one of Charlie's hands in mine, but I feel too awkward. I begin to stand while I search for the right words to say goodby."

"I guess I'll see you later then," I blurt nervously.

I search through my purse for some money, and I throw more than enough on the table for both Charlie and myself. Then I pivot, walk away from the table, and fight with that stubborn door again on my way out. I heave a huge sigh of relief as I hear the door scrape against its frame and come to a rest behind me.

For the first time, I hear another inner voice that takes me completely by surprise. And then I realize how good it feels, and how I don't hear my guilty voice at all right now.

You did it, Sam! ... That went far better than you expected ... You should be proud of yourself!

I'VE GROWN to respect Fatima's dedication to Team Reconciliation and their project over the past few weeks. Because she's a mature student with a lot of life experience, I suppose I shouldn't be surprised. It's not her fault that she got dealt an unlucky hand as a result of Eric Sanderson's random assignment of students to the four teams. But, I guess that's the whole point of the team building concept—how to mold a team out of raw human resources. All things considered, I think she's done the best she could do under the circumstances.

As I sit at the far end of the oval-shaped table, observing Fatima and Team Reconciliation in their weekly tutorial meeting, I can't help but feel sad that this team may not achieve their goal, despite Fatima's best efforts.

"I have to be honest with all of you," Fatima says. "The other three teams have come together, and are making much better progress than this team. We have virtually nothing to show for nine weeks, and we have to hand in our report and make our presentation in just three weeks!"

She looks around the table, making contact with each team member as she goes.

"Is there anybody in this room who isn't embarrassed by this team's performance?"

There is complete silence around the table. I notice Hunter begin to put his hand up, but he thinks better of it when Fatima gives him the evil eye.

"The next three weeks are going to be incredibly stressful, even if we do manage to come together," Fatima continues. "So, some of us have decided that we need to lighten the mood and have some fun—as a team—before we get down to serious work."

Fatima looks down the table at me, and I give her a nod that tells her she's doing a good job, and that I have confidence in her telling the team about our plans. She looks away and focuses on the team again.

"What we've come up with," she says, "is an international potluck dinner, to be held at my home this Saturday. We're asking each of you to bring one signature dish from where you grew up."

I watch the reactions of team members on their faces, ranging from Hunter rolling his eyes, and Terri giving an audible huff. The others, apart from Shanise and Katya, raise their eyebrows in surprise. Many of them shift in their seats and sit up to pay attention.

"And we would also like each of you to be prepared to tell the group a bit about your interests and hobbies, so we can get to know each other better," Fatima concludes. "Are there any questions?"

"Yeah, I've got one," Hunter says. "What's this dinner going to accomplish?"

"This type of gathering is something we did in my community, back home in Curaćao," Shanise counters. "It helps to bring people together for common causes. I think you will enjoy it."

"I'm with Shanise," Katya interjects. "Multicultural dinners and fairs are some of the most popular events in this community. Everybody who attends has a good time!"

"For once, I agree with Hunter," Terri says. "This group has nothing in common. This is just going to be a big, boring waste of time, if you ask me."

Recognizing the seeds of discontent being sown by Hunter and Terri, I feel my muscles beginning to tense and my stomach starting to churn. I also detect my angry voice and some of my newly found sense of self-confidence coming alive. I've heard enough, and I feel the urge to jump up and intervene.

Don't do it, Sam! ... It's Fatima's meeting ... It's up to her ...

My eyes connect with Fatima, who is looking at me for direction. I glare at Hunter and then at Terri, and then look back at Fatima. I nod to let her know that I'm not going to intervene, and that she's in charge.

"Let me be clear," Fatima says, wagging her finger at them. "We can not make participation in the dinner mandatory. But, this is a team event. And remember … our grades in this course are highly dependent on our participation in the overall project. So, any more questions?"

The room falls silent. Terri and Hunter look at each other, their faces showing surprise at Fatima's increasingly assertive responses to their negative attitudes.

I look to Fatima and nod my approval.

"Good," she says. "I am passing around a handout sheet with my contact information and directions to my home. Please text me to let me know if you are coming, and what kind of food you are bringing. And I will look forward to seeing you at my home on Saturday night."

CHAPTER 11—THE DINNER SOCIAL

UNIVERSITY STUDENTS like me aren't used to eating a feast like the one we just devoured. My relationship with food continues to evolve, and anything I know about cooking, I definitely didn't learn from Diane. In fact, when Uncle Bob and Aunt Melanie adopted me, I found the abundance of food and variety of tastes on their dinner table, to be quite overwhelming. Initially, I felt guilty eating anything besides goldfish crackers, because I'd learned very early that Diane would beat me if I touched whatever meagre food supplies were in our cupboards. It's taken me a long time to overcome that guilt, and to enjoy eating. So, I definitely don't take tonight's celebration of delicious foods from around the world for granted.

The other thing I don't want to take for granted is what is unfolding in Fatima's living room at this very moment.

"Oh, my God, Katya," I proclaim. "This apple cake … the shortbread crust and vanilla cream … this is to die for! Has anybody else tried this yet?"

"Not me," Uri says. "I'm having seconds of Arjun's mom's vegetarian korma … Can I come and live with you and your mom?"

Spontaneous laughter fills the room.

I can't believe this is happening right now! Laughter and Team Reconciliation don't go together, do they?

"I'm having more of your Israeli salad, Uri," Shanise shouts over the laughter. "I thought you said you could not cook."

"No cooking involved," Uri replies. "I just had to chop up the veggies, add the lemon juice, olive oil, and spices … and voilà!"

"Speaking of people who don't cook," I say. "How about Hunter's wild rice dish! I've never had it with apples, cranberries, and pecans before."

I catch Hunter blushing.

"I can't lie. That's all on my sister, cuz I never learned to cook," he admits. "So, where did *you* learn to cook mac 'n cheese like that? That was the cheesiest version I've ever had … and that's cheesy in a good way!"

He flashes a rare smile that catches me off guard.

"Let's not forget Shanise's stewed plantains and Mandy's sweet and sour pork," I say, trying to shift the attention away from myself.

Amidst the banter, Fatima's teenaged son and daughter, Hamid and Rasha, and her husband, Kareem, continue to take our non-alcoholic drink orders and cater to our needs.

My knees creak as I manage to get up from sitting cross-legged on the carpet, eventually making it to a standing position.

"Quiet, everybody," Shanise shouts. "Sam wants to say something!"

I look around the room at all the smiling faces, and then I clear my throat.

"I'd just like to thank our hosts, Fatima and Kareem, … and let's not forget Hamid and Rasha … for welcoming us into their home tonight, and for their wonderful hospitality. And Fatima, your spiced meatballs, wrapped in fried eggplant, were delicious."

I raise my plastic cup of ginger ale into the air.

"To Fatima, Kareem, Hamid, and Rasha!"

Everybody on Team Reconciliation joins in the toast and then applauds enthusiastically. Fatima places her hands together and gives a little bow to the team. Hamid and Rasha bow and then retreat to the kitchen, while Kareem carries a laptop computer to the far end of the room, where he starts connecting it to a flat screen TV.

"Thank you, everybody," Fatima says. "It is a pleasure to welcome you all here tonight. I too want to thank my family, as I am sure my children will not be so pleasant when it comes time to clean up tonight!"

The room erupts in laughter again.

"Thank you everybody for the delicious food you provided tonight," Fatima continues. "I felt like I was touring the world with your dishes from India, the Caribbean, Israel, Hong Kong, Germany, and elsewhere.

Fatima pauses to see if Kareem has the TV and computer connected. He nods to her to indicate that he's finished the task.

"Some of you have already let us learn more about you before dinner, by sharing about your hobbies. So, let us continue," Fatima says. "And please, feel free to keep eating … there is still lots of food."

A few members of the team get up for refills as Fatima speaks.

"Judging from some of the previews I have seen, I think you are in for some very pleasant surprises," she says. "Sam, would you like to start things off?"

Fatima looks in my direction, and Kareem brings me a remote control for the laptop. He presses the *play* button, which brings up a photograph of a homeless encampment on the TV screen.

"Thanks, Fatima," I begin. "Since some of you on the team have already been brave enough to share a little about yourselves tonight, I thought it was only fair that your TA should do the same."

I realize that the talking and laughing in the room has subsided, and all eyes and ears are focused on me.

"When I need to relax," I continue. "I like to get out my camera and snap some pictures, especially portraits of people I meet. Here's a few of my favourites."

I click on the remote control, bringing up the next photo. The black and white image shows a grizzled, elderly, homeless man, sitting outside a makeshift tent, heating some food over a small camp stove. The texture of his face is leathery, with deep grooves carved into his forehead and around his eyes. The corners of his mouth slope downwards, a telltale sign that he no longer has many teeth.

"Here's another one that I took at a homeless encampment, here in the city."

I hear whispering amongst the team members.

"You're very talented with your camera," Katya says.

"Thank you," I reply.

I continue pressing the remote control, showing a few more photos of a couple of my closest friends and also some other landmarks around the city. Finally, I reach the last of my slides. I pause to take a deep breath, and then exhale to calm myself. I press the remote one last time.

"This one is my new favourite," I say, as I bring up a portrait of Rose that I did at the *Healing Lodge*. "I was recently quite shocked to learn that this woman … my aunt … as well as my biological father … are Indigenous … Anishinaabe, to be more precise."

A brief hush descends on the room as the team members look around at each other with looks of surprise on their faces. Nobody looks more surprised than Hunter. Our eyes connect briefly, but I look away.

"You can imagine that I've been experiencing a lot of mixed emotions lately," I add. "Especially given this team's reconciliation project topic."

"That *is* a surprise," Fatima says. "Thank you for sharing it with us."

She looks around the room until she finds Hunter.

"Maybe this is a good time for our next surprise," she says. "Hunter, do you want to go next?"

Hunter, who is also sitting cross-legged on the floor, nods to Fatima and then to Kareem. I hand the remote control to Hunter.

"Before I turn on the video, you should know that this is a band that I joined a few months ago," he says. "I hope you enjoy this interpretation of one of my favourite songs."

He clicks the remote and starts the video. I see a five-piece band, all dressed in elements of traditional Indigenous attire, with Hunter sitting at a synthesizer keyboard. It takes a few moments for me to recognize the song—Green Day's *Revolution Radio*—since the arrangement is a clever blend of rock and hip-hop, infused with pounding Indigenous rhythms.

At one point, Hunter gets up from the keyboard and picks up a number of large hoops. He begins dancing a traditional Indigenous hoop dance to the song. I hear the team members whispering to each other. And then, out of the blue, Terri begins clapping to the rhythm. The remaining team members soon come together and join her. My eyes can't believe the transformation I'm seeing in Team Reconciliation.

Terri, of all people, applauding Hunter! What could top that!

When the video ends, the room erupts in enthusiastic cheering and clapping.

"Wow!" Fatima shouts over the cheering. "That was amazing!"

She lets the cheering and applause gradually die down.

"If you enjoyed that," Fatima says. "Then I think you will really enjoy our next performance. Terri, are you ready?"

Hunter passes the remote control to Terri, who gives him a pat on the shoulder and two thumbs up in the process.

"You all know that I used to be an exotic dancer, and that I now have my own exotic dance school and studio," she begins. "So, here's a little present from the teacher!"

She clicks the remote control and we're instantly transported to a stage with a large metal pole in the centre of the picture. A thumping rock rhythm comes from the TV's speakers, after Terri turns up the volume. Then, from one side of the screen, Terri emerges, dressed like the sexiest alien creature I've ever seen. I recognize the music as an Eighties dance classic from Uncle Bob's record collection. The team comes to life again, cheering and applauding.

Wow! Look at this crowd! And there isn't even alcohol involved!

Terri's video continues to showcase her stunning exotic dancing skills and her finely tuned physique, in an exquisite pole dance that rivals anything Jennifer Lopez has ever done on screen. When her performance finally ends, the team erupts again in uncontrolled applause. Fatima's neighbours must be wondering what's going on in their neighbours' home by now!

Just when I think I've seen it all, the seductive sounds of Middle-Eastern music start to float from a Bluetooth speaker on a living room bookshelf. I hear a rustling of fabric and look up to see Fatima at the top of the home's central staircase, costumed in belly dancing attire. Her head is covered, as is her face, but the fabric covering her face is semi-transparent, so we can see the seductive gleam in her eyes.

The team starts clapping in time to the music and shouting encouragement, as Fatima slowly descends the stairs, and then starts to weave her way seductively around the living room. I notice Kareem whisking their children into the kitchen.

As she dances her way to each team member, Fatima stops to gyrate her hips and shake her bosom seductively. I can't seem to stop staring at the hypnotic movement of her navel and her buttocks as her body twists and turns gracefully through the room. Her performance is absolutely captivating!

Suddenly, for the first time, with help from the universal magic of music and dance, I see Team Reconciliation starting to come together as one team for the first time in nine weeks!

FATIMA AND KAREEM help sort out our coats, as the team and I gradually say our goodbyes and thank them again for their hospitality. Terri, Hunter, and myself are the last guests remaining.

"Thanks so much to both of you, and the kids, for inviting us into your home," I say. "That belly dance, Fatima, was the high point of the evening!"

Fatima looks at Kareem, who is smiling and obviously proud of his wife's talent. Fatima turns her attention back towards us, and I see that she's blushing.

"That is not something I do in public very often," she says. "It was nothing compared to Hunter and Terri's videos. I wish we could have seen more of your talents."

"Actually, Hunter's taking me and Sam to a club downtown, where he and his band are playing live later tonight," Terri says. "Do you guys want to come with us?"

Kareem and Fatima laugh loudly at the suggestion.

"Thank you for asking," Kareem answers. "But I think we might have a revolt on our hands if we leave the kids alone to clean up. Maybe some other time."

"Looks like our Uber's here," Hunter says. "We have to go. Thanks again for everything."

I follow Hunter and Terri out of Fatima's house, and we hurry to the waiting Uber. Hunter jumps into the front seat, while I slide into the rear with Terri.

"Club Renaissance," Hunter says to the driver.

A moment later, we pull away from the curb and our driver points the car towards downtown. I can't help but feel like the whole evening has been a bit surreal. I don't think Fatima, Shanise, Katya, or myself really believed the dinner social would turn out anywhere near as well as it did. And, to top it all off, I'm riding in a vehicle with both Hunter and Terri, and neither one is insulting the other.

Am I dreaming? ... If I am, I hope it doesn't end too soon!

THE SOUNDS of pounding drums and electronic music reverberate through Club Renaissance, thanks to Hunter and his band—*Landback Promise*—who have taken over the stage. Terri and I watch as Hunter captivates the crowd on the dance floor with his innovative hoop dance.

"He's really good," Terri shouts.

"Yeah," I agree. "Who would have known that you had three incredible dancers on Team Reconciliation. It took a lot of guts for you guys to show your stuff to the rest of the team!"

I'm having a good time with Terri while Hunter is onstage. We're both relaxed and I feel like we've both let our defences down. A couple of juicy IPAs can have that effect on people.

"You two seem to be getting along tonight," I call out over the decibels. "What happened?"

"I'm embarrassed to admit it, but you, Fatima, Shanise, and Katya were right about the dinner social," she admits. "It was a damned good idea. And Hunter seems like a good guy, as long as he isn't preaching reconciliation to the rest of us."

I give Terri another dose of my evil eye.

"Okay, okay," she says. "I admit it … I can be a real bitch sometimes too. But, I don't think I'm a racist … not intentionally, anyway … I don't think anybody on the team is … what do you think?"

"I guess it depends on our individual perspectives," I reply. "What feels well-intentioned from one person, can feel extremely prejudicial and racist to another."

"So, now that you've found out that you're part Indigenous, is that going to change how you see reconciliation?" Terri asks. "Are you going to be taking Hunter's side now?"

Terri's question hits me hard. I'm totally unprepared for it, although I've probably been grappling with it subconsciously from the moment Diane told me about Charlie.

"I hope not," I answer, cautiously. "I've been telling people that I feel like I'm looking at the world through two sets of eyes now. I hope that means that I can see things from both sides … that I can still be objective."

Terri considers my answer and shrugs.

"Makes sense to me," she says. "I'll try to keep that in mind over the next few weeks."

All of a sudden, I feel like Terri was shouting her last few words at me. Then I realize it's because Hunter and the band just finished a set. The noise level in the room has fallen drastically, so that all I hear now is the sound of conversation, laughter, and the ringing in my ears.

"I gotta pee," Terri says. "I'll be back."

As she disappears towards the lady's room, I see Hunter making his way through the crowd towards me with a beer in hand. A deejay has taken over the stage, and the pounding rhythms of hip-hop elevate the noise level once again. Hunter slides into a seat beside me.

"What do you think?" he shouts. "Do you like our sound?"

"I do," I call out. "It's really unique. I think you guys have the talent to make it big!"

"I don't know about that," he says. "It helps pay the bills for now."

Our eyes make contact, and I see sincerity in his eyes.

"So you're half Anishinaabe," he continues, addressing the elephant in the room. "How do you feel about that?"

"Confused," I admit. "I'm having trouble finding the time to fully wrap my mind around it … things have been so busy at school."

"You can talk to me anytime, you know," Hunter says.

"Thanks," I reply. "For now, I'm seeing a lot of Aunt Rose on the weekends."

Enough about me … Change the subject, Sam.

"You and Terri really seem to be hitting it off tonight," I venture. "What's with that?"

Hunter takes a sip of his beer, and then takes a moment to think.

"I don't think she's a bad person," he admits. "She's sort of cool … especially for somebody her age … she really gets our music … I just get so frustrated with her sometimes, hearing the same old colonial myths about us over and over. How can I get her … and the others … to understand?"

I take a few seconds to reflect on his question.

"Keep your mind open," I answer. "Keep trying to focus on the things you have in common … and give her a chance. I think she really does want to learn … let her do it at her own pace."

Without warning, I see a familiar face in the crowd behind Hunter. By the time our eyes connect and I recognize the face as Uri's, I realize that Arjun and Mandy are right behind him. Uri leads the others over to our table.

"You guys showed up after all," I call out.

"We talked it over after we left Fatima's place," Arjun replies. "Uri convinced us that this is the place to be on Saturday night. Apparently, he's a regular."

"What can I say?" Uri bellows. "I already told you guys that I like going to nightclubs. This is the best one I've found around here."

"We enjoy playing this club too," Hunter says, shouting over the background music. "They're good to us, and they let us play here quite regularly."

"Besides," Mandy chimes in. "We wanted to see your hoop dancing in person. Your video was really awesome!"

"Thanks," Hunter says humbly.

"I thought Terri was coming with you," Arjun calls out. "Is she still here?"

"Lady's room … oh, here she comes now," I reply.

Terri weaves her way back from the lady's room. She stumbles and then slides awkwardly into her chair.

"You guys showed up after all," she shouts. "Wanna join us?"

It's apparent to everybody, except Terri, that we don't have a big enough table for all of us.

"We're probably just going to hang out at the bar, listen to the band and watch the hoop dancing," Mandy answers.

"What do you mean?" Uri bellows again. "I thought we came here to dance and have a good time. Loosen up a little. Forget about school for a while. Have some fun!"

Mandy shrugs and smiles.

"Okay, okay," she says to Uri and Arjun. "Let's go and order drinks."

"If we see a bigger table come open, we'll come and get you," Uri answers. "Have fun!"

"You too!" Terri calls out, as the trio heads toward the bar. She turns to me and Hunter.

"Another round?" she asks.

"Not for me," Hunter says, looking at his phone. "Gotta go up for another set. Will you guys be hanging around till we're done?"

He looks at me, in particular.

"Sure," I reply. "Why not!"

"We can share an Uber ride home," Terri adds.

"Then I'll catch you guys later," Hunter says, gulping the last of his beer. He gets up and works his way back toward the stage, while his bandmates grab their instruments and get ready to play.

I flag down a young server and motion her to our table.

"Two more IPAs," I say, and the young woman wanders away.

I smile at Terri as *Landback Promise* comes to life again in the background. Their drummer starts pounding out more traditional rhythms, while Hunter and the other band members start a traditional native chant. Our server returns with two more hazy, golden IPAs.

"To music and dancing!" Terri shouts. "Wanna dance?"

"I'd love to," I call out. "You can give me some lessons, and show everybody else how it's done!"

We break into laughter. As I get up from my chair, I immediately feel the effects of my first couple of beers on my body. I feel dizzy and I stumble. Terri catches me, and together, we weave our way out onto the dance floor, where Terri puts her hands on my hips and starts showing me how to move them.

"I'll turn you into an exotic dancer yet," she shouts, and we both laugh.

I have a feeling I'm going to regret this tomorrow morning! ... But, what the hell ... it's worth it ... the dinner was a big success ... we all deserve to celebrate ...

CHAPTER 12—WEEK ELEVEN

MONDAY MORNING, and I'm sitting in the chair in my office, my feet up on my desk, daydreaming and remembering the unexpected events from Saturday evening. Sipping my morning double-double, I feel more relaxed and more at peace this morning, than I have in a couple of weeks.

Maybe the stars are beginning to align for me, after all!

My phone rings, and the display shows Charlie's name. I sit up straight and remove my feet from the desk. My face lights up as I answer the call.

"Sam here," I say. "Good to hear from you, Charlie."

There's a pause on Charlie's end before he finally speaks. When he does, his speech is noticeably slurred.

"I'm sho shorry, Sham," he says. "I'm sho, sho shorry …"

My mood veers one-hundred and eighty degrees. I'm now buzzing with alarm.

"Charlie, are you alright?" I ask.

Another long pause on Charlie's end.

"Ya don' wan' me near ya …everythin' I touch just' turns t'shit," he mumbles.

I'm pacing back and forth now, alarmed by Charlie's negativity and his hopeless outlook.

"That's not true, Charlie," I say. "I want you back in my life! You're my father!"

"Ya done jusht' fine widout me … I'd jusht bring ya down," he says.

My mind is spinning out of control, struggling to find the right words to soothe him.

"Where are you, Charlie? I'll come right away! Let me help you," I plead.

"No use … s'not worth livin' no more … yer better off widout me …"

Out of nowhere, the line goes dead. Tears fill my eyes as I continue to pace frantically. I raise my phone and try calling Charlie back twice … there's no answer. In desperation, I stab at the button to phone Rose.

"Rose?" I shout. "This is Sam … Charlie just called me! … he sounded real bad … claimed his life isn't worth living anymore … help me! … you've gotta help him! … you don't know where he lives? …"

I feel lost … having difficulty finding words … desperate …

"Don't you know anybody who might know where to find him?" I plead. "I see … you can reach out to the community? … yes, that would be great!"

I feel my mind trying to disconnect from my body, so I look around my office frantically, looking for objects to anchor myself to reality. I scramble to remember everything Barbara taught me to do at times like this.

"Call me anytime … day or night! … thank you, thank you! … please find him!" I beg.

The line goes dead. It's all in Rose's hands, and there's nothing I can do now. I feel totally helpless and alone.

No, Charlie! … You can't do this to me! … Not again! …

I slump back into my chair, and I burst into tears. I feel totally, inconsolably, abandoned … feeling as though I'm three years old again.

THE ROLLERCOASTER ride that I call my life, continues to take my emotions to new peaks of joy and anticipation, and then drags them back down into valleys of fear, loneliness, helplessness, and sadness. At the moment, I feel like I've plummeted from one of the summits—my rise to the top fuelled by my meeting with Charlie and the success of the team's dinner social at Fatima's home, and the energizing night out with Hunter and Terri at Club Renaissance. But my sudden nose dive from the summit has left me in emotional limbo—fearing the worst for Charlie, and also afraid to allow myself to feel any joy or happiness—terrified that it will vanish at any moment, and plunge me right back down into another deep, dark, dangerous valley.

I glance again at my phone, laying on the table beside me, for the umpteenth time. I'm still waiting impatiently to hear from Rose, and the longer I wait, the more frantic I've become. The phone remains lifeless.

I'm desperately trying to force myself to focus on this critical meeting of Team Reconciliation's research group. I've left the discussion in Fatima's capable hands, and if she's aware that my mind is struggling to stay present, she isn't letting it show. The most significant thing I've noticed so far, is that there hasn't been any of the usual fireworks in this week's meeting, which would normally have jerked me from my daydreams by now.

"I'll continue to focus on *UNDRIP* and Section 35 of the *Constitution Act*," Hunter says, "Especially on how to put them into action that will result in real change for my people."

"Good! Thank you," Fatima says. "I am going through the ninety-four *Calls to Action*. I'm trying to link some of its main recommendations to *UNDRIP* and the *Constitution Act*."

She shifts her focus and looks across the table.

"What have you got for us, Terri?"

"I just finished working my way through the *Indian Act*," Terri replies. "To be honest, I'm not sure what to make of it, or how it fits with the *UNDRIP* or the *Calls to Action* yet. But, the more I read about it, the more uneasy I feel. I've just started reading Chief Joseph's book … hopefully he'll make the Act easier to understand."

I look up just in time to see Hunter and Terri exchange wary glances at each other. Despite the good times we all shared at Fatima's home and at Club Renaissance on Saturday night, I sense that there's still some lingering distrust hanging over them.

"Arjun?" Fatima says. "What about you?"

Arjun exhales slowly, his young face showing creases of concern.

"I've been looking at the historical treaties, as well as some of the modern treaties with First Nations," he begins. "I agree with Hunter, that acting on *UNDRIP* and Section 35 of the *Constitution Act* is absolutely essential for reconciliation … but, the more I study them and the *Indian Act*, the more unsure I am about how to do that."

He looks up and his eyes meet Hunter's.

"… The ninety-four *Calls to Action* feel really futile to me … it feels like they're just applying bandaids to First Nations people, when they've been metaphorically riddled by the equivalent of machine gun fire from the *Indian Act* for generations."

"Wow!" Hunter replies. "That's a pretty disturbing picture … and a bleak diagnosis, Dr. Arjun. What do you mean?"

"I just can't stop thinking," Arjun says, "that the whole system for dealing with Indigenous people needs rebuilding, from the bottom up."

"I'm starting to get the same feeling after reading the *Indian Act*," Terri interjects. "Even moreso after reading the introduction to Chief Joseph's book."

Hunter gives Terri a quizzical look, then turns his attention back to Arjun.

"So, what do you propose instead?" Hunter says. "Do we just throw out the whole Truth and Reconciliation Committee's report?"

"I'm not sure what I'm proposing yet," Arjun admits. "But I'm working on some ideas."

Fatima coughs as she tries to clear her throat. She shifts in her seat and takes a drink of water. Her sudden cough jars my wandering mind back into the room.

"You realize that this could be a big problem for us when it comes to making recommendations in our team's report!" she says. "Maybe we all need a couple of days to think about Arjun's observations … can the four of us meet again at the end of the week? … maybe Friday afternoon around 4 PM? … can everybody make it then?"

I watch as the members of the research subgroup check their schedules on their phones. One-by-one, they all nod affirmatively.

"What about you, Sam? Do you want to attend too?"

"I'm leaving Friday to go up north to visit my aunt," I answer. *They don't need to know about Charlie … What's going on in my life … And they certainly don't need a mentor who's head is only halfway into the game!*

"But, can I say something before we go?" I add.

"Of course," she replies.

"I just want to tell all of you that I'm impressed by the cooperation I've seen today," I say. "From what I've seen and heard, you still have a lot of work to do. But, if you keep working together like this, you might just be able to pull this project off in time! Keep up the good work!"

"Thank you, Sam," Fatima replies. "I agree, and I must say I feel more optimistic as well."

Fatima shifts her attention from me to the group.

"Okay," she says. "I will see you all here this Friday, when we must decide what to hand off to our Plan of Action committee."

Fatima and the research group begin gathering their things, actually chatting with each other as they start filing from the room.

For the umpteenth-plus time, I look down towards the table at my phone. Still no word from Rose, and the uneasy, sour sensation in the pit of my stomach continues to grow. Reluctantly, I pick up the phone, toss it into my book bag, grab my coat, and exit the room … my body walking on autopilot, while my mind remains stuck in emotional limbo.

THERE'S NOTHING like desperation to create motivation! In my case, it's serving double duty, distracting me from my worries about Charlie and Team Reconciliation, but also reminding me of my current precarious academic status. Yes, my own reality has kicked in since I promised to get my proposal submitted to Eric and the rest of my proposal committee … at just about the same time that the Team Building 201 class projects and presentations are due. Essentially, my whole academic career depends on what I get done over the next two weeks. No pressure here at all!

My fingers fly over the keyboard. Now that my thesis ideas have roughly coalesced in my mind, I'm in a groove and I feel an urgent need to commit them to paper.

My phone rings, and I jump, almost falling off my chair! My eyes dart to the screen and I see Rose's name on the call display. I lunge for the phone and tap the answer button in one frenzied motion.

"Rose!" I blurt. "Did you reach him?"

An agonizing silence follows, and I feel as if the bottom is dropping out of my stomach.

"I'm sorry, Sam," Rose says.

Her voice is somber, and I know instantly what she's going to say.

"It's too late," she continues. "I had a visit from the police last night."

My mind leaps straight into denial mode.

"The police?" I shout. "Please tell me he's alright! … Rose? …"

More silence, before Rose finally speaks again.

"It looks like it was an overdose … intentional," she says.

I hear the trembling in Rose's voice, and I hear her sniffling.

"He left a note for you," she says. "I'll save it for your next visit."

I feel my body going numb with shock. I'm losing track of time while I struggle to make sense of what I've just heard … feeling my mind trying to disconnect from my body … I fight to keep it present, and I feel a tear trickle down my cheek.

"Would you read it?" I ask.

"Are you sure?" Rose says.

I manage to answer between my own sniffles.

"Please … go ahead." I reply.

I hear Rose taking a deep breath and then letting it go.

"He says that his demons from the residential school were too much to live with," Rose explains. "He also says that he left you with Diane to protect you from him … and leaving this world now is his gift … to protect you from him in the future."

I feel the dam burst. Tears flood down my face, dripping from my chin.

"With his last words," Rose says, "he begged you to do whatever you can do to end the generational cycle of trauma."

I feel myself losing the battle … my mind is disconnecting from my body so quickly, that there's no time to remember the skills I learned from Barbara Way … I feel my tiny three-year-old self looking up at what appears to be a giant of a man … the giant is angry and his arm is raised, threatening to strike me … I hear my little voice screaming in the distance … and then I hear Charlie's booming voice …

"Would'ya shuttup, fer God sake!" he bellows.

I see his fist starting to come down in my direction … then suddenly, it stops … he freezes, for what seems like an eternity …

Without any warning, he wheels around, runs towards the main apartment door, flings it open wide, and runs out through the gaping space. The door remains wide open, and the room is suddenly silent. My tiny self is overwhelmed, first with fear, then short-lived relief, and finally a mixture of overpowering sadness, loneliness, … and anger.

I feel my three-year-old self frozen in time … that image of the wide open door … along with all the overpowering emotions … they all become engraved indelibly into my three-year-old memory at that moment.

CHAPTER 13—DARK PLACES

MY ANGUISH and grief are inconsolable as I sit on Barbara Way's couch. I can't stop wringing my hands, and my legs are vibrating up and down rapidly, doing their best imitation of a jackhammer. My breathing is shallow and rapid. The sharp pain in my chest, when I do try to breathe, feels like I'm having a heart attack. I feel helpless to stop the river of tears escaping from my eyes, and I'm sniffling non-stop.

"It's all … my fault!" I manage to say between gasps. "I told him … how angry … I've been … for all … these years … but I never … never told him … that I forgave him!"

I break into another bout of uncontrollable sobbing.

"You're angry at yourself," Barbara says. Her voice remains calm and soothing. "I know it's hard, but I need you to focus on the skills you've learned … look at me … focus on *my* breathing … breathe with me …"

I do my best to follow Barbara's breathing rhythm for a few breaths, and my weeping subsides slightly.

"Have you felt like cutting again?" Barbara asks.

I sniffle and wipe away some tears, before taking a slightly deeper breath.

"It's been a struggle … I wanted to … but I've managed …"

"Have you had any thoughts of harming yourself?" she asks.

Barbara's question strikes a nerve, and I jump to my feet, glaring at her.

"How can you ask me that?" I shout. "After what Charlie did? … Of course I haven't thought of kill … er, … hurting myself!"

"Sorry," Barbara says. "I know it's a sensitive issue for you right now, but you know I had to ask."

I sniffle again and wipe more tears from my face.

"I know," I answer. "It's just been hard."

I sit back down on the couch, and my legs start vibrating again.

"I understand," she says softly. "Try letting your mind go to your safe place … slow your breathing and let your mind go … let me know when you're there …"

I close my eyes and try willing my mind to fly away to the *Healing Lodge* … but I can't seem to do it. All I see are the same old dark, terrifying images. I start to panic and I open my eyes.

"I can't do it!" I shout. "All I see are the dark images … and his voice … so angry! … and my voices too … guilty and angry voices …"

"That's okay," Barbara says, her voice as reassuring as ever. "Then keep your eyes open … keep looking at me."

I feel my mind trying to disconnect again … losing touch with Barbara.

"Look at me, Sam!" she says, this time raising her voice. "Keep looking at me!"

I feel my head turning towards Barbara … she seems to be in a dense fog … I see her hands coming towards my face …

"Stay with me, Sam!" she calls. "How many fingers do you see? … count them, Sam!"

The muscles controlling my eyes feel like they're frozen … I squint once … squint again … gradually I see fingers coming into focus in front of me.

"Three? … no … four? … five?" I mumble.

"Five fingers," Barbara says. "That's good … stay with me! … now hear my breathing, Sam … breathe with me …"

Barbara's breathing gradually slows, and each of her breaths becomes slightly deeper, while mine initially feel tight and jerky.

But after a few breaths, I manage to fall in with her rhythm, even if my breaths aren't nearly as smooth.

"How are you feeling now?" she asks.

I pause, trying to make sense of what's going on inside my inner self.

"The voices are going away … they're more distant now," I answer.

"Good!" Barbara says. "Just one more breath … nice and deep …"

I follow Barbara's lead and manage to inhale more deeply. My chest still feels a bit tight, and my breathing still isn't smooth, but there's no more pain.

"How are you feeling now?" Barbara says.

"Better … I think … very tired," I reply.

"That's alright," she says. "Do you feel like trying to go to your safe place again?"

I close my eyes and allow my mind to start reconnecting with my body. By no means do I feel back to normal … but the scary images are no longer threatening to intrude.

"Sure, I think I'm okay," I answer.

"Alright … What's the most peaceful part of your safe place?" Barbara asks.

"The campfire … by the pond," I answer.

"Let your mind start there," she says. "Just imagine your adult self being there by yourself … enjoying the peace and quiet … taking nice, slow, deep breaths … what do you hear? … what do you see?"

"It's night," I reply. "I hear the water lapping against the shore … leaves crunching under my feet when I walk … coyotes in the distance … an owl … and I see the campfire … I sit … watching the coals glowing orange …"

I feel my breathing and my heart slowing down … the tension lifting somewhat from my chest … then from the rest of my body …

"Now," Barbara interjects. "Try having your adult self welcome some of those inner voices to be with you."

I go silent, while I imagine my inner voices joining the adult me … the terrified infant … three-year-old me … my angry and guilty voices … my older survivor voice … my caregiver voice …

"Are they all there?" Barbara asks.

"Yes," I answer calmly.

"How do the infant and three-year-old voices feel?" she asks.

"Lonely and scared," I reply. "They need a hug."

"Can they ask your caregiver … and maybe your survivor voice … if they can give them a hug?" Barbara asks.

Still breathing slowly, I do as Barbara suggests.

"How do you feel?" she asks.

"Better," I say. "Not quite as scared … or alone … or angry."

"Good," Barbara says. "So, over the next few days, what are you going to do to keep yourself stable?"

I pause for a moment, breathing in and then exhaling. I feel the tightness in my body continuing to release, little by little, with each new breath.

"Remember to breathe … go to my safe place … and find my caregiver and survivor voices?"

"And what do you do if the angry and guilty voices are too scary?" she asks.

"Open my eyes … and ground myself?" I say, tentatively.

"That's right," Barbara replies. "And what do you do if you can't keep yourself present? Or if you feel like cutting or harming yourself?"

"Phone you … I promise … I'll call you if it's not working," I answer.

I know the drill … I know what to do when I'm here with you … But, it's not the same when you're not around … When I'm all alone … That's when things get really scary … Too scary! …

DEEP DOWN, my inner survivor voice knows that wanting to be alone with my grief right now is the worst thing I can possibly do. But that voice, as well as my caregiver voice, are being drowned out. All I can hear inside my head right now is my lonely, abandoned, terrified three-year-old child, along with a heavy dose of my guilty and angry voices.

It doesn't seem to matter what I do—trying to distract myself by going for a long walk, listening to music, or reading—those taunting inner voices follow me wherever I go, and I can't get them out of my head. I've had to use Barbara's breathing techniques so many times to control my panic since seeing her yesterday, that I can't count them all. And trying to send my mind to my safe place hasn't worked well at all—the second I close my eyes, my brain flies back to three-year-old times, with all the dark shadows, shouting, anger, and that graphic image of Charlie walking out the door.

Your life is just one giant shitload of stress, Sam! ... It's all too much! ...

Desperate to do something to reduce my growing panic, and to calm my chaotic flashback images and inner voices, I grab my computer. My fingers start pounding out a desperate email message.

Eric:
Charlie killed himself and it's all my fault
I'm sorry everything is just too much for me and I can't deal with school and all the other shitty things in my life so I have to quit school and get away from it all because things are too hopeless for me to go on anymore.

Sam

I feel my entire body shiver.

Run yourself a hot bath ... Relax ... Shave your legs ... Maybe that will help ...

I undress as far as my underwear, but I break down into another round of inconsolable weeping. I only get as far as plopping my butt down on the edge of the bathtub, bawling my eyes out, hearing my guilty and angry voices shouting out loud, beating myself up. I find myself staring at the safety razor that sits beside me on the side of the tub.

You just HAD to tell him that you've been angry at him for years! ... How could you be so stupid, Sam? ... It's all your fault that he's gone now! ...

I can't stand the emotional pain anymore, and I feel myself losing control of my body again. My hand reaches for the razor, which I open to remove its single blade. I set the empty razor back on the tub's edge, while I stare at the light reflecting from the blade's cutting surface. Or, closer to the truth, I feel like I'm staring *through* the blade, while my mind is stuck in my three-year-old hell. I'm vaguely aware that I'm holding out my left wrist. My absent gaze shifts to the blue blood vessels I see there. Tears splash on my wrist as my stare locks in on the largest, most visible artery.

I shift my body while I watch, totally fascinated, as the blade hovers over that bulging blue vessel, poised to strike a long, fatal gash—but my thigh knocks the razor off the tub's edge, sending it to the tile floor with a sudden clatter.

Hurting people ... That's all you'll ever be good for ... Causing other people pain ... No fuckin' point in you living ...

Then my eyes spot the old scars on my thighs ... and I remember pain ... and relief ... from years ago.

Something deep inside of me ... my survivor voice? ...catches my attention.

You're stronger than that! ... Charlie wouldn't want you to do this! ... Not on your wrist! ...

My hand moves slowly … deliberately … but not towards my wrist. Instead, it inches towards my already scarred thigh. I draw in a deep breath and grit my teeth … and then the blade breaks the skin and draws fresh blood from the flesh of my thigh … and I feel an excruciating, searing pain …

Slowly, I exhale … I stare at the crimson dribbles of blood creeping across my thigh, and dripping slowly onto the edge of the tub and down to the floor. My thigh screams with physical pain … yet I also feel a liberating wave of emotion and endorphins rushing through my body … my brain yields to the illusion that I'm in control of my emotional pain … a look of relief gradually replaces the grief on my face.

In the distance, I hear my survivor voice calling to me. I hear it again, but this time my caregiver voice has joined in. I feel my survivor voice coming alive, shouting aloud, calling to my angry and guilty voices.

Shut up! … It was NOT her fault! … You're wrong … Don't blame her for Charlie's pain! …

Then I hear my caregiver's calm, empathic voice speaking to my inner three-year-old from a distance.

It wasn't your fault, Sam … You didn't cause Charlie's pain … Leaving this world was his choice … He thought it was a gift … He wasn't thinking straight …

I feel as if I'm frozen in time again. I tilt my head to the side, trying to hear another distant voice … it's my inner three-year-old calling out to me.

He did it because he loves me … He's not angry with me … His spirit told me so … He wants me to live …

I take a deep breath, and then exhale slowly. I drop the razor blade to the floor. My facial expression begins to release some of the tension that's been stored in it, slowly replacing it with relaxation. I take a couple more calming breaths, while my mind anchors itself back in the present and starts thinking coherently again. I reach over to the bathroom counter for my phone and tap on my recent calls list with my index finger. It rings three, four, then five times before I hear a click on the other end.

"Rose? … It's Sam … Is it still okay if I come up to the lodge? … I really need help … I shouldn't be alone …"

CHAPTER 14—LIGHT IN THE SHADOWS

FALLEN LEAVES crunch beneath our feet as Rose and I walk along beside the stream. Being here at the Healing Lodge for the past day has been just what I needed to start healing, after the shock of Charlie's death. The crunching and swishing of the leaves, the gentle gurgling of the stream, and the sounds of chickadees, cardinals, crows, and owls in the forest have helped to calm my inner voices and get myself anchored again.

"It's almost time for the next full moon," Rose says, as we emerge from the forest and she gazes up into the clear November sky.

"It's hard to believe that a month has passed since I was here for the *Full Moon Ceremony*," I say.

"The next ceremony—the Freezing Moon—will be Sunday night, the day after Charlie's funeral," Rose adds. "Unfortunately, the forecast is for snow."

However, tonight it is calm, the sky is clear, and the temperature has dipped below zero. We're far enough from the lodge and its lights, that the night sky is now clearly visible. I see our breath as we stand, staring upward at the moon and stars.

"Look," Rose says, as she turns and points towards the northern sky. "The Aurora's going to be beautiful tonight. We call it Wawasayg"

I follow Rose's arm and immediately see an iridescent green glow appearing above the treeline.

"Legend has it," Rose says, "that our world used to spin perfectly upright long ago, with temperatures staying the same around the world, year round. That is, until there was a great flood that killed most plants and animals. However, the Creator saved one northern tribe from this flood."

"Sounds a lot like Noah, in the Bible," I say.

"Quite similar," Rose says. "But in this legend, as the waters receded, its tremendous weight threw the world off balance, causing long, dark, cold periods in the North and South."

"That's how the four seasons began," I observe.

"That's right," Rose says. "So, when the Creator's chosen tribe could no longer feel the sun and its warmth, the Creator told them to gather their families and possessions, and to migrate across the barren, ice-covered northern lands to a new land. But many in the tribe became lost in deep crevices in the darkness. So the tribe prayed to the Creator for help."

Rose pauses as part of the Aurora dances high into the sky, casting an eerie green glow over the clearing and the light dusting of snow on the ground.

"So the creator covered the barren northern land in great crystals of ice," Rose continues, "which extended into the sky and captured the rays of the sun, refracting them up into the sky to light his chosen peoples' way. Those people continued to marched southward, eventually arriving at the warmer, fertile plains in the south. They were the ancestors of our many First Nations."

"And we've been able to admire the beauty of the Northern Lights ever since," I add. "They're absolutely remarkable!"

The muffled sound of my phone, ringing in my coat pocket, shatters our peace and quiet. I reach into my pocket, pull out my phone, and see that it's Eric Sanderson calling. I look at Rose apologetically.

"I'm sorry, I have to take this," I say. "It's my supervisor."

Rose nods her understanding, and I walk away towards the clearing and the ceremonial firepit.

"Hi Eric," I say. "I've been meaning to call you."

"Thank God, you're still alive!" he blurts. "Your email … I was worried sick!" he exclaims.

"I'm sorry if I scared you," I reply. "I wasn't myself when I sent it."

"It certainly didn't sound like you," Eric says. "The important thing is that you're alright now. Have you reached out for help? … the hospital? … or Barbara Way? Are you feeling any better?"

"Yes, thank you," I answer. "I've been staying with my aunt at the Healing Lodge. The peace and quiet up here, and being with Rose, has been really helpful."

"I'm glad to hear that," he says. "I want you to know that I spoke to the department chair, and we're okay with you taking a leave of absence … all the time you need. I hope you didn't mean what you said in the email about quitting."

"I appreciate that," I answer. "I've thought about that a lot, and I've talked it over with Rose. I think I need to come back soon, if you'll have me. If I take a leave, I'm afraid I'll lose any motivation I might have to come back. I'd like to at least finish the term … if you'll have me. I think I owe it to you and the four teams … I'm hoping it will help to distract me from my other issues."

"Are you sure?" Eric says. "Will you still be seeing Barbara regularly?"

"Yes," I reply. "I'll continue to see Barbara every week, and I'll be spending weekends up here at the Healing Lodge, at least until the end of the term."

"Okay," he says, his voice still sounding doubtful. "As long as we know you've got lots of support."

"I'm sorry I missed this week's tutorial," I say, changing the subject. "How are the teams doing?"

"Don't worry about missing the session," he says. "You didn't miss much. Most of them are doing just fine."

"What about the reconciliation team?" I ask.

"It's hard to say," Eric replies. "I gather from Fatima that they're still behind, and still pulling their research together.

They're going to meet again on Friday afternoon. I don't think they need you to be there."

I look over towards Rose as she stands, still gazing up at the great natural spectacle in the northern sky.

I feel myself sigh.

I wish I could just stay up here until Charlie's funeral on Saturday ... But I feel compelled to make sure Fatima and the team are still on track ...

"I think I'm well enough to drive back tomorrow," I say. "I can catch up on my proposal for a couple of days, and then meet with the team on Friday, before I come back here for Charlie's funeral."

"Are you sure?" Eric asks. "Take the whole week off if you're not feeling up to it."

He may be a pain in the ass at times, but Eric's a good guy at heart. I could have done a lot worse in choosing a supervisor.

"Yeah, I'm sure," I say. "I'll check in with you on Thursday or Friday. Will that work?"

"Yup," Eric replies. "Just take care of yourself, and let me know if anything changes, okay?"

"I will," I say. "Talk to you later."

"Bye," he says, and the call ends.

I walk back to where Rose remains transfixed by the Wawasayg.

"I never get tired of watching this," she says. "Is everything okay?"

"It's fine," I say. "Eric's really understanding, and he told me I could take as much time off as I need. But, I told him I think I can finish out the term. I'm going to go back for a couple of days. I think I need to meet with the reconciliation team on Friday."

"You know you're welcome to stay as long as you want," she says. "How has that team been doing lately? You haven't said anything about them since you got here. Is Hunter getting along with the rest of the team?"

"They've been much better since we had that dinner social," I answer. "Hunter seems to be listening more respectfully to the others after that night. And the rest of the team seems more respectful too. I think they're starting to feel like they can trust one another."

I hold up my gloved hand and manage to cross my fingers for Rose to see. We both chuckle.

"Let's just hope it continues!" I say

I pause for a moment to take in more of Mother Earth's light show. I see and hear the slow, steady rhythm of my breathing, and I feel my heart beating the same slow rhythm in my chest. I let myself enjoy the sensation of relaxation and calm throughout my body.

"Rose, thank you for being here for me," I say. "Just hearing your calm voice … letting me join in the prayer groups … giving me space to wander around with my camera to enjoy Mother Nature … it's helped so much!"

"You're my brother's daughter," she says. "You're family, and I'm glad I'm here to help. Besides, it's been good for *me* to have *you* here too. Are you sure you feel healthy enough to go back?"

"I do," I reply. "I've been able to do a lot of thinking while I've been here. I realize how easy it is for those inner voices to spin out of control, and how close I came to ending my *own* life."

I feel myself swallow while I gather my thoughts.

"Now I feel a lot more empathy for Charlie … I've got my own traumatic past … different than his … but traumatic nonetheless … so I think I can understand why he did what he did."

"I'm glad to hear that," Rose says.

"But most importantly, understanding Charlie's actions has helped me to understand that what he did, wasn't my fault."

I wrap my arms around Rose. We squeeze each other tightly in a long embrace, before I finally let go.

"What would you like to do now?" Rose asks. "Go back to the lodge for a cup of tea before bedtime? Or maybe we could build a fire and stay here for a while longer."

I pause to ponder my choice.

"It's a beautiful night," I say. "How about a fire? I'll bring more wood if you want to get the fire started … I want to enjoy this as long as I can."

THEY SAY, whoever *they* are, that it's always darkest just before dawn. I really hope *they* are right! I think I've been able to see some daylight over the past few days, after teetering on the brink of self-inflicted oblivion. My body may be physically present at this meeting of Team Reconciliation's research subgroup, but my mind is still only halfway present—at best. Coming back to school and being able to concentrate, was a lot harder than I expected. My mind continues to replay recent events … my visit with Charlie … the hope I felt after that visit … the life-altering phone call from Rose about Charlie's death … the sudden hopelessness … sitting on the edge of my bathtub … the razor … the excruciating pain in my thigh … the blood dripping down my leg … the weird sense of relief … being at the Healing Lodge with Rose … and the meeting hasn't even started yet!

Fatima's mood is serious as she looks around the table at the other members of the research group—Hunter, Terri, and Arjun. Then she turns her head and looks to the far end of the table, where I'm seated.

"We missed you earlier this week, Sam," she says. "We are sorry you were ill, and we hope you are feeling better."

"Thanks, Fatima," I say, not wishing to say anything more about Charlie and my personal life. "I'm feeling a bit healthier and stronger every day."

She smiles and nods in my direction, then turns her attention back to the group, her face once again serious.

"Our presentation is less than two weeks away," she says. "That gives us exactly one week, at the most, to get a plan of action to the presentation group. So, how are things progressing? … Hunter, can we start with you?"

I watch Hunter closely for his reaction, my fingers crossed.

This is it! … If he hasn't made any progress, they're never going to make it in time!

"It's going to be tight getting all my information ready by then," he says. "There's so much in the *Truth and Reconciliation Report,* the *UNDRIP* declaration, and *Section 35* of the *Constitution Act,* and so little has been done to put them into action. But, I think I can do it."

The wrinkles in Fatima's forehead and around her eyes deepen, conveying her concern at Hunter's report and his limited confidence. She turns to Arjun.

"Arjun, how about you?" she says.

"I've found some interesting historical information about treaties and self-government," he replies, then he turns to Hunter.

"Correct me if I'm wrong," Arjun says. "But are you still suggesting that the best approach to reconciliation, and towards creating change and practical benefits for First Nations, lies in translating *Section 35* and *UNDRIP* into changes in existing legislation?"

"That's one possible approach," Hunter answers. "But our elders are increasingly resorting to court challenges and lawsuits to hold the Government accountable."

Arjun pauses to consider Hunter's response to his question. He jots down a note for himself, then he turns his attention back to Hunter.

"I agree that *Section 35* and *UNDRIP* are extremely important documents," Arjun says. "But it seems to me that their recommendations are quite broad, and possibly hard to translate into legislation and practical benefits for communities. Thanks for making that clear."

Arjun turns back to Fatima.

"I still need to review the *Calls to Action* over the next week, but I think I can be ready."

Fatima's face relaxes somewhat at this piece of hopeful news. "Terri?" Fatima asks.

"I've finished working my way through the *Indian Act* and Chief Joseph's book … it was tough reading, and I have to admit it's been a real eye opener."

I notice looks of surprise on both Hunter's and Fatima's faces. Even my own curiosity is awakened by the unexpected tone of Terri's announcement. Almost immediately, my mind is one-hundred-percent back in the room.

"What do you mean by that?" Fatima asks. "Can you elaborate?"

"Well," Terri answers slowly, referring to her notes. "The Act isn't really a coherent Act at all. Initially, it was just a consolidation of existing, unrelated regulations that were passed in the decade after Confederation. Most of them were passed when the Indians … as they were called then … came to be seen as an obstacle to settlement or development."

Terri pauses to look down at her notes again, then she takes a sip from a bottle of water.

"My overall impression is that the Act is incredibly paternalistic and demeaning," she continues. "It treats Indians like children, who must put out their hands and beg whenever they need money for anything. And, ironically, even though the clear goal of the *Indian Act* was to assimilate Indigenous people into the colonial mainstream, most of the Act's provisions actually discouraged them from participating in the larger Canadian society! I had no idea … I'm going to have to work hard to be ready by next week."

"Do you think we should recommend that the Act be amended?" Fatima asks.

"Actually," Terri replies. "It *was* already amended back in 1951, and then again in 1985 to bring it into line with the *Constitution Act*. There were minor changes, but the Act still treats Indians, and especially the women, as second-class people. My first impression is that further amendment isn't the way to go, but I don't know what else to suggest at this point."

"Thanks, Terri," Fatima says. "We will have to answer that question by next week."

She pauses to look at each member of the group, and then she looks at me. I've raised my hand slightly, signalling Fatima with my index finger that I'd like to have a word with the group.

"Sam," Fatima says. "You have something to say?"

"Yes, thanks," I begin. "I'm sorry I couldn't be here for your last meeting. But I'm proud to see all of you starting to trust each other, and to see that you're applying what you've learned in class. Keep up the good work. I know your team can do this!"

"Thank you, Sam," Fatima says. She acknowledges me with a nod before turning her attention back to the group.

"So, it is time for all of us to dig deep, and to show our commitment to each other and our project," she says. "When we meet this time next week, we need to show Sam that we have delivered results. We cannot let her down. And more importantly, we must not let ourselves and our teammates down!"

Amen to that! I just hope they believed my little pep talk a lot more than I do right now!

As the group packs up their belongings and the meeting comes to an end, my mind leaps to the next item on my life's agenda … saying goodbye to Charlie.

I hope Rose is right … That once I get past tomorrow, I'll be able to see some light at the end of this dark, shadowy rut that I've been stuck in for the past week!

THE REALITY that today is Charlie's funeral, hits home as I wheel my trusty Yaris into the parking lot of the local Community Centre, which I see is located at the far end of the lot. I find a Yaris-sized parking spot close to the building, park, and turn off the ignition. I pause for a few moments to reflect, taking slow breaths while I let the reality of Charlie's death sink in. Tears soon fill my eyes.

It's okay to grieve, Sam ... Okay to let the tears flow ... There was nothing you could have done to stop him ...

After a few minutes, I wipe the tears from my eyes and pull myself together. I step out of the car and start walking towards the Community Centre. As I draw close, I see Rose come out to greet me.

"Boozhoo, welcome!" she says.

We wrap our arms around each other and embrace.

"I'm glad you made it back safely," Rose adds. "How are you doing?"

"Not great today," I say, my voice a somber monotone. "But better than a few days ago."

"Come!" she says. "The ceremony is about to start, so you got here just in time. I'm glad you came … the ceremony is important for helping you on your healing journey."

She puts her arm around my shoulder and we walk together towards the building's entrance. As we near the door, I see an odd object—seemingly made from birch bark—hanging by the door.

"What's that?" I ask.

"It represents a snake," Rose replies. "It hangs by the door to keep the spirits away."

She opens the door and we enter the Community Centre. My facial expression quickly changes from sombre to surprise, when I see how many people have gathered for Charlie's ceremony.

"You're surprised to see so many people?" Rose asks.

"I am," I say. "I thought he hadn't lived here for many years."

"We're still a close community," she answers. "Especially when it comes to acknowledging the school survivors."

We're greeted by the steady rhythm of ceremonial drums, coming from the front of the hall. Rose takes my hand and leads me towards the drumming, stopping at a table near the drummers. My eyes begin to water and I feel a tear escape, making its way slowly down my cheek, before I wipe it away.

"The drumming is to make contact with The Creator," Rose says, raising her voice over the rhythms, "to help send Charlie's spirit to the spirit world."

"It's beautiful," I reply. "I love that constant rhythm … it leaves me feeling peaceful and calm."

The drummers continue as Rose guides me to our seats. While we're standing, I see Charlie's open casket, just a few paces away. I watch as a few people approach it, and then solemnly drop something into the casket. Alarmed, I lean towards Rose and speak into her ear.

"What are they dropping into the casket?"

Rose manages a slight smile.

"That must seem strange to you," she says. "They're birch bark matches … to light the deceased person's way to the spirit world."

The drumming ceases, and a man approaches a podium at the front of the room, where he speaks into a microphone.

"He's our spiritual leader," Rose whispers.

"Boozhoo!" he begins. "We come here today on the fifth day of grieving for our brother, to send him on his journey to the spirit world. I would like to invite his sister, Rose, to join me in cleansing this sacred space, our hearts, and our minds."

Rose pushes back her chair and makes her way to join the leader. Together, they each light tobacco and sage in a clay bowl, causing fragrant smoke to rise into the air. They each take a large feather, waving them gently in a circular motion to spread smoke over their torsos, heads, and out into the room.

"Creator," the leader says. "We ask that you cleanse us and our sacred ceremony, and that you guide the deceased, as he makes his way safely to the spirit world. We ask that you free him from his painful earthly memories of the residential school, and that you help other survivors, and their future generations, heal from the intergenerational trauma of the schools and their role in the cultural genocide against us."

The reality of the ceremony hits me hard. I feel an overwhelming rush of mixed emotions … sadness for the loss of Charlie and the opportunity to connect with him … trying to imagine the terror of what it would have been like if I'd been dragged from the safety of my uncle and aunt's home … what it would have been like to be taught that everything I knew was wrong … but also a new feeling … one of peace and acceptance from having so many other people around me, all grieving for Charlie at the same time. Despite my tears, I allow my eyes to roam over the crowd as Rose makes her way back to our table.

I notice the door at the auditorium's rear begin to open. I gasp, as Hunter unexpectedly slips into the room. Shocked, I feel my body freeze momentarily, wondering what to do next. As the spiritual leader continues talking about traditional Anishinaabe views of life and death, I slip from my chair and hurry to the back of the room.

"I didn't expect to see you here!" I whisper, as I get close enough for him to hear.

"I needed to be here," he whispers. "Helping to send your father on his journey … it's the least I can do. I'm sorry for your loss."

I take his hand and lead him back towards our table. We arrive just as the leader and Rose smoke an offering of tobacco for the spirit of the deceased. After she has passed the pipe back to the leader, Rose's eyes meet mine. She smiles at me and Hunter. I manage a quick smile in return, then I lean towards Hunter and whisper in his ear.

"I appreciate you coming all this way. Your support means a lot. Thank you!"

The offering now complete, the leader begins speaking to the crowd again in their traditional Anishinaabe language. Rose leans over and whispers in my ear.

"He says that Mother Earth has taken back his physical body, and The Creator is now taking back his spirit," Rose says. "Notice that we never mention your father's name, as this helps us all let go of his spirit … and free his spirit for his journey."

The spiritual leader continues his story.

"He says that the deceased person's spirit will now travel westward, across vast prairies, and up steep mountain slopes, until it reaches the high clouds. There, a bright light will guide his spirit into the Spirit World, where the spirits of our ancestors are waiting."

As the leader finishes his story, the ceremonial drummers and singers break into another traditional song. This time, many of the attendees join in the chant. My spine tingles, and I'm filled with awe at the spectacle I'm witnessing.

"We have one more thing to do before the ceremony concludes," Rose says.

She reaches into a bag beside her chair, and she removes a small bundle, wrapped in yellow cloth, which she places on the table.

"It is a final offering of food to the spirit of the dead person, to nourish him on his journey," she explains. "After the feast is over, we will smoke a final offering of tobacco to end the ceremony."

The drumming and singing comes to an end, and Rose stands to join the leader at the podium. She hands her bundled food offering to the leader, who holds it in the air for everybody to see.

"May this offering of food nourish the deceased person, and give his spirit safe passage to Gaagige Minawaaanigozigiwining, that he may live in the land of everlasting happiness," he says. "We invite all of you to stay with us and join in the ceremonial feast."

As the spiritual leader brings the ceremony to a close, the crowd begins to push their chairs back, stand up, and start mingling, Rose leans towards me and we give each other a warm embrace. Afterwards, we both wipe some lingering tears from our eyes and cheeks. She looks at Hunter and gives me a quick wink.

"Are you going to introduce me to your guest?" she says, smiling.

This is embarrassing ... Now everybody is going to think we're an item.

I pause briefly to think.

"Ummh … this is my, uh, friend … Hunter," I say to Rose. "He's part of that project at the university that I told you about."

Sensing my discomfort, Rose does what Rose does best, helping others feel welcome.

"Nice to meet you, Hunter," she says. "It was so good of you to drive such a great distance to be here today, and to take part in our ceremony."

"I wouldn't have missed it, after Fatima told me what happened," he replies. "I get so tired of hearing stories like this about school survivors, over and over again. It's what makes me so angry sometimes!"

Rose nods her understanding, then she turns her attention back to me.

"What did *you* think of the ceremony, dear," she asks.

I pause again, trying to sort out my mixed emotions.

"I couldn't help feeling sad," I say. "But I think I also feel a bit of closure … some acceptance of what happened. And I think … maybe … that he's finally going to be in a better place in the spirit world. So, yes … I liked the ceremony a lot."

Rose looks towards the rear of the auditorium, where women have started setting out large platters and trays of food.

"I hope you'll be staying for the feast," Rose says to Hunter.

"I wouldn't miss it," he replies.

"I should go and help," Rose says. "I'll join you two later at our table."

She rushes away to help the other women, leaving Hunter and I standing in awkward silence.

"When did Fatima tell you about the ceremony?" I ask, finally.

"After yesterday's meeting," he answers. "I could tell you weren't yourself during the meeting. You hardly said a word … In fact, you didn't even scold me like you usually do!"

Smart ass! Am I really THAT easy to read?

"Very funny," I say. "You didn't have to come all this way, you know."

The smile on Hunter's face turns more serious.

"I haven't had a chance to talk with you much since you told us about your ancestry," he says. "And then … well, with your dad's death … I figured all of this must be a big shock for you. I've had my share of family funeral ceremonies for survivors too, you know. I understand."

Wow! Somebody, besides Rose, who really gets what I'm going through.

"Thank you," I reply. "It means a lot to know somebody understands what I've been experiencing for the last few weeks."

Hunter reaches out and rests his hand on my shoulder.

"You can talk with me anytime, you know … about *any* of this," he says.

This is getting awkward … I feel like giving him a hug … But he's one of my students … What do I say?

I briefly put my hand on top of Hunter's, and I give it a pat to show that I appreciate his concern. Then I pull my hand back away from his.

"Maybe in a couple of weeks, after the course is over," I say. "Until then, let's just say I appreciate the offer a lot. Okay?"

He gives me a knowing nod.

"I see Rose waving at us to come and get some food," he says. "Have you eaten traditional Anishinaabe food before?"

"I have," I answer. "After my first *Full Moon Ceremony*, about a month ago. But it was more like a lunch than a full meal."

"Well, let's go and I'll introduce you to a full funeral feast," he says. "It's probably similar to my Haudenosaunee tradition, so I think you'll really enjoy it."

"I'm sure I will," I reply. "Especially now that I have a friend I can share it with. You lead the way!"

CHAPTER 15—WEEK TWELVE

GETTING THROUGH Charlie's funeral ceremony was a major hurdle for me. I feel like it finally allowed me to let go of a lot of my past anger towards Charlie … and towards myself too. I also feel like my guilty inner voice isn't as loud as it was over the past week. Being with Rose, being accepted into the Anishinaabe community for the ceremony, and being accepted without judgment by Hunter, all helped my inner three-year-old to be more open to my inner caregiver. I think I can actually see some light at the end of last week's very dark tunnel. I've even given Fatima permission to tell the rest of the research group about Charlie's passing.

"On behalf of the whole team," Fatima says. "I would like to express our sympathy for your recent loss. We're glad to have you back."

"Thanks, Fatima," I reply. "I appreciate your kind words."

I take a moment to nod to Terri and Arjun, and then to Hunter, who gets a small smile. I see him try to return the smile, but something about it seems strained.

That's odd … I wonder what's bothering him?

"I was glad to see some progress last week," I continue. "I'm proud of each of you and your hard work, and I'm very much looking forward to hearing how you've been doing this week. I know you've got a lot to cover, so I'll hand things back to Fatima."

"Thank you, Sam," she says. "Who wants to go first?"

Arjun raises his hand.

"I'll go," he says. "I stumbled onto a 2016 public opinion poll, mentioned by the Truth and Reconciliation Committee, that's quite significant."

He shuffles some papers on the desk in front of him, until he finds the one he's looking for.

"Ah, here it is," he says. "It found that sixty-eight percent of all Canadians feel that minorities should be doing more to fit in with mainstream society, rather than keeping their own customs and languages."

"I don't find that surprising at all," Hunter says, grimacing slightly.

"Me neither," Fatima adds.

"Just wait, there's more," Arjun replies. "Another 2016 poll showed that the vast majority of Canadians report that they know virtually nothing about residential school survivor abuse, or about the loss of Indigenous language and culture. And more recently, a poll just before the 2021 Federal Election found that Truth and Reconciliation was only a high priority for seven percent of Canadians. A year later, when housing affordability, spiralling inflation, and a crumbling healthcare system were foremost in peoples' minds, Truth and Reconciliation wasn't even in the top ten national concerns of the average Canadian!"

Hunter emits an angry huff.

"I didn't need a few opinion polls to tell me that," he says, sounding somewhat strained.

"Well, I'm ashamed to admit that I've been one of those people for a long time," Terri says.

Hunter's head turns abruptly towards the woman who has been a thorn in his side for weeks. His face conveys a look of complete, but also pained, surprise.

"But it's not just me," Terri continues. "I see it all the time with friends and other people I meet. There's a significant undercurrent of pushback in non-Indigenous people these days. They feel like they're being told how reconciliation is supposed to proceed, and they feel like they have no say about the issue. And they're very afraid that they'll be branded as racists if they express a different opinion."

I can't help myself. I feel an immediate need to encourage the healthy discussion I'm hearing for the first time.

"So, if that's true," I say, jumping into the discussion, "what does that mean for this group?"

"I think it means that we have to make recommendations that will resonate with *both* Indigenous *and* non-Indigenous people," Arjun interjects.

I see some of the same old frustration showing in creases on Hunter's forehead.

"I'm sorry," he says loudly. "That's bullshit! We're the ones who've been wronged for seven generations. We should have the right to say what should change!"

Terri turns to Hunter.

"I agree," Terri says. "But you also have to deal with the realities exposed by those polls. And also deal with the realities of the *Indian Act* … it's so misogynistic, racist, and patriarchal, I think our team has a duty to educate non-Indigenous Canadians about it, and to recommend significant changes to the whole system."

"That's easy for you to say," Hunter replies. "Where would *you* start?"

"Well, first I need to apologize to you for things I've said to you before," she begins. "You were right … we *don't* have an Indian problem in Canada … we have an *Indian Act* problem! That's where we need to start."

"That's interesting," Arjun says to Terri. "The more I read the *Calls to Action*, the more I see the *Indian Act* as a giant impediment … so many different branches of the Federal and Provincial Governments have to be involved in order to translate the recommendations into action through the *Indian Act* and other legislation. More importantly, I think the *Calls to Action* contain some very important and interesting clues for creating an alternative to the *Indian Act*."

Arjun turns his attention to Hunter.

"I also stumbled on something else in my reading that's worth considering, if we're talking about changing to something other than the *Indian Act*. There was an Indigenous World War I veteran … I think his name was Loft … Lieutenant Fred Loft …"

Arjun shuffles more papers until he finds the one he's looking for.

"Here it is. He was upset about how Indigenous veterans were treated after the war," he says. "He proposed something that he called a *League of Nations of Indians of Canada* … a unified group of Indigenous communities, communicating and working together to address Indigenous issues."

"We already have that with the Assembly of First Nations," Hunter answers, pausing to catch his breath. "As far as I'm concerned, the first thing the AFN needs to do is to make the Federal Government accountable for addressing each of the ninety-four *Calls to Action*."

"That's true, and I completely agree," Arjun says. "But, from what I've seen and read, the AFN is little more than an Indigenous lobby group that has no legal status, and limited political power. And they're still working within the *Indian Act*!"

Arjun pauses briefly, allowing the rest of the team some time to digest his information.

"Maybe we need to think outside the box … outside the *Indian Act*," he continues. "What if we created a new Nation of Indigenous First Nations? An entity with self-government and *real* political power?"

"You mean something like Nunavut?" Fatima asks. "A new territory?"

"Perhaps," Arjun says. "But when I read the issues that need to be addressed in the *Calls to Action*, most of them relate to issues that fall within provincial jurisdiction in the Constitution …

education, health, social services, community infrastructure, justice and policing, resources … so why couldn't the 'nation of nations' be a new province?"

The room goes silent while we all digest Arjun's suggestion.

"I think," Arjun continues. "That the *Calls to Action* are inadvertently giving us the clues and a roadmap for how to replace the *Indian Act* with a whole new level of Indigenous self-government … at the provincial level!"

"Territory … province … what's the difference?" Hunter asks.

I catch Hunter wincing, as if he's in pain, and I see that his face has virtually lost its colour.

"As I understand it, the Territories are still accountable to the Federal Government in many ways," Arjun continues. "A province would be more independent from Ottawa. What does everybody else think?"

"I think it is an interesting idea," Fatima says. "But we are just the research group. I think you need to translate that into a Plan of Action."

She looks up at Hunter and then Terri.

"That would be you, Hunter, and Terri," she says. "And I think Arjun should join you."

"How could anybody make a single province out of over sixty First Nations, and over six-hundred-thirty First Nations bands living across one thousand communities?" Terri asks, looking in Arjun's direction. "I think we need to meet again soon to talk about how this would even work. Can we meet in the next two or three days?"

"I think I can find the time," Arjun says.

All of a sudden, Hunter lurches unsteadily to his feet. His face is white as a ghost, and he's clutching his stomach.

What's happening? What's wrong with him?

I feel my stomach start churning, full of anxiety and concern.

"I'm sorry, I think I'm going to be sick!" Hunter blurts.

He bolts unexpectedly from the room, leaving the rest of us staring at each other, and looking totally stunned.

"What the hell?" Terri exclaims.

My feelings exactly ... What the hell? ... What else could possibly go wrong? ... Another hurdle? ... And just when I thought I was beginning to see some daylight ahead ...

EVERY TIME I feel like I'm starting to move forward a step, it feels like the gods are conspiring to set me back two! And then the second-guessing starts ... mostly from my guilty inner voice ... although I think I'm starting to see that voice in a different light these days. I realize now it's much more than just feeling guilty ... it's a deeper, more insidious feeling of not being good enough ... of always judging myself ... of feeling like I'm to blame whenever something goes wrong ... whether it's to me, or to anybody close to me.

So here I sit in my office, in front of the computer again, suffering through another case of writer's block. I just can't seem to put my heart into my thesis proposal. Instead, I realize that I'm becoming more and more preoccupied with Team Reconciliation ... and with the whole concept of reconciliation and the treatment of Indigenous people ... my people!

There, I've said it ... *my people*! It's starting to make sense why I feel like I'm now seeing the world through two sets of eyes ... I'm conscious that I'm starting to feel my Indigenous heritage creeping into my identity ... my inner caregiver starting to feel more like Aunt Rose every day ...

A knock on my door breaks my train of thought and drags me back into reality.

"Come in," I call out.

The door opens, to reveal Terri and Arjun. Both team members are out of breath and have concern etched deeply on their faces.

"Have you heard from Hunter since he left the meeting?" Terri asks.

"We were supposed to confirm a time with him for meeting today, but he hasn't replied to any of our texts, phone calls, or messages!" Arjun adds.

I reach for my phone and scroll through my contacts list until I come to Hunter. I tap on his information and wait … my phone rings and rings until it goes to voicemail.

"Hunter, here," the recording says. "You know the drill—leave a message."

I frown, not just because I'm frustrated by the message, but I feel a growing sense of concern over Hunter's apparent disappearance.

"Do you know if anybody else on the team has a different number?" I ask.

"We called Fatima," Terri says. "But she has the same number we have."

I take a moment to think, and then I turn to Terri.

"He lives with his sister, remember?" I ask. "We dropped him off at her place after we watched his band at the club last Saturday. Does anybody know *her* number, or where she lives?"

"I don't think so," Terri answers. "And I'm afraid I had so much to drink that night, there's no way I can remember where he lives!"

I feel myself blush.

You were also in fine drinking form that night yourself, Sam!
"Yeah, me too," I admit.

"You're our TA … you're technically on staff, right?" Arjun says. "Can't you just call the registrar's office for his address?"

"I seriously doubt it," I answer. "Would you want them giving out your contact information to anybody who asks?"

"I didn't think about that," Arjun admits.

The room goes silent while the three of us think. Then a fleeting image emerges from the recesses of my mind.

"Wait! There was something," I say to Terri. "A big hill or a mountain … somewhere near his house. He didn't live far from the club … do you remember seeing anything like that?"

Terri shakes her head, looking dejected.

"Maybe I was just seeing things," I suggest. "Maybe it was nothing."

"Or maybe it wasn't," Arjun replies. "Looks like there's only one thing to do. We know he doesn't live far from downtown and the club. So, we drive around the inner city and look for Sam's mountain, until we find his sister's place!"

"Are you crazy?" Terri asks. "That could take hours … or days!

I stand up and grab my jacket from its hook on the back of the door.

"He's right," I say. "Do we have any better ideas? How else are we going to find him?"

I pause to get my thoughts in order, and to come up with a plan.

"Arjun, you know the city, so you can ride shotgun with Terri. I'll take the areas west of the club, and you guys can search to the east. We've got each other's numbers if we find anything."

Arjun and Terri look at each other and then at me, giving me nods of acknowledgment.

"Sounds good!" Arjun says. "What are we waiting for!"

I feel adrenaline rushing through my body … my heart is pounding, ready to meet the challenge … but also out of fear that something terrible has happened to Hunter …

Where are you, Hunter? Why aren't you answering our calls?

I CONTINUE to drive my car back and forth through the inner city, feeling a lot like an *Amazing Race* contestant who's doing one of the show's infamous 'needle-in-the-haystack' challenges. I drive

through the park, feeling a certain irony at seeing traces of
Hunter's red paint, still marring Queen Victoria's statue. I pass the
bus and train stations, and I think maybe he parked there and went
somewhere for the weekend … until I remember Hunter doesn't
have a car, and my hopes sink again.

I pass the arena and the downtown market, my eyes scanning
every face in hopes of seeing Hunter's face and his black braids.
As I leave the downtown area, I see mostly businesses and
churches on the busy main street, so I turn onto a side street and
begin driving up one street, and then down another, in an effort to
do a more systematic grid search. It doesn't help that many of the
streets aren't laid out in a uniformly rectangular pattern, so it's
easy to miss portions of streets that intersect at odd angles.

*Who designed this city anyway? And what were they smoking
at the time?*

I pull into a strip mall's parking lot, stop the car, and pull out
my phone. I tap Arjun's number and wait for my call to connect.
He picks up after only a single ring.

"Arjun," he says. "What's up, Sam?"

"Nothing, so far," I concede. "What about you guys?"

"Same here," he says, dejectedly. "We haven't seen anything
yet that looks remotely like a hill or a mountain."

I look at the time on my phone.

"I'm getting hungry," I say. "Let's give it another hour …
maybe we can meet somewhere downtown for a bite of lunch after
that?"

I hear Arjun talking in the background to Terri.

"Sure, that works for us," Arjun replies. "Happy hunting."

"You too," I say. "Talk to you later."

I end the call and then wheel my little Yaris back into another
community of older, wood frame houses. Signs of a new revival in
the neighbourhood … colourful coats of paint, new landscaping,
and young families on the street with children … are mixed with

older, run down, and poorly maintained houses … signs of poverty and decay.

As I cruise each street, I slow the car at every intersection, looking right and left for any signs of the elusive hill or mountain. And then I start second-guessing myself again …

Maybe you were just seeing things, Sam! … You had way too much to drink that night! … It's crazy to think you're going to find his sister's place!

I reach the main route out of downtown again, turn right, and then right again at the next street, doubling back from the direction I just came from. It's a long street, with a vacant lot and a field on my left, and businesses to my right. I accelerate past the businesses to the next intersection, where I fall back into my routine of slowing the car, and then looking both right and left for any signs of my target.

I accelerate past intersection after intersection, until I see a T-intersection, and the end of this current street, only a few blocks ahead. As the intersection grows nearer, I see an old red-brick building on the left, and I remember that it used to be an old food processing plant. I slow down and carefully scan the residences on both sides of the street, while the old plant and the intersection grow closer.

As I enter the last block before reaching the plant, a dark shadow slowly emerges on the right. My eyes grow wide in anticipation. The shadow grows larger, and I suddenly realize that it belongs to a huge pile of crushed concrete on the site of the old processing plant. I feel my heart start pounding in my chest. I slow my trusty Yaris to a crawl as I enter the last block before reaching the plant. I scan every house for anything that might be the least bit recognizable.

And then I see it … something familiar! One of the homes is painted in bold blue with orange trim. And on the porch, I see and remember a telltale sign … a small tribute to residential school victims … a few pairs of children's shoes … and a teddy bear wearing an orange t-shirt.

This is it! I'm not crazy after all!

I turn the wheel abruptly and park, then I grab my phone and tap Arjun's number.

"Arjun? Sam!" I shout. "I think I found it!"

MOMENTS LATER, I see Terri's car in my rearview mirror, speeding up the street towards me. Terri swings her car to the curb behind me. She and Arjun exit the vehicle and walk briskly towards me as I climb out of my car. I point to the blue and orange house beside us.

"Look familiar?" I say to Terri.

"Yup, but where's the mountain," she asks.

I cross the street to get a better angle for viewing the pile of crushed concrete.

"Come over here and take a look," I say. "It's a deserted packing plant that they're demolishing. They must be reclaiming the old concrete."

Arjun and Terri both join me for a better view.

"I can't believe it. You were right!" Arjun says. He looks back across the street to the blue and orange house. "Is anybody home?"

"I don't know," I say. "I thought I'd wait until you both showed up. Let's find out."

We cross the street together and walk up the sidewalk to the front porch, pausing briefly to look at the tribute. We climb the steps and I ring the doorbell. A moment later, a young woman comes to the door and opens it a crack.

"Can I help you?" she says, tentatively.

"I hope so," Terri says. "We're looking for a friend who's gone missing. Would you happen to be Hunter's sister?"

The woman looks at us suspiciously. I don't blame her … three perfect strangers standing on her porch … and me, with my purple hair and nose ring!

"We're from the university," I explain. "Hunter is part of a team project that has to be completed by next week. I'm the team's teaching assistant. He's an important part of the team, so it's vital that we reach him!"

Still suspicious, the woman takes a moment to decide if she can trust three total strangers. Finally, she decides to open the door wider.

"I'd like to help you," she says. "But Hunter's appendix ruptured. He's in serious condition in the hospital."

Arjun, Terri, and I stand in shock, lost for words.

Oh, shit! … I hope he's going to be okay! … This cannot be happening!

CHAPTER 16—PLAN OF ACTION

I HAVE a new appreciation for anybody who has had to live in limbo … hearing, out of the blue, that a friend or loved one has been in a sudden, unexpected accident, or has become seriously ill … wondering if they'll ever see that person again! I haven't ever experienced illness or death in my life before … until Charlie's unexpected death and Hunter's sudden illness shattered my sheltered existence twice, within a matter of only two weeks.

Finally hearing from Hunter's sister—and hearing that his condition has improved significantly enough that he can now see visitors—has ultimately released me from this latest purgatory. Hunter's doctor grudgingly gave us permission to meet with him, but she was stern in her warning to keep the meeting brief.

It's difficult to see Hunter this way, sitting semi-reclined in bed, with an intravenous drip suspended from a bedside pole. His face is pale and his voice is weak. It's hard to believe it's really him, when we're used to seeing and hearing his strong voice, and feeling his strong sense of conviction.

"Run that by me again," Hunter says to Arjun. "How can you make over six hundred First Nations into a single province?"

"Well, each First Nation is a distinct community, right?" Arjun replies.

Hunter nods his head slowly in acknowledgment.

"So, think of each First Nation community as a municipality, with its own elected government, much like any town or city in Canada. And much like Westbank, in British Columbia," Arjun continues. "Except Westbank has a self-government agreement with Ottawa that treats them like a municipality, but also gives them jurisdiction over many areas such as resources, agriculture, education, health, culture and language, and policing … much like a province."

"And get this!" Terri exclaims. "That agreement actually has clauses that leave the door open for another level of self-government, which is exactly what we're proposing! It also gives Westbank the same power to negotiate deals with other governments, that existing provinces already have."

"Okay," Hunter says. "But you still haven't answered my question: How can you make over six hundred First Nations into one province?"

Arjun smiles and nods his head in understanding.

"I get it," he says. "If you think about the traditional notion of a province as being encompassed within physical boundaries, like the walls of a box, it doesn't make any sense at all … but, what if you think outside the box? What if the provincial boundaries are virtual?"

Hunter exhales, then he shakes his head from side to side.

"Just listen, Hunter," Terri pleads. "Here's the best part! The Westbank agreement ends the *Indian Act*'s influence over their lands and people! It allows Westbank to negotiate annual transfer payments, just like the rest of the provinces!"

"So, we could just negotiate one big transfer payment for all six hundred First Nations?" Hunter asks.

"Exactly!" Arjun replies. "The new Indigenous provincial government would get to decide where and how it wants to spend the money, and how it wants to address any unresolved Truth and Reconciliation issues in their communities. No more negotiating with multiple agencies in Ottawa to fix each of the separate ninety-four recommendations. No more bandaid cures from Ottawa. And no more *Indian Act*!"

Hunter pauses for a moment to think.

My God! Is he actually thinking seriously about this?

"I'd have to think about it some more … but it sounds like a possibility," Hunter says, finally. "What about the issue of *Clear Consent* that's part of the UN Declaration? Indigenous people need to have the right to give or withhold consent on any issues that directly affect our lands."

"Is that like a veto?" I ask.

Hunter pauses to take a deep breath. It's obvious that he's tiring fast.

"Call it what you like," he says. "We just want the right to *Clear Consent*. And what about outstanding land claims?"

"It doesn't look like that was an outstanding issue in Westbank," Arjun replies.

"Well, it damn well *is* an issue for First Nation communities!" Hunter exclaims, trying to dig deep to make himself more forceful. "There's no way First Nations can sign onto this if we don't resolve where our territories begin or end!"

Arjun and Terri look at each other for a reply to address Hunter's concern.

"What if we proposed a special court or tribunal to get land claims out of the existing court system?" Terri says. "We could speed up the settlement process."

Hunter pauses and gasps a short, sharp breath.

"Are you alright?" Terri asks.

He exhales slowly.

"Yeah," Hunter answers, cautiously. "Still some pain from the surgery … I'm okay … about the land claims … I think we already have a system of special claims tribunals. But, I think they only deal with claims related to existing treaties. There's still more than a hundred outstanding claims related to our traditional lands."

Hunter pauses again, taking a long breath to gather his strength.

"At the pace Ottawa is going, it will take generations to settle all of the claims!" he says.

Arjun and Terri look at each other again, and they take a moment to think.

"How about this?" Arjun says. "Maybe we could propose a new type of tribunal that's focused solely on speeding up the resolution of outstanding land claims?"

Hunter flashes a look of exasperation, followed by wincing in pain.

"You settlers …," he says. He turns his head and looks at me sheepishly. "I mean, non-Indigenous people … you just don't get it, do you! We don't rush into solving everything as quickly as possible, like you do. We take our time … we think ahead about the impact of our decisions for seven generations into the future … we will take as long as it takes to do what's best for our future generations."

He's getting tired and frustrated … And he's losing patience with Arjun and his proposal … I have to say something!

"I'm sure there must be some kind of solution," I say, no longer able to stay neutral. "Especially if Westbank and other First Nations can find one. Can we agree to let Arjun and Terri look into other modern treaties for ideas?"

Hunter looks at me, and I see that he's completely exhausted. He exhales slowly.

"Sure," he says to me. "Whatever … sorry, Sam … I think I'm done for today."

I sigh, relieved that Hunter still seems to be on board with the project, but still concerned about his health. Hunter grabs his right side and winces in pain, just as a nurse comes into the room. She notices him wincing.

"Okay, everybody," she says, sternly. "Your friend is still exhausted and weak. Time to wrap it up!"

"The team's running out of time, Hunter," I say quickly. "Are you okay with Arjun and Terri working out more details over the next couple of days … while you're recovering? We need to get this to the presentation team as soon as possible!"

Hunter is still noticeably uncomfortable, but he gives me a weak nod. I look at Arjun and Terri.

"Can you guys go ahead?" I say. "I'll catch up in a minute."

Arjun and Terri glance at each other. Taking my hint, they nod back to me.

"Rest up," Terri says to Hunter. "Get yourself healthy. We'll check in with you in a couple of days."

Arjun and Terri exit the room, leaving me alone with Hunter and the nurse. I exhale and smile at Hunter.

"It's nice to see you guys pulling together as a team," I say. "I have a good feeling about how this is going to turn out!"

I rest my hand on Hunter's shoulder. He tries to smile, but it turns into another big wince. The nurse steps in, thermometer in hand. She gives me a disapproving look.

"Time to go, dear," she says.

An awkward silence ensues. There are things I still want to say to him right now.

So much to say about my new Indigenous identity ... Things we have in common ... I wish I could stay and talk with him ...

I take my hand from Hunter's shoulder and give his hand a brief squeeze. With tears starting to form in my eyes, I hurry from the room before anybody sees them.

I RECEIVED the text message from Hunter's sister within hours after Terri, Arjun, and I had visited him in hospital. It confirmed my biggest fears, after seeing him grimacing with pain yesterday ... Hunter's condition has gone downhill again. As a result, I resign myself to the fact that Hunter probably won't be healthy enough to be much help to the Plan of Action team. My first instinct, early this morning, was to call Fatima to tell her the bad news. We agreed to call Terri and Arjun, to ask them if Fatima and I could sit in on their planned meeting for dealing with Hunter's

Plan of Action concerns. I thought I'd wait until we met with them in person to break the bad news.

Fatima is seated on the other side of my desk. Both of us have deep furrows of concern on our foreheads and around our eyes, when we hear the knock on my door.

"Come in!" I call.

Terri and Arjun realize something is seriously amiss, as soon as they see the grave looks on our faces.

"What's wrong?" Terri asks. "Does this have anything to do with Hunter?"

I nod my head, finding it difficult to speak. I pause to take a breath and clear my throat.

"Yes," I reply. "His sister texted me this morning … he's developed a serious post-surgical infection."

"Oh, no!" Arjun says. "Is he going to be alright?"

"He's taken a serious turn for the worse since we saw him," I answer. "He's on heavy-duty antibiotics, and his sister thinks they'll be keeping him in hospital for at least a couple more days."

"What are we going to do?" Fatima asks. "The Plan of Action group needs to get their research and recommendations to the Presentation group by the end of the week!"

"That only gives us about three days at most!" Terri cries out. "And it's essential to have Hunter's input to ensure that we have an Indigenous perspective!"

"Yeah, I think I've found some ways to address his concerns," Arjun adds. "But I need to run things past him, so that the team arrives at an unanimous recommendation."

I pause to think, and then I take another slow breath.

Come on, Sam! … Pull yourself together … It's time to be the mentor you want to be!

"Before we declare this a catastrophe," I say, finally. "We need to remember the real goals of this course. Dr. Sanderson wants to see that you've learned and applied the team building skills that he's been teaching."

I look around the room and my eyes meet with each of the team members.

"The content of the project," I continue, "isn't as important as the process of learning to trust each other, to feel comfortable with disagreement, and to find some sort of logical consensus that you all agree upon! Each team's topic is just a vehicle to help achieve those goals."

"But we all want to do the best work we can," Fatima counters. "We do not want our presentation to make us look like fools!"

"Fatima's right," Arjun says. "If Dr. Sanderson didn't care about the content, he wouldn't have assigned such controversial topics. And I can't afford a bad grade in this course, or it will ruin my GPA for getting into med school!"

"I never thought I'd hear myself saying this," Terri adds. "But we owe it to Hunter to make sure we do justice to Indigenous grievances and the need for change."

"I understand you guys completely," I reply. "And you need to know that I'm so proud of the personal growth I've seen in every member of this team over the past two or three weeks. I believe in you guys!"

"Thanks for the vote of confidence," Terri says. "But seriously, what are we going to do?"

I take a moment to think, and then I turn to Arjun.

"You guys have done some great research," I answer. "And you, Arjun, have come up with a really unique possible solution. But we know that Hunter has concerns about unsettled land claims and the need for Indigenous consent. Right?"

Arjun nods in agreement.

"So, have you thought more about it since we saw him?"

"We're tossing around a couple of ideas," Terri says, jumping into the conversation. "And we think they're workable. But, what if Hunter thinks they're unacceptable?"

"Then all we know is that they are not acceptable to Hunter," Fatima says. "We should not assume that he speaks for all Indigenous people. So, we can only control what we can control."

"Fatima's right," I say. "All you can do, is do your best to anticipate Hunter's concerns and try to address them honestly. Do you think you can do that?"

"I guess so," Arjun replies.

I take a deep breath, push my chair back and stand up.

"You guys have all come a long way as a team since the dinner social," I say. "You've learned to trust that your teammates have the same goals. But it's time that you all learned to trust yourselves and your abilities as well."

I pause for a quick gulp of water.

"God knows I'm nobody to preach about self-confidence," I continue. "But you need to know that you guys have helped inspire me to be more confident in myself. I just want each of you to have confidence in your own abilities … to finish this project, and make it great."

I stop to look around the room at each team member again.

"So, use what you've learned in the lectures, and use what you've learned from your research and from Hunter," I say. "Control what you can control, and finish this project … without Hunter if necessary. I know you can do it!"

"Thank you for your faith in us, Sam," Fatima says, then she turns to Arjun and Terri. "Let us remain positive and pray that Hunter makes a full recovery."

Confidence, Sam! … Have confidence!

"I agree," I add. "We all know Hunter's a fighter, so let's not write him off this project yet!"

TERRI BRINGS two lattés back to the booth in a campus coffee shop, where Arjun has his laptop open in front of him. Scraps of paper with scribbled notes litter the table beside the computer. Terri sets the cups down and slides into the booth, opposite Arjun.

"So, what do you think about this *Clear Consent* issue?" Terri asks. "Why is it so important to Hunter?"

"I think it comes from the UN Declaration on the Rights of Indigenous People," Arjun says. "Let me see …"

He swipes and clicks on his computer's trackpad for a moment or two.

"Here we are," he says. "It seems to come up in a number of situations … removal of Indigenous people from their lands … removal of cultural artifacts from their lands … loss of traditional lands … development projects on Indigenous lands … the declaration says that states need to obtain 'free, prior, and informed consent' from Indigenous people in any of these situations."

"Oh, yeah. I think I heard something about this on the news a while ago … haven't people been criticizing the Trudeau Government for not endorsing that declaration?"

"I think you're right," Arjun says. "Let's see here …"

He does some more swiping and clicking on his trackpad.

"Yeah," he continues. "It says here that the Government has interpreted *Clear Consent* to mean that they only have a duty to consult with Indigenous people in these situations. But Indigenous people interpret *Clear Consent* to mean that they have the right to say no, even when they *are* consulted."

"Ohhhhh … I get it now," Terri says. "That *is* a big difference of opinion … It sounds a lot like a veto to me!"

"And it seems like that's what concerns the Government," Arjun adds.

"If that's Hunter's big concern … that *Clear Consent* means having a veto … I don't think I could live with that," Terri replies. "And neither could a lot of other Canadians! What if the Government absolutely needs a highway or a pipeline to go across Indigenous land? The Indigenous people could just say no to that?"

"I guess so," Arjun says. "Look at all of the Indigenous protests over the past few years … over pipelines, logging, fishing, land developments …"

"So, what are *we* going to do?" Terri asks. "Do *you* agree they should have a veto? How do we address that in our project? Hunter will be pissed at us big time if we don't give the new province *Clear Consent*, as they interpret it!"

"I agree with you," Arjun says. "I don't think that the power of veto is a good thing anywhere or anytime. But, remember what Sam said. If Hunter isn't well enough to continue, the decision is up to us. We just have to make a logical case to justify our recommendation."

Terri shakes her head and smiles.

"Isn't this ironic?" she says. "If Hunter is well enough, he's going to demand the right to consent to our recommendations, or withhold his approval. *He* wants to have *Clear Consent* power over *our* project!"

She stops and shakes her head again while she pauses for a moment to think.

"Is there anything else we could suggest that might get him to move on this?" she asks.

Arjun pauses to mull over Terri's question.

"The only thing I can think of right now," he says. "Is finding a way to resolve outstanding land claims. That seems to be his other big pet peeve."

Terri brings her hand to her chin, unconsciously rubbing it as she thinks.

"Okay," she says, finally. "Because both of us disagree with the notion of a veto, we'll recommend that the Federal Government only has a duty to consult with Indigenous people in those situations. But, in return, we'll recommend some kind of new tribunal to keep land claims out of the courts, and to speed up the claims settlement process."

Arjun takes a moment to type a note into his laptop.

"Good," he says. "But there's one more thing that still bothers me. And I know he's going to ask the question."

A puzzled look crosses Terri's face.

"What's that?" she asks.

"What's the incentive for both Ottawa and Indigenous peoples to buy into a radical idea like ours?" he asks. "If we can't answer that, the idea would never gain any real traction!"

Terri frowns and is momentarily tongue-tied.

"Shit!" she says, finally. "I never thought of it that way. If we can't answer that question, it doesn't matter whether Hunter approves or not!"

"Exactly!" Arjun says. "Sam expects us to make logical recommendations, regardless what Hunter says. And we can't do that unless we answer that question!"

THE LAST two days have been a giant blur for me. Unable to concentrate on my thesis proposal after my meeting with Fatima, Arjun, and Terri, I decided to pack up my laptop and notes, and I headed for the peace and quiet of the Healing Lodge and Rose's soothing presence. But, try as I might, I couldn't stop myself from being preoccupied with Team Reconciliation and their project. Deep down, I couldn't shake the feeling that their topic is more than just a night class assignment, and their success means more to me than just a checked box on my academic resumé. Instead, as I drove home after those two days at the lodge, I started to feel like I'm seeing the team's conflicting opinions through my two sets of eyes, and I'm beginning to sense that I'm helping with something that has real significance.

A flood of mixed emotions overwhelms me as Arjun, Terri, and I walk into Hunter's hospital room. I didn't think it was possible for him to look weaker, or more pale, than he did two days ago, but I couldn't have been more wrong! The relief I feel at seeing him alive, pales in comparison to my alarm at seeing his physical condition. Although his doctor expressed her grave reservations over allowing us to discuss the team's project with him, Hunter's stubborn nature prevailed in the end.

Now, Arjun, Terri, and I stand beside his bed while Hunter reviews Arjun and Terri's draft recommendations. Every couple of moments, Hunter pauses to breathe deeply, trying to muster the strength to make it through the document. With every passing minute, I feel the tension in my body, as well as my breathing and heart rates, increasing dramatically. My hands are sweaty, so I try to surreptitiously wipe them dry on my blue jeans.

Hang in there, Sam! ... He's in good hands ... He's going to be alright ... He'll recognize how hard Arjun and Terri have worked!

The silence is broken when Hunter throws the recommendations down on his bed. The old familiar look of defiant anger shows in his eyes. His teeth are clenched and the muscles in his neck are standing out.

"I would *never* present this to another Indigenous person without adding a condition for Indigenous *Clear Consent* in *any* negotiations with governments!" Hunter declares.

"But we *have* included the concept!" Terri replies. "It's only fair that governments should have to consult with Indigenous people about how their land is used."

"Consult!" Hunter says, doing his best to raise his voice. "It's just a settler word for paying lip service to our concerns, and then overruling us like you've always done!"

He pauses to gather some more strength.

"We demand the right to say no to deals that aren't in our peoples' interests!"

Hunter picks up the document and throws it on the floor in disgust.

"*Please* read the rest of the plan!" Arjun answers. "We've added recommendations to speed up land claim resolutions that should appeal to *both* Indigenous and non-Indigenous people."

Oh, no! ... This is going downhill fast! ... Do something, Sam!

"Okay, you guys!" I say, jumping into the fray. "That's enough!"

I turn my attention to Hunter.

"I get it, Hunter!" I cry out. "You know my eyes are open now to the intergenerational trauma that our peoples continue to suffer. But you have to understand ... non-Indigenous people see *Clear Consent* as a potential veto against the rest of the country in future issues. And vetoes never work! They only serve to make groups more defensive and divisive, with little or no incentive to listen, negotiate, and compromise."

I feel my body trembling ... fearing that my plea won't be heard and this negotiation might fall through.

"Just look at what vetoes have done to cripple the UN Security Council! Do I need to remind you of Russia's vetoes that paralyzed the Council's attempts to deal with the invasion of the Ukraine?" I say. "I'm begging you ... please read the rest of this roadmap for self-government! Arjun and Terri have worked hard to incorporate some of your other ideas!"

My eyes make contact with Hunter's, silently pleading my case.

"I'm sorry, Sam," he says.

Hunter sucks in a breath and holds it while he winces in pain. He exhales slowly as his pain gradually subsides.

"I can't deal with this now! ... Please ... leave me alone ..."

I feel emotionally drained ... and I feel a sense of hopelessness creeping in.

Damn! ... Please! ... Don't let this end this way!

HUNTER'S TEXT finally arrives just after lunch.

I've read the whole thing again. Bring the others & visit later this PM.

I'm so full of anticipation, and my hands are trembling so much, I can barely type out my response.

Thanks! We'll be there!

The next three hours feel like an eternity to Arjun, Terri, and me. We don't think the rest of the team would be comfortable with Hunter's interpretation of *Clear Consent*, so we're at a loss as to what we'll do if he doesn't see Arjun and Terri's roadmap as a good compromise. We toss around a few other ideas in case we get desperate.

We arrive at Hunter's room at about 5:15 to find him sitting up in his bed, the proposed Plan of Action in hand. He makes eye contact with me and clears his throat to speak.

"I just can't accept this, Sam!" he says, his voice tired and weak. "And it's not just the *Clear Consent* issue!"

He holds up the plan and points repeatedly at it with his finger.

"What's with making entry into this new 'First Nations Province' contingent on settling land claims?" he asks. "This is like putting a gun to our heads and saying 'settle or else'!"

"It's not meant to be that way at all," Arjun says. "It's an incentive … for *both* Indigenous and non-Indigenous people alike! The faster the land claims get settled, and the faster the new province gets off the ground, the sooner your people will have what you've always longed for … a uniform, workable framework for self-government … and the sooner Ottawa can start handing off the responsibility for Indigenous issues to Indigenous people. It's a win-win for everybody!"

"My people would rather wait another seven generations, than rush into another bad deal with the colonial powers!" Hunter says, trying his best to raise his voice.

Enough! ... He's just not going to bend at all ... Do something, Sam!

"Hunter, listen to me!" I plead. "How long do Indigenous peoples *really* want to wait? You've had over one-hundred-fifty years of the *Indian Act*. How many more generations can afford to put up with that? How many more generations are going to have to go without adequate housing or safe drinking water?"

I step forward and rip the Plan of Action document from Hunter's hand. I start waving it angrily in front of his shocked face.

"Getting rid of the *Indian Act* and replacing it with a workable framework for self-government is the single biggest thing that non-Indigenous people can offer to start atoning for the injustices and intergenerational trauma the Act has caused!" I say, my voice about as loud as I dare in a hospital.

"And you've got to remember," Terri adds. "Even though most non-Indigenous Canadians are horrified by the residential school revelations, and they want to see reconciliation in some form someday, it's simply not a high priority for them. You can't ignore that reality! Whatever the Indigenous strategy has been until now for selling reconciliation to the non-Indigenous population— whether it's seeking apologies or seeking rulings and reparations through the courts—the polls show that it's not working. You're not reaching a significant number of them!"

"Terri's right," I say, trying my best to contain my frustration, and to keep the ball rolling. "It's time for Indigenous people to strike while the iron's still hot ... while Canadians are still outraged by what happened in the residential schools. Over time, even with more revelations, it's going to become old news for the rest of Canada. It's sad, and it's not right, but that's the way the news cycle goes!"

"And as far as court challenges and lawsuits goes," Terry adds, "they're costly and time consuming—it could take years, or even decades, for First Nations to achieve results if they go that route.

Even worse, the legal process is an adversarial process that promotes attitudes of *us versus them*. But, on the other hand, Arjun's framework is a collaborative approach that could help to bring First Nations and non-Indigenous people together, and significantly speed up the reconciliation process!"

I see Hunter growing more fatigued, and having more difficulty maintaining his attention. Arjun picks up where Terri and I left off.

"If Indigenous people can convince the rest of the country that replacing the *Indian Act* with a new Indigenous Province will help non-Indigenous people solve their so-called 'Indian problem'," he says, "it may be your best chance to get self-government, and to help your people improve their economies and their social conditions! And that will allow all Canadians—Indigenous and non-Indigenous Canadians alike—to start living in a state of mutual respect!"

While Arjun tries to hammer home our arguments, I find myself staring out the window, thinking about his plan. Something about what he's been saying is eating at me, but I can't put my finger on exactly what it is. The words 'Indigenous Province' are echoing through my mind.

Province ... Jurisdictions ... Provincial powers ... Holy shit, that's it!

"Hold it, everybody!" I shout, barely able to contain myself. "We've lost track of the most important part of Arjun's plan."

"What do you mean?" Hunter says quietly.

"As a province," I begin. The new 'Nation of First Nations' ... a new Indigenous Province ... would automatically have jurisdiction over most of the matters that are outstanding in the *Calls to Action* ... they would have a *de facto* veto and jurisdiction over those matters, simply by virtue of being a province within the Constitution!"

I take a quick breath to re-energize myself.

"The matter of *Clear Consent* would become a non-issue for the majority of issues! And in the event of a disagreement with Ottawa, the issues would be settled by the courts, like they are now with the existing provinces."

An uneasy silence descends on Hunter's hospital room. I watch as Arjun and Terri look at each other, then I turn to Hunter, waiting breathlessly for him to speak.

"Okay," Hunter says slowly. "If that's the case ... if I drop my objection to your definition of consent ... and if I accept that you recommend speeding up the land claims ... what else would you offer us?"

Arjun and Terri look hopefully at each other, and then at me.

"Well," Arjun replies. "Indigenous people would still have a good argument that, with only about five percent of the population, they still wouldn't be well represented in the Federal Parliament. What if we also proposed electoral changes ... a system of proportional representation, like in many European countries, where every Indigenous vote would count the same as every non-Indigenous vote?"

I feel my entire body trembling with anxiety while Hunter pauses to think.

"And don't forget," Terri adds. "A new Indigenous Province would also get its fair share of representation in the Senate, just like other provinces do right now!"

Damn, look at how much you've learned! ... I'm proud of you, Girl!

Hunter lets out a huge sigh. He's clearly exhausted and reaching the limits of his energy and resistance.

"Important question," he says, almost in a whisper. "Why should we join an Indigenous Province? ... Why doesn't each First Nation just declare itself to be an independent nation, with each Nation having a new, modern treaty? ... Why even stay in Canada?"

"Good point," Arjun says, giving Terri a quick glance. "I've thought about that a lot. But just think about it for a moment. It will be tricky enough having virtual provincial borders around over six hundred Indigenous communities, with the new province dealing separately with Ottawa and the existing provinces."

He pauses for each of us to really think about the ramifications.

"But I can't begin to think about how complicated it would be to share infrastructure and services between six hundred independent Indigenous countries, the provinces, and Canada!"

Hunter sighs, and the room goes silent while he ponders the team's arguments.

"You know, there's one other big issue that nobody on this team, including me, has raised yet. What about the growing number of urban-Indigenous people in this country who live off-reserve, like me and my sister?" he says. "We already have trouble accessing key programs that are administered through the *Indian Act.* And even though we're allegedly able to access the same federal and provincial programs as other Canadians, those services usually aren't culturally appropriate or easy for us to access."

Terri and I look at each other with blank stares on our faces. Then we turn to Arjun to see if he has an answer.

"You're right," Arjun replies. "I've encountered that issue in my research, but I decided to ignore that group because they fell outside the *Indian Act.* I probably shouldn't have dismissed them so easily, and that was wrong."

"So, what would you propose to do about it?" Hunter asks.

Arjun takes a long pause while he contemplates the question.

"I don't think there's an easy answer," Terri says, breaking the silence. "It seems to me that this is where the ninety-four *Calls to Action* still have a significant role to play. Implementing those recommendations will still be necessary for eliminating systemic racism in existing government programs, and for making them more accessible and culturally appropriate for urban-Indigenous people. And, over time, we can hopefully all learn from newer programs developed by Indigenous people within our proposed province, and extend that learning to existing government programs, to provide more appropriate service for the urban-Indigenous population."

"Don't forget," Arjun adds. "The proposed new Indigenous Province would also have self-determination—the right to define who is a citizen of each First Nation. This could allow some urban Indigenous people to qualify for citizenship and services provided by the new province."

I turn to Hunter and our eyes meet.

"You know that my perspective on Indigenous issues and reconciliation has changed a lot over the past couple of months," I begin. "Arjun's ideas are really good. I think that creating one large Indigenous Province is the best alternative I've heard."

I put my hand on Hunter's shoulder.

"It's not a total solution for the *Indian Act* problem … it's more like a fresh starting point for reconciliation. But, it's far better than continuing to deal with the *Indian Act*," I say. "And it's far more practical than having a fragmented collection of independent First Nations, each one dealing separately with Ottawa, the other provinces, and other nations. I think it would be a good deal for our people that's worth considering seriously."

Hunter exhales slowly again.

"Alright," he whispers. "I agree … it's a starting point … it's not a perfect solution … but, I guess nothing is …"

Arjun, Terri, and I let out a collective sigh of relief. The worry on our faces is replaced by smiles of accomplishment and satisfaction. Arjun, Terri, and I step up, and we each give Hunter a quick high-five. My eyes connect with Hunter's, and I feel our new connection … one of friendship and respect … growing stronger.

"Get this to Fatima and the others," he whispers. "Tell them I'll be there … tell them to knock it out of the park …"

CHAPTER 17—THE PRESENTATION

TEAM CLIMATE CHANGE remains standing in front of the class as the audience applauds their presentation. The lecture theatre is packed for the final presentations by each of Eric Sanderson's four teams. I'm seated in the second row, behind Team Reconciliation, with Rose beside me. As Eric gets up from his seat in the front row and makes his way to the lectern, Rose leans towards me and speaks into my ear.

"They've all done very well," she says. "You should be very proud of your students."

"I am," I reply. "They've all worked hard this term."

Rose notices that I've started wringing my hands, and my feet are starting to vibrate up and down.

"Are you nervous, dear?" she asks.

Nervous? ... Is she kidding? ... I'm so emotionally involved with Team Reconciliation ... I can't wait for this to be over!

"Just a little bit," I lie.

"Thank you, Team Climate Change," Eric announces. "I think everybody will agree that your presentation was both informative and sobering. Good job!"

Uri leaves his seat in front of me, and I watch him jog quickly up the stairs, two at a time, until he reaches the top row. He stops at the top row and glances to his right. My eyes follow, and I catch my breath as I see him give Hunter a high-five!

Oh, my God! He made it for the presentation!

I have to resist the urge to leave my seat and run up the stairs myself.

"And now, the final presentation of the evening," Eric says. "And potentially, one of the most challenging and controversial of our four topics … Team Reconciliation."

Eric extends his arm, motioning to the front row and welcoming the team. Fatima leaves her seat and walks up to the lectern as Uri beams the first slide of the team's presentation onto a large screen behind the lectern. The slide shows the overall organization of the presentation.

"First," Fatima begins. "I would like to acknowledge that this presentation is taking place on land located within the Haldimand Tract, land that was granted to the Haudenosaunee of the Six Nations of the Grand River, and is within the shared traditional territory of the Neutral, Anishinaabe, and Haudenosaunee peoples."

Fatima pauses and looks to the second row, where Rose and I are seated.

"I would also like to welcome our special guest, Rose Sinclair, who is the aunt of our esteemed TA, Samantha Bower, and a member of the Anishinaabe Nation."

Fatima nods to acknowledge Rose, then turns back to the assembled students.

"Since our time tonight is limited, let us begin."

Fatima clicks a remote control to bring up the next slide, introducing the history of Indigenous/colonial relations up to Confederation in 1867.

"What is Reconciliation?" she asks. "It is a big, overwhelming question and a difficult concept to define."

She clicks the remote once more, this time bringing up her next slide, which she reads to the audience.

"The dictionary tells us that the word reconciliation means to settle or resolve differences, and also to restore harmony or friendship. This implies a process with at least two parties involved, with differences existing between parties, and with a goal of restoring or improving harmony between those parties. But how does that definition apply to Canada?"

Fatima pauses while she turns around to face the crowd.

"Before we can even begin to answer that question, we need to put it into an historical context. Following the British victory over France in the Seven Years' War in 1763, the British Government's relationship with Indigenous peoples in North America was relatively respectful."

She pauses to catch her breath, steady her nerves, and to slow herself down.

"In a Royal Proclamation that same year," she continues, "King George III reserved any lands for Indigenous Peoples' continued use, that had not been previously ceded or sold by them. He recognized the need for colonizers to coexist peacefully alongside their Indigenous neighbours."

Fatima continues to present more historical background on subsequent years, leading up to the decades just prior to Confederation in 1867. At this point, Shanise takes over the presentation.

"However, by 1844," Shanise says. "The demand for land for new settlers and the need for infrastructure development, led to the gradual emergence of a new attitude. The Colonial Government now saw Indigenous people as an impediment to development, and as a growing problem."

Shanise pauses to look out over the audience.

"This led to the 1844 Bagot Report, which recommended that control over all Indian matters should be centralized. It also recommended that Indian children should be sent to boarding schools, to encourage their assimilation into European-style culture. Thus, the Bagot Report provided the initial framework for the *Indian Act*, and eventually, for the residential school system."

Shanise brings up her next slide in the background, titled *Confederation and the Indian Act*.

"By 1876," she continues. "The *Indian Act* legislation rested on the emerging principle that aborigines, as they were previously called, were to be kept on reserves to be taken care of by the government, until such time as they learned and assimilated into European culture."

Shanise clicks up another slide, titled *Legacy of the Indian Act*.

"But, while the Act was allegedly designed to 'take care' of Indigenous people, in reality, it was a racist and patriarchal tool to erase Indigenous culture and indoctrinate the people into European-style society," she says. "It's provisions included the creation of reserves, denying women status, allowing for expropriation of portions of reserves for Public Works, renaming individuals with European names for the purpose of registering Indians and enabling assimilation, and many other provisions to control the lives of Indigenous people."

Shanise pauses for a moment to take a sip of water.

"And of course," she continues. "The most devastating legacy of the *Indian Act* was the residential school system."

Shanise nods to Mandy in the front row, who comes up to the lectern and takes the remote control. She clicks to bring up the next slide, titled *The Residential Schools*.

"Thanks, Shanise," Mandy says. "By now, you've all heard about the residential schools. Like me, you've probably wondered why some Indigenous parents would have voluntarily sent their children to the boarding schools. The reality is that *some* parents did … they saw it as a way to educate their children so they could benefit from the colonists' economy."

Mandy steps away from the lectern and moves to the other side of the classroom.

"But, large numbers of children were also rounded up against their parents' wills, as a way of speeding up the assimilation of Indians into the new European-style culture."

She looks up at her audience and pauses for a moment.

"The stories of survivors paint a bleak, devastating picture of abuse, trauma, and children who felt defective or foreign if they returned to their homes and dared to speak their native languages," she continues. "The psychological damage of this trauma led many survivors to resort to alcohol or drugs, suicide, or caused them to unknowingly perpetuate a cycle of intergenerational abuse and trauma within Indigenous communities."

Mandy brings up the next slide, titled *The Need for Reconciliation.*

"So, this brings us back to our big question, and the purpose of this presentation," she says. "What is reconciliation? … Our team believes it is the process Canada must go through to acknowledge and reconcile the damage and trauma inflicted upon Indigenous people as a result of the *Indian Act*!"

She starts walking back, slowly and deliberately, towards the lectern.

"And that brings us to the Truth and Reconciliation Commission and its 2015 report," she says.

I watch Mandy, admiring the way she commands her stage, while she summarizes the history of the TRC Report, and its recommendations.

"The report recommends changes across a wide range of issues, including health, education, policing and the justice system, resource management, child welfare, language, culture, and many more," she continues. However, a closer examination of the ninety-four *Calls to Action* shows that they are each addressing different symptoms of the wide-ranging damage caused directly by the *Indian Act*."

Mandy pauses one last time, ready to deliver the final point on the slide.

"While our team absolutely agrees with every one of the ninety-four recommendations, we also see them as mere bandages for the *Indian Act*," she says. "And, instead of trying to patch up the effects of the *Indian Act*, we feel that the entire Act must be scrapped and replaced, before reconciliation can move forward and become a reality!"

Mandy nods to Katya in the front row, who leaves her seat and makes her way to the lectern, where she takes the remote control from Mandy.

"Thank you, Mandy," Katya begins, with her distinctive German accent. "So, if we conclude that we must replace the *Indian Act* in order for reconciliation to happen, what do we replace it with?"

She clicks up the next slide, titled *Replacing the Indian Act*.

"When our team examined the *Calls to Action* closely, we saw clues that suggest a possible answer," Katya says. "A large number of the recommendations call for changes to systems Mandy mentioned previously: health, education, policing and the justice system, resource management, social welfare, and so on—all areas that fall under provincial jurisdiction under the *Constitution Act, 1982*."

Katya looks up at the audience and pauses briefly.

"And that brings us," she says. "To the story of Lieutenant Frederick Loft, an Indigenous World War I veteran. Like many other Indigenous veterans, Loft was disillusioned by the treatment of veterans after the war. So, he proposed a 'League of Nations of Indians'."

Katya brings up a new slide, titled *A Nation of Nations*.

I listen closely as Katya presents the details of Arjun's novel variation on Lieutenant Loft's original idea.

Wow! ... The Presentation Team has done an amazing job of condensing all of that information ... They've made it so understandable and easy to follow!

"Thus, to summarize," Katya says, finally. "The proposed new Indigenous Province would treat First Nations communities like municipalities. And the agreement that creates it would be modelled after the *Westbank Self-Government Agreement* and other modern treaties. The new province would be partially funded with transfer payments, just like Westbank and the other provinces and territories are funded now."

Katya pauses for a breath and a drink of water.

"Once the legislative framework for the new Indigenous Province is in place," she continues. "We will have created a doorway of opportunity for each First Nation to walk through, that will allow them to leave the *Indian Act* behind, and walk into a new relationship with the rest of Canada. But, let us be clear: Creating this virtual province will not be easy … and it will be costly! And not all First Nations are ready to do this yet. To become ready to join the new province, each community will need to do three things."

Katya looks up at her audience again.

"First, communities will need to create their own unique constitution that specifies how they will be governed internally. Second, they will need to work with Ottawa to resolve any outstanding land claims," she says. "And finally, each nation will have to mobilize grass roots campaigns to overcome the fear of change that exists within many First Nations communities, before they can build the confidence to vote in favour of leaving the dysfunctional, co-dependent relationship they've had with Ottawa because of the *Indian Act*. First Nations community leaders will need to increase awareness that other First Nation communities, who already have self-government agreements with Ottawa, are doing better socially and economically, than those who don't.

"Thus, the transition to the new province will be gradual," she continues. "Starting with just a few First Nations at first, and gradually taking in more communities over time. Until a First Nation fulfills these conditions for joining the new framework, it would still be subject to the *Indian Act*."

Katya pauses again, and then walks slowly and deliberately to the centre of the room.

"But it isn't only First Nations communities who must prepare for a new Indigenous Province. Non-Indigenous Canadians must also learn just how racist, patriarchal, and dysfunctional the *Indian Act* is. They too must mobilize grass roots movements to endorse the legislation for creating the proposed new province," Katya continues. "There would obviously have to be some amendments to the *Constitution Act* to go along with the necessary legislation to create the new Indigenous province. And non-Indigenous Canadians would need to commit to speeding up the process for resolving all outstanding Indigenous land claims, as soon as possible."

"Our team concludes," Katya says. "That the new virtual Indigenous Province would provide First Nations with the opportunity for self-government and self-determination, the opportunity for economic growth and independence, the opportunity for social change, and a superior modern framework that would create a fresh starting point for implementing the recommendations of *UNDRIP* and the Ninety-Four *Calls to Action*, and for reconciling the appalling, traumatic legacy of the *Indian Act*."

She brings up the last slide—the definition of reconciliation that Fatima displayed at the onset of the presentation, then steps back to the lectern and makes eye contact with her audience again.

"So how does our team's findings and conclusion relate to our definition of the word *reconciliation*? We have shown that European colonization, and especially the Indian Act, has created a society rife with systemic racism that has inflicted enormous trauma and harm on Canada's Indigenous Peoples, especially over the past one-hundred-fifty years. But the reality is that both Indigenous and non-Indigenous Canadians are here to stay. So we must learn to work together to settle and resolve our differences— to restore friendship and harmony between Indigenous and non-Indigenous cultures, and to build a new and better nation."

Katya pauses to take a breath and to survey the crowd.

"Since reconciliation requires participation by at least two groups, it can never be a one-way street. There can be no reconciliation without listening, dialogue, negotiation, and compromise from all parties involved. Our team believes that our proposed framework fulfills the definition of reconciliation, and would provide Indigenous Canadians with an opportunity to move forward in a new relationship of increased trust and mutual respect with the rest of Canada—a relationship that would allow us to rebuild the foundations of our country in a way that truly fulfills Lieutenant Loft's dream. Thank you!"

Katya steps back from the lectern.

Oh, my God! They did it! Who would have thought this was possible three weeks ago!

A feeling of satisfaction and pride sweeps through me, and I jump to my feet to applaud. In front of me, the rest of Team Reconciliation stands to applaud Katya and their own efforts. And then the rest of the audience behind me begins to rise to its feet, applauding enthusiastically. I turn to Rose, my face beaming with joy. She smiles and nods her head approvingly at me. Finally, I turn my head and look up to the top row of the lecture hall at Hunter. He's on his feet, applauding. As our eyes meet, he grins and gives me two thumbs up.

Eric Sanderson leaves his seat and makes his way from the audience to the lectern, where he bows to Katya and applauds. He motions for the rest of the team to join Katya at the front of the room.

"A big thank you to Team Reconciliation, for a job well done," he says.

He waits patiently for the applause to wane.

"This brings our first ever team presentations in this course to a close," he says. "I think you'll agree with me that all four teams did an exceptional job!"

Eric waits for another round of applause from the students to die down.

"Before I bring the evening, and the course, to a close," he continues. "I'd just like to thank one more person … your TA,

Samantha Bower … I know she went far beyond the call of duty many times to help all four teams this term. Let's show her your appreciation.

Oh, no … Don't start blushing … Don't embarrass yourself in front of them again!

It's no use. I feel my face starting to flush and grow hot. I turn to face my students, smile, and give them a wave. And as I wave, I see the genuine looks of appreciation on their faces. Any remaining feelings of self-consciousness immediately start to fade away, and my blushing recedes with it. Instead, it is replaced by a rather foreign, but pleasant, inner sensation … my growing sense of self-confidence and pride!

And I didn't even dump all of my belongings all over the floor this time!

"Thanks, Sam!" Eric says, then he looks up at the rest of the class. "And thanks to all of you for taking this class! Good night, and good luck on your exams!

AS THE AUDIENCE members stir, gradually rise to their feet, and start to disperse, I stand up and turn to Rose.

"Thank you so much for coming!" I say. "It means a lot to me … so, what did you think?"

Rose smiles and nods her approval.

"A very creative and interesting idea … definitely something for our people to think about … and non-Indigenous folk too," she replies. "But, what impressed me the most, was how you helped bring that diverse group of people together … eight people from different ethnic groups … different ages … I'm very proud of you!"

"Thanks, but I didn't do much … they did the work."

Over Rose's shoulder, I see Eric packing up and readying to leave the lecture hall.

"Will you excuse me?" I say to Rose. "I have to talk to Dr. Sanderson before he goes."

"Of course, dear," Rose says. "I need to get going anyway. Run along … I'll call you soon."

I kiss Rose on the cheek.

"You've got the copy of the team's report that I gave you?" I ask.

Rose pats the bag she's carrying.

"It's in here," she says. "I'll let you know when I've read through it."

"Okay, talk to you later!" I say, as I make my way from our seats and hurry toward the lectern.

"Eric! Do you have a minute?" I shout.

He raises his head after hearing his name, and he smiles when he sees me.

"Sure, what can I do for you?" he says.

"I just wanted to thank you for standing by me this term," I begin. "I really appreciate it. I learned a lot about myself, and I think I've finally decided what I want to do about school."

Eric raises his eyebrows, seemingly surprised that I've finally made up my mind.

"I'd like to apply for a transfer to a Clinical Psych program," I say. "And I'd like to study the effects of Residential School trauma on First Nations people. Can I count on you for a reference?"

Eric grins and his eyes sparkle.

"Of course!" he says. "I'd be more than happy to do that for you. I'll be sad to lose you as my grad student, but I'm glad you've figured out what you want.

"Thank you," I say.

From high up in the lecture theatre, I hear Hunter's voice calling.

"Sam! Up here!"

I turn and look up. He's standing up in the top row, still looking pale and weak, waving to me. I turn back to Eric, and he winks at me.

"Come by my office and we'll talk more about it, once your exams are done," he says. "I think somebody else wants to talk to you now."

I smile at Eric, then I hurry up the stairs to meet Hunter. I'm out of breath and puffing by the time I reach the top of the theatre.

"You made it!" I blurt between breaths.

"I wouldn't have missed it," Hunter replies. "The team knocked it out of the park, thanks to you!"

"Why is everybody congratulating me?" I ask. "I didn't do much. It was you guys who did all the work."

"Don't be so humble," he replies. "Without your patience and guidance, we may never have seen eye to eye on anything."

I notice Hunter shuffling his feet, and he looks away briefly, avoiding my eyes. He swallows and clears his throat.

"Ummh … So now that the course is over, any chance you'd be interested in going for that cup of coffee?"

Oh, boy … What do I say? … I really want to stay friends, but not like that …

I feel like I'm taking an eternity to answer. Finally, I put on a serious face.

"As friends?" I answer. "Two friends who've learned to understand and respect each other?"

Hunter pauses briefly, then he shrugs his shoulders and nods that he understands.

"Fair enough," he says. "As friends."

I pause again, but after a moment I break into a full smile and start to chuckle.

"Forget about the coffee … are the doctors letting you drink beer yet?"

"Are you going to rat on me if I do?" Hunter says, smiling.

"Who, me?" I answer. "And while we're at it, maybe we should discuss what you're going to do about that court appearance tomorrow."

He flashes a big smile.

"Whatever you suggest, counsellor! But, I should tell you … rumour has it that the charges against me are probably going to be thrown out."

"Really?" I blurt. "Where did you hear that rumour?"

Hunter flashes a sly smile in my direction.

"Let's just say that the Crown may have realized that it's going to be dealing with much bigger Indigenous court challenges and law suits in the near future. They've got bigger fish to fry than me."

I feel a great sense of relief wash over my body after hearing Hunter's news.

"Well, in that case," I reply, smiling broadly. "Sounds like we have even more to celebrate!"

We break into spontaneous laughter. I open the door for my convalescing new friend and we leave the lecture theatre, making our way slowly, but joyously, towards the Grad Students' Lounge.

SO, THAT'S the chain of events that finally led me to discover what had been missing from my life. If Diane hadn't opened Pandora's box by telling me my dad was Indigenous, and if I'd never met Aunt Rose or that ragtag assortment of eight night class students, I'd probably still be searching for answers in Dr. Way's office. Do I know all the answers yet? Of course not. But now, I feel blessed to have two sets of eyes for seeing the world that, working together, have helped me to start integrating my previously chaotic inner voices. At least I can now say that I respect myself, I have much more self-confidence and pride, and I know myself far better than I did before this term began.

But, more importantly, I've found a new sense of direction and purpose in my life's journey. Thanks to Team Reconciliation, I'm beginning to feel that I have something to offer to both my Indigenous and non-Indigenous Canadian brothers and sisters, as we all try to reconcile the past, and as we strive to move forward into the future together with mutual respect.

EPILOGUE

ERIC SANDERSON watched with a feeling of pride as Sam walked away, thrilled to know that she would be applying to Clinical Psych programs, and knowing that he had played a small part in helping her plot a course for her future. As she ran up the stairs to meet Hunter, Eric spotted a middle-aged blonde woman in heels and an expensive blue suit, carrying a dark blue overcoat, carefully descending the stairs and looking his way. She smiled and waved, and he returned her smile.

"If it isn't the Honourable Juliet Pereira," he said, jokingly. "To what do I owe the honour of meeting with the newly-appointed Minister of Intergovernmental Affairs?"

"I could never pass on a chance to visit with my favourite professor," she replied, still smiling warmly. "Besides, how could I resist your rather cryptic message to my secretary about a 'mystery presentation' that I don't want to miss."

The old friends embraced and exchanged a quick European-style kiss on the cheek.

"I'm surprised you could make it on such short notice," Eric said. "I'm sure you're incredibly busy these days."

"You lucked out," Juliet replied. "I had a joint announcement with the Provincial Jobs Minister for a new auto battery plant in my constituency this morning. The timing was perfect."

"So, what did you think of that last presentation?" Eric asked.

"Very interesting! You say those students are all undergrads?"

"Every one of them, with the exception of their TA, Samantha."

"I'm amazed at their maturity and creativity," Juliet said. "But I'm even more impressed at the racial diversity in the team, and how they were able to come together. As the daughter of Portuguese immigrants, I can appreciate how difficult that must have been at times for them. It's good to see them taking an interest in politics."

Eric nodded his head in agreement and chuckled.

"It wasn't easy, I can assure you," Eric answered. "They displayed just about every kind of dysfunction a team can have for a couple of months, but they somehow managed to get their act together and overcome it with Sam's guidance. Believe it or not, she found out that her biological dad is Indigenous shortly after they started the project. It was a real rollercoaster ride for her, but she was determined and she pulled through. Her identity and self-confidence improved a lot over the past few weeks."

"Wow! That must have made working on the project far more difficult for her. Now I'm even more impressed," Juliet replied. "In fact, if you think the group wouldn't mind, I'm sure their report would make interesting and thought-provoking reading and discussion for the PM and cabinet. Do you think you could get me a copy?"

"I thought you might be interested," Eric said. "I've got a PDF copy I could email to you, or you could have my printed copy … I've got it right here in my briefcase."

"I'll take the paper copy if you're willing to part with it," Juliet answered.

Eric dug through his briefcase, pulling out a file folder with the team's printed report. He handed it to the Minister.

"That's perfect," she answered. "I think we want to read and discuss this before any of the opposition parties catch wind of what's inside. I'd appreciate it if you don't send that PDF file to anybody else. I'll owe you!"

"No problem," Eric replied. "Besides, sharing new ideas is what universities are for, isn't it? Just make sure the team and the university get credit if you decide to turn any of this into policy."

"Agreed," Juliet said. She followed up by shaking Eric's hand and sneaking a quick look at her watch. "Sorry, I gotta run to catch a plane back to Ottawa. Thanks Eric!"

The two friends embraced once more and gave each other a goodbye peck on the cheek, before the Minister made her way up the stairway and exited the lecture theatre. Eric closed his briefcase and took one last look at the now empty theatre before heading up the stairs himself, whistling contentedly as he went.

ROSE LEANED into the wind and pulled up her collar to keep out the brisk northwest gale that was blowing off of Lake Huron. Flakes of snow were beginning to swirl in the air as she reached her car in the visitor's parking lot behind the Social Sciences Building. She shivered as she dug into her bag to find her keys, then she unlocked the car and climbed in behind the wheel. She turned the ignition and allowed the car to idle to warm it up.

As she waited, she noticed a black Lincoln limo pulling up in front of the Social Sciences Building's rear entrance. A distinguished looking blonde woman in a dark blue overcoat exited the building and hurried towards the limo, grabbing Rose's attention. The face looked achingly familiar, but somehow out of context, and Rose wracked her brain searching for a name to put with the face. The woman was carrying a file folder that appeared to contain a sheaf of papers—a sheaf that looked only too familiar. She reached into her bag and pulled out the sheaf of paper that Sam had given her—Team Reconciliation's full report—almost identical to the package the woman was carrying.

She's got a copy of the report too!

At that moment, Rose's brain finally made the connection.

Juliet Pereira! She's a Federal Cabinet Minister!

Rose turned on an inside light and thumbed quickly through the report to the recommendations section near the end. She took a few moments to review the section, then she put the report back in her bag. She shook her head slightly from side to side, as if in disbelief.

"Does it take recent immigrants from other countries, with fresh sets of eyes, to open our own eyes and to be able to come up with new ideas like this?" she mumbled aloud to herself. "Are they the only ones who can see these issues more objectively, and think outside of the box?"

Rose reached into her bag again, scrounging around until she found her phone and pulled it out. She opened her contact list, tapped on a contact with her finger, and then waited.

"Hello?" she said, after the call connected. "It's Rose. I was going to drive back to the *Healing Lodge* from the university tonight, but I wanted to talk to you first."

She listened to the person on the other end of the call for a moment.

"Yes, it's about that project that my niece's students did on reconciliation … I have something that we're all going to want to read and think about … And I think I just saw a Federal Cabinet Minister carrying the same document … Sure, I can stay the night … Okay, I'll be there in an hour …"

THE END

ACKNOWLEDGMENTS

During the writing process, there are always many people whose contributions help to grow an idea into a story. I would like to thank my friends and neighbours who shared their thoughts and questions about the Reconciliation process in Canada during our precious few summer get-togethers during the pandemic, and to the many Facebook friends who completed my online survey about their knowledge of Reconciliation during the summer of 2021. I would also like to thank Kelly Welch for sharing ideas and suggestions for developing Samantha Bower's character, as she goes on the journey of discovering her Indigenous identity. To Jennifer Henry and Graeme Menzies, a big vote of thanks for the interest you showed in my initial ideas—your feedback gave me the confidence that I had an idea that was interesting enough to pursue further. To Anne Ellis and Bryan Hinkowich, thank you for volunteering to read the first draft, and for your encouragement, comments, and suggestions. To Peter Menzies and Lianne Viau, thank you for your suggestions for people to contact for finding Indigenous feedback about the story. Most of all, a huge thank you goes out to my loving wife, Peggy, for her ongoing patience and support during the writing process, and for her time and her critical eye during editing.

Last, but certainly not least, a huge vote of thanks goes to you, the reader, for reading *The Night Class*. Independent authors, like myself, depend on your reviews and your word-of-mouth recommendations of our books to others. So, thank you for purchasing this book and for recommending it to your friends, neighbours, colleagues, and even your book club and your local library. And finally, thank you for taking a few minutes at the end of this book to review it, and to tell potential readers what you liked best about this story.

OTHER BOOKS BY DAVID ALEX JONES

(Written as Alex Jones)

Walls (The Survivor Trilogy, Book One)

Angela's Eyes (The Survivor Trilogy, Prequel)

Faces (The Survivor Trilogy, Book Two)

Spirits (The Survivor Trilogy, Book Three)

Visit David Alex Jones' web site to find out where you can purchase his other books:

http://www.davidalexjones.com

Be sure to check out the Excerpts for *Angela's Eyes* and *Walls* at the end of this book.

ABOUT THE AUTHOR

David Alex Jones is a retired Clinical Psychologist who lives in Ontario, Canada. In his writing, he combines his understanding of human identity and personality, his passion for helping victims of trauma, abuse, and Post-traumatic Stress Disorder, and his love of reading fiction, to create a unique brand of psychological suspense and political commentary. His writing is rich with complex characters and controversial social issues, resulting in an abundance of internal and interpersonal conflict, dysfunction, and tension. Dave also enjoys spending time with his grandchildren, travelling with his wife, photography, and home brewing craft beer.

CONNECT WITH THE AUTHOR

Independent authors, like David Alex Jones, provide readers with quality books at low prices. We can do this because we don't pass along the costs of traditional publishing houses to our readers. In doing so, we take on the responsibility for marketing our own books. Thus, we depend on our readers to visit our social media sites and our web sites to make us more visible on search engines like Google. Every "Follow,", "Like", and "Click" on our sites helps raise awareness of our writing and spreads the word!

Dave thanks you in advance for taking the time to follow him on Facebook, Instagram, and Twitter, and for visiting his website to stay current on events and news about his books. Be the first to find out about upcoming offers and projects, and discover his new blog: *The Null Hypothesis*. Here's how you can connect with him on social media:

Facebook: https://www.facebook.com/DavidAlexJonesWriter

Instagram: https://www.instagram.com/d_alexjonesauth/

Twitter: https://twitter.com/Alex_J_Writer

Web Site: http://www.davidalexjones.com

Email: dave@davidalexjones.com

SUGGESTED READING

Craft, A. & Regan, P. (Eds). *Pathways of Reconciliation.* Winnipeg : University of Manitoba Press, 2020.

Government of Canada, Crown-Indigenous Relations and Northern Affairs Canada. *Westbank First Nation Self-Government Agreement (2005).* https://rcaanc-cirnac.gc.ca/eng/1100100031766/1543001371378

Government of Canada, Department of Justice. *Constitution Act, 1982.* https://www.justice.gc.ca/eng/rp-pr/csj-sjc/constitution/lawreg-loireg/intro.html

Government of Canada. *Indian Act, 1985.* Justice Laws Website. https://laws-lois.justice.gc.ca/eng/acts/I-5/FullText.html

Government of Canada. *Nisga'a Final Agreement, 2000.* Justice Laws Website. https://laws-lois.justice.gc.ca/eng/acts/N-23.3/FullText.html

Government of Canada. *Nunavut Act, 1993.* Justice Laws Website. https://laws-lois.justice.gc.ca/eng/acts/N-28.6/index.html

Hall, Anthony J. (2006, February 7). *Royal Proclamation of 1763.* The Canadian Encyclopedia. https://www.thecanadianencyclopedia.ca/en/article/royal-proclamation-of-1763

Joseph, B. *21 Things You May Not Know About the Indian Act.* Port Coquitlam : Indigenous Relations Press, 2018.

Joseph, B. & Joseph, C. *Indigenous Relations: Insights, Tips & Suggestions to Make Reconciliation a Reality.* Port Coquitlam : Indigenous Relations Press | Page Two Books, 2019.

Truth and Reconciliation Commission of Canada. *Truth and Reconciliation Commission of Canada: Calls to Action (2015).* https://publications.gc.ca/site/eng/9.801236/publication.html

United Nations, Department of Economic and Social Affairs. *United Nations Declaration on the Rights of Indigenous Peoples (2007).* https://www.un.org/development/desa/indigenouspeoples/wp-content/uploads/sites/19/2018/11/UNDRIP_E_web.pdf

Wilson-Raybould, Jody. *From Where I Stand: Rebuilding Indigenous Nations for a Stronger Canada.* Vancouver : Purich Books, 2019.

Wilson-Raybould, Jody. *True Reconciliation: How to Be a Force for Change.* Toronto : McClelland & Stewart, 2022.

* * *

BOOK CLUB GUIDE

BOOK CLUB DISCUSSION QUESTIONS

1. The author provided his reasons and his goals for writing *The Night Class* in the book's Foreword. Do you think he achieved his storytelling and educational goals?

2. Many would say that, because the author isn't Indigenous and isn't a woman, Sam's story isn't his story to tell. What do you say about that opinion?

3. The author wrote *The Night Class* in the first person, from Sam's perspective. Why do you think he chose that point of view?

4. The author states that *The Night Class* is full of metaphors. What metaphors do you see? Can you see what purpose each one serves?

5. The story is set within a university night class. Why do you think the author chose that particular setting?

6. Do you think Sam's traumatic childhood, and her subsequent mental health struggles, were accurately portrayed and believable?

7. What did you learn, if anything, about the history of Indigenous/Non-Indigenous relations from reading *The Night Class*?

8. Do you feel that the author treated First Nations' traditions thoughtfully and respectfully? Did you find those scenes to be believable?

9. Do you feel that you are more able to empathize with the plight of First Nations people in Canada after reading *The Night Class*?

10. The author presented a rather unconventional possible pathway for future reconciliation in Canada. What do you think of the solution he presented?

A BOOK CLUB CONVERSATION WITH THE AUTHOR

In conversations with family and friends about my experiences while writing "The Night Class," especially with those people who read the first draft of the book, many of them made similar comments or asked me similar questions about the book, and about reconciliation. So, I thought I would spend some time sharing my thoughts about those issues with my readers. In doing so, I may be shedding some light on a few of the Discussion Questions that I posed to readers in the previous section. However, the additional issues I've chosen to discuss will hopefully give readers more insight into the origins of the story and its characters. By doing so, I hope it will help to generate more conversations within your book club about both "The Night Class" and about the process of reconciliation with Indigenous peoples.

* * *

What prompted you to write *The Night Class*? Where did the idea come from?

As I explained earlier in the book's Foreword, I had become disillusioned over the years about the whole relationship between

First Nations and the rest of Canada. All of my reading and research led me to the conclusion that Canada's *Indian Act* is the primary reason for the dreadful state of that relationship. When it comes to writing fictional stories, I usually have a general idea of the journey I want my characters to take, and I depend on making a detailed outline of the entire story before I start writing. However, in the case of *The Night Class*, the ending—the surprise solution that my characters proposed for replacing the Indian Act—actually came to me first, about five years ago.

But once I had an ending, I was forced to work backwards—to figure out what to do with that proposed solution. Since I'm neither a political science or sociology scholar, nor a constitutional expert, I don't have the credentials necessary for writing a non-fiction textbook about Indigenous relations and reconciliation. Furthermore, I'm sure if I attempted such a book, it would likely put most of you to sleep quickly. First and foremost, I'm a psychologist and a writer of fiction; so what was I going to do with my idea for helping to move reconciliation forward through a fictional novel and its cast of characters? I knew there had to be a story there somewhere, but I struggled for about four years to find a socially acceptable and empathic way of presenting my idea through storytelling.

My breakthrough came to me (as it usually does) when I allowed my mind to wander while going for a walk on a nice sunny day in May during the pandemic. Where else is the ideal setting for a story with a philosophical and political commentary about reconciliation, if it's not in a university—a place of learning? From there, I more clearly defined the setting as a night class, with an assigned team project that had a definite, time-limiting deadline, in order to provide drama and tension for my readers. Once that seed of an idea came, the ideas for characters and scenes for the thirteen-week course timeline came quickly, and I was able to start outlining the rest of the story.

Where did you get the ideas for the characters in *The Night Class*?

As I indicated above, the seed idea for *The Night Class* began as a political commentary about the painfully slow progress in reconciliation with First Nations people in recent years. But I also needed to build a story around the university night class and the students who were assigned to do the reconciliation project, that would incorporate political commentary seamlessly into it. The idea for a young woman (Sam), who had grown up believing that she was caucasian, but who unexpectedly finds out that she is half Indigenous, was born out of the necessity to have a main character who could empathize with both First Nations and non-Indigenous people. Thus, Sam is a metaphor for Canada and its mixed Indigenous and non-Indigenous identity.

The team of eight students who make up Team Reconciliation, was created as a metaphor for Canada's multicultural mosaic of First Nations people along with non-Indigenous immigrant groups. To create dramatic tension in the story, it was essential to have a First Nations character (Hunter), as well as a conservative caucasian character (Terri), who would butt heads frequently. These two characters are metaphors for First Nations culture and colonial culture. The remaining team members were selected as a metaphor for the wide range of different cultures existing in Canada—people who came to Canada from all over the globe for a variety of reasons.

Finally, since the story sees Sam as a victim of intergenerational trauma, and she understandably struggles with her mental health, it was necessary to create two dysfunctional parents—her father

(Charlie), a residential school survivor, and her alcoholic and drug-addicted white mother (Diane), as well as an empathic therapist (Barbara Way) who is part of the post-colonial establishment and culture.

What is the the role of Rose Sinclair, Sam's aunt, in the story?

The role of Rose Sinclair, Sam's newly-discovered aunt, is so important that her character is worthy of a separate discussion. Years ago, I met a young woman who revealed that she had recently discovered that her dysfunctional biological mother was Indigenous. This came as quite a shock to the young woman. You are right in assuming that bits and pieces of Sam's character were suggested by that young woman's story. But the important part of that young woman's story was that she began seeing a tribal elder in order to learn more about her Indigenous heritage, and about where her mother had come from.

I only saw that young woman once or twice after this revelation, but I do know that the combination of what she had learned from traditional psychotherapy, plus the traditional Indigenous knowledge she had gained from her elder, helped her to solidify her identity and increase her ability to cope with life's stressors. So, given that healing is a necessary part of the reconciliation process, it was essential for me (and for Sam's character growth), to have a wise, Indigenous elder who could act as a counterbalance to the traditional form of psychotherapy that Sam was receiving, and to show that both approaches to healing have value for Indigenous and non-Indigenous people alike.

What was the biggest challenge in writing *The Night Class*, and how did you overcome it?

I think that my biggest challenge in writing *The Night Class* was balancing the need to introduce information about the Indian Act, other important documents such as the *UNDRIP*, the Truth and Reconciliation Commission's *Calls to Action,* and some history of how Indigenous/Non-Indigenous relations developed after initial colonial contact, with the need to keep the action interesting and moving at a quick pace so readers don't become bored. I needed to find ways to show the information to readers through Sam's story, rather than falling into the trap of lecturing readers—I didn't want the story to seem "preachy." I could easily have included a lot more detail about history and documents to help fill out the book and make it longer, but I purposely limited the amount of information I introduced. By doing so, I kept the book's length slightly shorter than that of most novels to keep the story from bogging down due to information overload. I like to think that, in the end, I managed to find a good balance between informing and entertaining my readers.

In the Epilogue, the story ends with two events, both having ambiguous endings. What prompted you to write that particular ending?

For writers, it is always a scary thing to hand over our stories—our labour of love—to the outside world for constructive criticism. When I sent out the first draft of *The Night Class* to real people for comments and feedback, there was only a single event in the Epilogue, where Rose sits in her car with a copy of Team Reconciliation's report, and she phones a mystery Indigenous person to arrange a meeting. I was uncomfortable with that ending, because it left me feeling like I was projecting a colonial agenda on Rose's Indigenous character. The initial readers didn't provide any negative comments about the first draft's ending, but they didn't rave about it either. However, after I revised the ending and added a new scene where a Federal cabinet minister also ends up in possession of the same report, it allowed readers to wonder about how both Indigenous leaders and non-Indigenous leaders might react to a proposal, such as the one posed by Team Reconciliation in the story. When I passed along the new ending to initial readers, they much preferred it to the original ending. Thus, I am a lot more confident that the current ending will be a more realistic and satisfying conclusion to the story for my audience.

What's next for you after releasing *The Night Class*? Do you have any other projects in progress?

The ideas for my next project, tentatively titled *Constitution Avenue*, involve themes surrounding freedom, democracy, and constitutions, which have come to the fore because of COVID pandemic restrictions, the January 6th Capital Riot in the U.S., and the so-called Freedom Convoy that occupied the streets of Ottawa for many weeks before it was disbanded by authorities. At this point, I have a list of characters, as well as a long list of possible scenes that need some elaboration. However, I hope to start putting words on the page over the coming winter, once *The Night Class* is released in early December of 2022. My goal is to bring *Constitution Avenue* to readers sometime in 2024, but it is a very ambitious project.

ANGELA'S EYES: EXCERPT

The Survivor Trilogy (Prequel)
by David Alex Jones
(Originally as Alex Jones)

PROLOGUE

I REMEMBER THAT DAY, almost one year ago, like it was yesterday. My eyes were wide open and alert to my surroundings, as they had been every day since I stole 4.7 million dollars from Soren Kristiansen and went on the run, vanishing from the lives of everybody I knew and loved. From that day on, my eyes have kept a constant vigil. I've been paranoid of every person I see, unable to trust a soul and waiting for the day when Soren eventually finds me.

The setting sun was sinking behind the towering landscape of downtown Los Angeles, the daytime heat giving way to long, late afternoon shadows. I sat on the grass in San Julian Park, leaning up against a cinderblock wall, trying to blend into the shadows. This had become my usual afternoon and evening routine - hiding in plain sight in this small green oasis amidst the most unfortunate of humanity. As usual, the park was crowded with people; leaning up against trees, laying on the grass, or sitting cross-legged on the ground. In the park and out on the street, throngs of other street-people staked their claim to a small square of sidewalk or grass to set up temporary sleeping quarters for the coming night. They unpacked portable tents or cardboard boxes from the shopping carts that contained the sum total of their possessions. The small mass of humanity in East Los Angeles was winding down another day of subsistence survival in the unseen underbelly of America.

Many of the park's residents knew each other well, jabbering casually with each other. I knew many of them by sight, as they knew me. But I rarely allowed myself anything more than raising my eyebrows in acknowledgement, or a curt greeting to any of them. I wasn't willing to risk conversation or the possibility of revealing anything about myself to anybody.

I liked San Julian park. It was a place where I could sit in the shade when it was warm, or find some sunshine when it was cool. I could keep my back to the cinderblock wall or the trunk of a tree, where I could keep a wary eye on every person who passed or entered the park. I blended in well, wearing the same pair of torn jeans, threadbare t-shirt, hoodie, and well-worn boots that I wore each time I visited the park. My shoulder-length blonde hair was purposely tousled and unkempt, and there wasn't a trace of makeup on my face. On that spring day, I wasn't wearing the grey hoodie I'd been wearing through the cooler winter months, but I was glad I still had it with me, using it to cushion my behind from the hard ground.

I first noticed the woman with the camera while she worked her way down the opposite side of the street. I'd never seen her in the area before, so she roused my attention immediately. She had an old-school SLR with a large telephoto lens attached, and she appeared to be taking candid photographs of people from a distance. The hairs on the back of my neck tingled. I riveted my eyes on her as she moved slowly towards the park.

The residents of skid row were used to seeing photojournalists who sometimes ventured here to document their existence. But this woman was different. She spent more time composing and taking each shot, manually focusing and setting the shutter speed and aperture for each exposure. She was completely engrossed, but relaxed at the same time. She was doing this for art and her own relaxation.

She was tall and thin, with an olive complexion and short dark hair. As I studied her carefully, she looked down at the SLR and checked its settings. Apparently satisfied, she raised her head and started surveying the area for potential targets. She noticed San Julian Park and started moving in my direction. I reached beneath me for my hoodie, wondering if I would be less noticeable if I pulled the hood over my head.

I decided against doing anything to attract attention, averting my eyes and hoping she wouldn't see me. It was time to leave the park. I stole a quick glance in my peripheral vision, hoping to see that her camera was focused on other residents of the park.

It was too late. I felt fear take control over my body. Instead of getting up and running, I froze. She had already spotted me and our eyes met. Automatically, she raised the camera and focused the large lens on me. Before I could look away, I saw the the camera's shutter opening and closing, capturing on film the fear and distrust on my face and in my eyes. It was all over in a couple of seconds. She lowered the camera away from her face and our eyes met. She could tell that I was different from the other residents of the park - she knew I didn't belong here. If I stayed where I was any longer, I knew she was going to come closer to start asking questions.

It was time to go. I reached for the used plastic grocery bag full of personal belongings beside me, and rose quickly to my feet. I pulled the hoodie over my head and lowered my eyes, walking briskly past the mystery woman and onto the asphalt pathway that led to the park's only exit at the corner of the green space. I turned right and quickly crossed St. Julian Street. Once across the street, I hunched down and slid behind a large blue dome-tent - somebody's lodging for the night. Shielding myself from the woman's view, I moved quickly along East 5th Street, leaving the park and the woman behind.

Now, hiding from the world in my makeshift bed in the darkness of a Las Vegas floodway, I recall the ominous feeling I had about those photos. Somehow, I knew they were going to come back to haunt me. I didn't know when or how, but I knew the day would come. I couldn't risk having anybody seeing them. As far as the rest of the world was concerned, I was dead. I walked away from everything - my two kids and my parents - and I ran away from my job. As far as anybody was concerned, I had simply vanished from the face of the earth.

My premonition came true three weeks ago. Suddenly seeing my face in the background of a TV news report took me by surprise, but it wasn't a total shock. I recognized the look of fear and distrust in my eyes in the candid portrait. The same feeling of fear swept through my body as I realized the implications of what I saw. With one quick glimpse of myself on TV, my entire world had turned upside down.

Since that day, my mind has been spinning - continually replaying the events from eighteen months earlier. Could I have done anything differently? How did I, Angela Baranyi, an innocent, religious, hard-working single mother of two, ever manage to get involved in Soren Kristiansen's web of dishonesty, deceit, and crime? How did I become a criminal myself? No matter how many times I analyze the events in my mind, I haven't come up with any good answers to those questions. But the events keep replaying in my memory, like a nightmare that never ends …

* * *

WALLS: EXCERPT

The Survivor Trilogy (Book One)
by David Alex Jones
(Originally as Alex Jones)

PROLOGUE

"In the internal 'houses' of people who survived childhood trauma, there are often many thoughts, feelings, body sensations and emotions that are … kept secret from the self and from others, as if they are kept behind locked doors and thick walls."

— Sandra Paulsen, PhD
Looking Through the Eyes of Trauma and Dissociation

FROM BEHIND THE WALLS she had erected in her mind, Francesca Capellini was struggling to comprehend last night's real-life nightmare.

As though she was on autopilot, her lean, naked, 41-year-old body had been swimming mechanically, back and forth, through the cool cleansing salt water of the swimming pool for the past forty-five minutes. As she swam, her mind battled within itself to try to understand, but also to forget, the terror of last night.

The sun was low in the eastern sky, just beginning its ascent over the California desert and the isolated estate, high in the hills over Palm Desert, where Francesca and her husband, Philippe, lived their reclusive, luxurious lives.

She struggled to stay in the moment, and to keep herself focused on the calming sensations of the water flowing over her skin.

Her efforts to keep her mind present were in vain. It drifted back to her youth in Manarola, Italy. In those days, she had learned to find escape from the loneliness of her home, and from the shame of the sexual advances and humiliation of her older sister's husband, Paolo. Rising at dawn, stripping off her clothing, and swimming in the Mediterranean off the rocks surrounding the village's small marina, it was the one place where she felt free and could cleanse herself of the shame that seemed to cling to her after he had humiliated her or used her young body.

The memories of those dark times from her past began overwhelming her brain. Walls came up in her mind to block them, but it was too late. Those haunting memories from her past connected with images and sounds from the surreal events of the last few hours. The sensory overload of those old memories, plus the nightmare of the past few hours, was working its way up and over her walls, creeping into her consciousness. She saw ghostly images of the young Columbian man shouting at Philippe and heard distant screams of anger from Philippe in reply. Then there was the anguish and fear she'd heard in the young woman's cries. It was as if she was living it all over again. The images, screams, and cries from last night flooded into her consciousness as she swam.

Francesca felt cold fear course through her body. Her muscles tensed, her heart pounded, and her strokes became more labored.

Then, there was only darkness.

In her mind, Francesca felt the cold desert air of the February night chilling her to the bone. Her muscles were trembling, but she couldn't tell whether it was from fear or the cold. She was vaguely aware of sitting in the passenger seat of a car in the darkness.

In the distance, she heard a seemingly endless cycle of sounds: a shovel sinking into the gravel, occasionally striking a stone, a human grunt, then a brief pause before debris could be heard hitting the ground nearby in the darkness. The rhythm repeated itself until she had no sense of time.

Suddenly, the shovelling stopped and the implement dropped to the ground.

A voice with a heavy French accent barked out of the darkness in frustration.

"Are you going to help, or must I do everything myself?"

Francesca forced herself out of the car and moved reluctantly around to the trunk, where Philippe waited impatiently.

"Lift his legs!" he commanded.

Philippe grabbed the man's upper body. As Francesca's arms circled a pair of rigid legs, she caught a glimpse of the victim's lifeless white face. She gasped, her lungs and her legs momentarily paralyzed as she stared at the ghost-like visage.

Philippe tugged on the body. Francesca's legs and lungs jumped back to life. She struggled with the lifeless weight, doing her best to look away at the ground as they staggered towards the shallow pit in the desert floor.

There was a dull thud as the man's body slid out of her frozen hands and dropped into the makeshift grave. It was all she could do to keep from vomiting as she forced herself to repeat the same repulsive process with the young woman's corpse.

Francesca's body continued swimming on autopilot. She felt filthy and nauseated, trying desperately to refocus her mind on her swimming, and to bring it back into the present. As she glided out of the shadows and into a sunlit area of the pool, the brilliant morning sun blinded her, bringing her body and mind out of the darkness simultaneously.

Where did Philippe say he was going?

One part of her identity vaguely remembered them showering to remove all traces of the grime, sweat, and evidence after returning from the desert just before sunrise. Philippe was agitated as he followed her out to the pool afterwards. He was incoherent, and rambled on about having to go to Tijuana to dispose of the South American couple's rental car.

Then he abruptly left her alone, and Francesca started swimming.

As she swam, her mind escaped to Manarola, to the memories of swimming along the coastline of northwestern Italy. In her mind, she was rolling over and floating on her back. She felt as if she was twelve years old. The buoyant Mediterranean waters kept her afloat as she gazed up at the azure sky and the vibrant yellow, green, and pink buildings of the town, perched on the rocky cliffs. Her gaze swept to the green terraced vineyards that carpeted the hillsides along the five-mile stretch of coastline between the five peaceful little villages that made up Cinque Terre.

Twelve-year-old Francesca rolled over onto her stomach again and continued to swim for a few more minutes in the direction of Corniglia, the next village. In her mind, she heard the laughter of dolphins playing in the distance. Suddenly, a pair of the sleek mammals breached beside her, heckling and laughing at her each time they surfaced, then swimming circles around her. She envied their freedom and their playfulness. Yet, while swimming, she felt as free as the dolphins.

Then, as quickly as they had appeared, the dolphins disappeared. In her mind, she turned around for the imaginary swim back to the rocks and the marina at Manarola. Her strokes quickened for the return swim. She was late and had to get herself dressed and ready for school.

Getting ready? For school?

Francesca's mind became confused as reality jumbled together with her childhood memories. She started to remember Philippe's ramblings, and it dawned on her that the part of her identity that was a forty-one-year-old adult had to get ready for work at the hotel today.

Philippe Morel's French accent was much thicker than usual. He was mixing French words into his English, a sign of the intense anxiety and agitation he was feeling.

"Francesca, *ma chère*. You must go to work as usual today. You have to be calm. You must not show any sign that anything is different. Do you understand?" he said.

"And … and tell Carmen that I have the flu. I cannot come in today. You and Carmen will manage the guests as usual," he said.

The hotel. The guests.

Francesca struggled to keep herself connected to reality. She became vaguely aware again of the rhythm of her strokes and the gentle flow of cool water caressing her skin. Both sensations were helping to calm her and bring her back gradually, bit by bit, into the present. She noticed that the yellow streaks of sunlight had spread and were bathing much of the far side of the patio in light. The air was getting warmer. She realized it was time to shower, dress, and to drive into Palm Springs to the hotel.

Francesca pushed the nightmare of the tragic murders into the dark recesses behind her walls. She coasted to the end of the pool nearest the house and pulled herself up onto the deck. Her body was covered in water droplets, causing her skin to cool rapidly. She shivered as the hairs on her arms stood upright and her nipples became firm and erect. She always felt sad to end her swims, but she also loved the feeling of the nerves in her skin coming alive. It made *her* feel alive.

She reached for a large bath towel and hurriedly dried her shivering body.

Pull yourself together Fran.

She was finally starting to access the businesslike part of her personality that always helped her to manage in times of stress. This was the part of her identity she liked the most. It was a part of her that her American friend and mentor, Susan, had taught her during her teen years in Cinque Terre. It was the part that helped her feel strong when the darker parts tried to take over. It was

Susan who first called her Fran, and it was Fran who became the businesslike, responsible part of herself.

She started to plan what she would wear and thought about the things she needed to do when she arrived at the hotel. She was beginning to win the battle within her mind for now. As she had learned to do in her youth, she pushed those parts of herself that were feeling afraid, dirty, and ashamed back behind her walls.

Fran continued to reassure herself while she quickly showered, rinsing the salt from her skin.

Philippe is right. Just focus on your usual routine and do not worry about anything. Philippe will take care of this mess. Everything will be alright. You will see. He will take care of you. He always has.

Fran emerged from the shower, dried quickly, and hurried into the large closet to choose some cool and casual clothing. She preferred to wear more informal attire to the hotel, which she helped Philippe manage and also worked as a part time massage therapist.

She looked for something white. Something that would help her to feel clean. She settled on a simple white low-neck cotton tank top that tastefully framed her breasts and décollage. Along with the tank top, she chose a pair of white capris and a gold belt. She picked out a pair of white running shoes with gold trim that matched her belt. Once the large items were selected, she quickly grabbed some white bikini panties, a white camisole, and a sheer bra with white lace trim that went well with the low-cut tank top.

As Fran slipped into her clothes and looked at herself in the mirror, she nodded approvingly. She felt and looked crisp and clean. Professional, but still casual. Finally, she reached for a bikini and a cover-up in case is was warm enough to give massages outside on the patio.

A glance at the clock told her that she had to hurry with her hair and makeup. Fortunately, her dark Mediterranean complexion looked good without much makeup and her short black hair was easy to maintain. She hastily applied a touch of lipstick and eye shadow, then the slightest hint of her favorite Italian perfume, and she was ready to go.

Fran paused and took a single, deep breath to calm and center herself.

It worked. Her businesslike persona was ready to go. She chose a matching white purse, swiftly transferred her belongings into it, and headed for the garage.

Although Philippe insisted on addressing her as Francesca, and preferred that she dress with class and style in a way that befitted the wife of a wealthy art agent and dealer, she often longed to be less ostentatious and formal. In her choice of a personal vehicle, a silver-blue Prius, Philippe allowed her to have some input in the decision for once. But when they went out in public, Philippe would still insist that they be seen together in his luxury Mercedes or a chauffeured limo.

Fran opened the driver door and slid into the Prius, once again pausing to catch her breath. There were only a handful of places where she felt she could be herself: when she was swimming, on those rare occasions when Philippe allowed her to go out by herself with her camera, when she felt her clients losing themselves in relaxation from one of her massages, and when she was alone in her Prius, as she was now.

She turned on the vehicle and heard the soft whine of the electric motor as she silently backed out of the garage. She felt a slight vibration from the gasoline engine as she shifted it into gear and drove slowly towards the main gates of their estate.

On either side of the massive wrought iron gates, in both directions, stretched an imposing ten-foot high, stucco-covered wall topped with coiled razor wire. Philippe maintained that it was necessary to keep their estate secure from outside intruders. She knew that it could also keep people securely imprisoned inside.

Although she had some freedom to come and go, she knew that Philippe was always aware of where she went. He ensured she didn't have the resources to go far on her own. In return, Philippe had always kept her safe. Until last night.

Fran reached for the remote control to open the gates. As she did, she felt a wave of nausea growing in the pit of her stomach. Her muscles tensed, her heart raced, and her chest tightened. Once again, she struggled to control her breathing. As the Prius gradually accelerated through the opening and the gates closed behind her, she realized she was driving out into a world that was suddenly dangerous and starting to careen out of control

* * *

www.ingramcontent.com/pod-product-compliance
Lightning Source LLC
Chambersburg PA
CBHW070444120726